Wha

Audrey Stone was color, life, vivacity.

On a visceral level, she rattled him, made him wish for youth, innocence, oblivion. Relief from too many problems.

He wasn't a man who caved in to his needs. He was strong. Or had been. He needed that strength back. And to do that, he needed to break this obsession with Audrey.

***Because of Audrey* returns to Accord, Colorado, where one man learns the truth about himself thanks to one incredible woman.**

Dear Reader,

When the idea for the heroine of this book, Audrey, popped into my head, she came fully blown—a complete character who was self-confident, happy with her quirky ways and not the least bit afraid to be different from those around her.

I had a lot of fun writing a strong individual who couldn't be forced into a mold.

I also had fun dressing her. This woman has a generous figure. She's not worried about her weight. She's never dieted. She embraces her image by playing with it, by emphasizing her assets. She sews her own retro clothes or buys vintage Chanel.

When developing a suitable hero for her, I came up with a wounded man. Where Audrey is confident, Gray is a ball of anxiety. He didn't used to be, but a lot has happened to him lately. Too much. As well, there was that pivotal event in his past, the memory of which he buried so deeply he doesn't think it ever happened. While he forced it out of his mind, Audrey embraced the experience and used it to create who she became later.

She is here to help Gray to remember and to heal.

I enjoyed writing a story about how one event changed two people so differently and delving into the ways in which people not only survive, but thrive.

Enjoy,

Mary Sullivan

Because of Audrey

Mary Sullivan

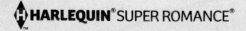

Recycling programs
for this product may
not exist in your area.

ISBN-13: 978-0-373-60807-2

BECAUSE OF AUDREY

Copyright © 2013 by Mary Sullivan

Printed in U.S.A.

ABOUT THE AUTHOR

Mary has an abiding respect for the imagination. She just didn't know it until she decided to stop telling herself to quit daydreaming and to start writing down those stories rattling around in her brain. Boy, is she glad she did. This is her ninth Harlequin Superromance book and the ideas don't quit. New stories continue to pop into her head, often at the strangest moments. Snatches of conversations or newspaper articles or song lyrics—everything is fodder for her stories. She takes a simple idea, a character, a sentence and through effort, patience and a fertile imagination turns it into a novel. She loves to hear from readers. To learn more about Mary or to contact her, please visit her at www.marysullivanbooks.com.

Books by Mary Sullivan

HARLEQUIN SUPERROMANCE

Other titles by this author available in ebook format.

This book is for Brenda,
who has been there through thick and thin
and who never fails to offer a compassionate ear.
I adore your intelligence and humor.
Quite simply, you rock.

CHAPTER ONE

HIDDEN BEHIND THE safe harbor of a tree, Audrey Stone studied the men invading her land and knew that bringing the handcuffs had been smart.

She'd parked her Mini on the shoulder down the road out of sight. No sense warning these guys she was coming.

Trees appeared like ghostly Ents out of the morning mist that rose from low-lying patches of land. She had no problem with fantasy. The thought of talking trees appealed to her. She talked to her plants, didn't she? She believed they listened.

The construction workers had already unloaded their massive yellow equipment. Wary, she inched between a bulldozer and an earthmover, her pulse pounding like a jackhammer, her steps muffled by damp early-morning August earth.

When she saw the digging bucket of a backhoe, its horizontal stabilizers already deployed, hovering dangerously close to the fragile glass roof of one of her greenhouses, she swore. Oh, her babies. What if Noah hadn't noticed these men on his way into town and called her? They would have destroyed her work without her knowledge. All of it down the tubes with the casual flick of a machine's lever.

Thank God she'd arrived in time.

She ignored her racing heartbeat and scooted through the busy workers until she reached the front door.

Someone shouted, "Hey, you! What are you doing?"

Protecting my livelihood.

She snapped one end of the handcuffs to the door handle then locked the other around her wrist. A split second later a hand landed on her shoulder.

A man spun her about—the foreman, maybe?— and frowned when he saw what she'd done. "What the hell's going on?"

She had no doubt who was behind this. She should almost have seen it coming. She tried not to think of Gray, though, and the sorrow he engendered in her.

"Unlock yourself and get the hell out of here," the construction worker ordered, pugnacious in his anger.

"No."

"Gimme the keys." He waggled his fingers. Considering that they were on the end of a very muscled arm, she almost gave in.

"No," she said again, glancing through the window of the greenhouse, gaining strength from her seedlings, her future.

"Call Grayson Turner," she said, infusing her voice with as much authority as she could muster.

The construction worker scratched his head and pulled out a cell phone.

A second later, he said, "Boss, you gotta get out here. We have a nutcase who's locked herself to one of the greenhouses."

Audrey bristled at the characterization of her as a nutcase. She differed a little—okay, a *lot*—from the average woman, but she wasn't crazy. Just worried. Scared. Desperate times called for desperate measures.

If she were lucky, her plants hadn't been traumatized by the offloading of the heavy equipment so close to home. She had only four more weeks to nurture them to perfection, and now this. She'd almost lost them because one man couldn't be bothered to check his family's records.

Grayson Turner could have everything else on earth, but not this little piece of paradise. Audrey needed it, wanted it and owned it. Period.

Her slice of land might be modest by most standards, but pride of ownership blazed through her.

While the worker reported to Gray on the phone, Audrey's gaze shifted to her fields, to the dewy promise of life in the burgeoning grasses surrounding her. If love were visible, had a color, it would be green. She loved this land.

She breathed deeply of air scented with the damp freshness of morning dew. How ironic that the man who'd inspired her love of nature and the outdoors should be the one who could destroy her.

The foreman hung up, crossed his muscled arms over his chest and stared her down, as though he could change her actions by the force of his willpower.

Not a chance.

No beefy construction worker, or backhoe or business mogul would stop her from protecting her babies, even if said businessman did hold the key to a corner of her heart she'd locked away nearly thirty years ago.

Be still, my hammering heart. He's only a boy you used to know. He has no power over you.

Even so, she held her breath while she waited for Gray. She knew from experience that trouble wouldn't be far behind.

GRAYSON TURNER RACED his father's Volvo along the back road that bordered his parents' land outside of Accord, Colorado, biting down on his frustration. What now?

He'd been back home only three months, and already his stress level was through the roof. He still remembered that disturbing call from Dad's office manager.

"He's slowing down, Gray," Hilary had said. "He comes in only two, three hours a day. He's not here long enough to make decisions that need to be made." Shocking, considering that Dad used to practically live there, putting in twelve-and thirteen-hour days when Gray was growing up.

"The decisions he's making are hurting the company," Hilary had continued. "You need to take care of this."

Hilary had worked for Dad for thirty years and knew Turner Lumber inside out. If she said Gray needed to be here, then he needed to be here.

So he'd come home. He should have done so years ago, but Marnie... No, he couldn't go there.

His attempts at dragging the family business into the twenty-first century were being scuttled at every turn, mainly by Dad. Gray had an agricultural conglomerate lined up and was ready to hand over a boatload of money to him for the land, a decision with which Dad had agreed, and what should have been a straightforward mission to tear down the old greenhouses on the property was being held up.

Who would lock themselves to a Turner greenhouse? What had Dad done? Offended a tree hugger? Eaten a piece of meat?

Joking aside, what *had* his father done? Anything was possible these days.

Cool it, Gray. It could just as easily be a squatter. Dad doesn't have to be blamed for everything.

Leaving a trail of dust in his wake, Gray shot down the dirt driveway and pulled up in front of the largest greenhouse, barely registering the idle workers and the one woman leaning against the front of the building.

He opened his door and set a foot onto the ground. *Darkness. Suffocation. Clawing panic.*

Not this again. He shook his head to free himself of the debilitating feelings. He had work to do and no time to figure out what the hell was wrong with him, and what it had to do with Accord.

The car accident had happened in Boston, so why was it affecting him more in his hometown than it had in his adopted city?

He swiped the back of his hand across his sweaty brow and took control of his unruly, nameless fears, got out of the car, and there he was, feet on terra firma, on Turner land, and disaster hadn't struck to warrant the panic. All of that worry for nothing.

Time to deal with the nutcase his foreman had called about.

Silhouetted against the building, her posture dramatic, one arm chained to the door and the other spread across the glass as though one of the workers were threatening her with a sledgehammer, stood a full-figured woman who looked like she'd stepped out of an old movie set.

It took him a moment to recognize her, to remember her from high school.

Audrey Stone.

That darkness, that suffocating panic, slammed into his chest with the force of a wrecking ball. He reached to loosen his tie so he could catch an ounce of oxygen, a fragment of air, anything to stop the dizziness and nausea.

What the *hell* did the accident have to do with this woman? He hadn't seen Audrey in years. He'd never had a relationship with her. They'd never dated, had never been friends.

Audrey didn't look a thing like Marnie, and in fact was Marnie's antithesis. Marnie would never have done something this rash. This emotional. So why did Audrey bring up this crippling hangover from the accident?

He undid the top button of his shirt and sucked in a deep breath.

Better.

Ramming his shaking hands into his pants pockets, he studied the woman chained to his greenhouse and forced himself to rise above his distress to view her objectively. Studying her would give him a minute to collect himself.

He'd avoided her in high school. Looked like he wasn't going to be able to now.

Audrey had changed. She'd been strange back then, in Doc Martens, studded dog collars and spiky black hair, but she'd traded it all in for a more sophisticated weirdness. She wore a suit—a cropped jacket and skirt, and looked like something out of a sixties society photo, *Mrs. S—Lunching with Friends.*

He stepped closer. Fire-engine-red lipstick that matched a ridiculous little hat perched on her head defined a sinfully full mouth. Black eyeliner framed violet eyes. A cap of black curls surrounded a pale face.

Jackie O meets Betty Boop.

Gray knew both characters well. Mom had a lifelong obsession with Jacqueline Bouvier Kennedy Onassis, and Dad loved old cartoons, but come on, these days who dressed like an uppercrust fifties or sixties housewife out on the town?

As had happened in high school, his feelings about Audrey couldn't be clearly defined—sometimes anger, sometimes confusion, often panic. They flummoxed him and made him a little crazy. He was a good judge of character, but who was Audrey, really, and why did he feel so strange around her?

And why did she bring up these memories of the accident?

Why would *who* she was even matter to him? It wasn't as if she was anything more than another of the town's citizens, a satellite floating around the edges of his world.

Calmer now, he stopped in front of her. If his stance was aggressive, so be it. He was in no mood to beat around the bush. "What are you doing?"

"Protecting my property." Her body might have Betty Boop's curves, but her voice had none of her squeaky breathlessness. No-nonsense and down-to-earth, it had an intriguing depth.

"You've got stuff in our greenhouses?" So this situation wasn't Dad's fault. Audrey was nothing more than a garden snake variety of trespasser. Harmless. "That's squatting."

He turned to his foreman. "Cut off the handcuffs. Escort her from the property."

"This land belongs to me." For a short woman,

she had a big voice. Must be those well-endowed…
lungs. "If any of you puts a hand on me, I'll call the
police and have you charged with both assault and
trespassing. Get off my land now."

Gray stilled. "*Your* land? What are you talking
about?" His foreman was right. She was a nutcase.

With her free hand, she reached into a boxy white
purse hanging from her handcuffed wrist and pulled
out a paper, the nerves underneath her defiance betrayed by the wavering of her hand.

He snatched it, read it…and stopped breathing.
A photocopy of the sale of a swath of land to her, it
looked legit.

Impossible. The air around him became thin. Man,
he was getting tired of being dizzy.

Dad, you didn't—

You couldn't have—

He had.

Dad had sold a piece of their land to Audrey Stone
in…Gray checked the date…January, seven months
ago, and not a corner plot, or a slice of land from one
of the boundaries, but a chunk right in the blasted
middle of the land Gray wanted to sell. Correction,
needed to sell.

His jaw hurt with the struggle to maintain control, to keep the panic at bay. "How did you get this
out of my father? What did you do, threaten him or
blackmail him with something?"

"I *asked* him. Politely. He said yes. It's legal."

"We'll see about that." He strode away and

whipped out his cell. Dad's lawyer answered on the second ring, none too pleased to be disturbed at breakfast. Too bad. This needed to be handled. Two minutes later, Gray had an appointment to see the man in his office this morning.

He hung up and gestured to the construction crew. "Clear out. Remove the machinery."

If this sale was legitimate, they were trespassing.

They grumbled but obeyed. Today's debacle was going to cost Gray a bundle. If the sale of land to Audrey had been fraudulent in any way, Gray would sue for damages.

He turned to the woman unlocking herself from the greenhouse door. If he were a violent man, he'd knock her ridiculous red hat from her head.

"This isn't over."

"Yes, Gray, it is." She'd just won a battle and should have looked triumphant. Her solemn frown, though, didn't reflect victory.

The few times he'd run into her over the years, he'd gotten the feeling she knew something he didn't. What? Her knowledge, and his ignorance of it, angered him, made him want to lash out. She was nothing more than a resident in the town he'd grown up in, so why this sense of…drama, of history?

He jumped into his car to drive home, to find out from Dad what kind of whim or idiocy had led him to sell a valuable portion of their land, but not at all sure he'd get an answer that would satisfy him. Dad had always been too softhearted, and was growing worse with age.

When Gray realized he was counting telephone poles, he pulled onto the shoulder, put the car into Park and reached into the glove compartment. Counting, for God's sake. In the months since he'd returned to Accord, he'd started counting everything, from how many times he chewed his food before he swallowed to the number of steps between his bedroom and the bathroom. Wasn't that a sign of OCD personality or something? He'd never done it in his life before. Moving back home had screwed him up. He loved Accord. He'd had a good, solid childhood, so why did returning give him the heebie-jeebies?

Granted, he hadn't been himself since last year's accident, but he'd been recovering. So, why had coming home left him reeling? Why had it brought all of those bad associations, which had finally been healing, back into play? Moving away from Boston, away from the scene of the accident, should have made him better. So, why had coming *here* made him worse?

He pulled out a pack of cigarettes, cursing when his hands shook. After lighting one, he blew smoke out the open window. Before last year, he'd never smoked.

Times had changed.

He'd changed.

While he smoked, he struggled for equilibrium.

Rather than calming him, the nicotine riled him— and that pissed him off. He had to stay calm. Turner

Enterprises needed a strong hand at the helm. Obviously, Dad was no longer up to the task. *He'd sold that piece of land.* Sheer lunacy. That strong hand would have to be Gray's, but for the first time in his career, he was afraid he wasn't up to the job.

The cigarette tasted like crap and was making him nauseous. Not surprising, given that he'd run out the door before having breakfast. He flicked the butt onto the road.

Pull yourself together, Turner.

Before he knew it, he was lighting up a second cancer stick. It tasted as bad as the first. He tossed it out the window, too, and crushed the pack of remaining cigarettes in his fist. He needed to pick up gum or something. Inhaling tobacco was a dumb idea. Weak. Spineless.

He drummed his fingers on the window well. The scent of pine and cedar from the woods lining the road drifted in on a breeze and blew the smoke out of the car.

He started the engine, pulled a U-turn and returned to the greenhouses to have it out with Audrey. Better to push his anger on her than on his aging father.

AUDREY SHOULD HAVE been reveling in her victory—after all, she had won—but instead she watched Gray drive away and wished she could turn back history to better times. But too many years had passed. Maybe Gray wouldn't want to go back to those times.

Maybe he was better off not remembering. He'd certainly shown no sign of recalling much about her, let alone how much they'd meant to each other all of those years ago. As much as *she'd* tried to forget, in many ways it seemed she was still that girl she'd been when she was only seven. And, today, seeing Gray again, all of the sadness of that time—the trauma, the tragic ending, the sad goodbye—still lingered.

When the backhoe leaned too close to the glass roof after pulling in its stabilizers, she shouted, "Careful!" then tracked its laborious journey to a flatbed and waited until every piece of machinery and every last construction worker was gone.

At last, in peace and quiet, she entered the greenhouse.

"Hey, kids, Mama's here," she said, aware of how odd she sounded and not caring a whit. Life was made to be grasped with both hands and lived to the fullest. If she happened to live hers strangely, so be it. As soon as she'd graduated from high school, she'd decided to embrace her individuality, and embrace it she had. With gusto.

She'd been different from others back then, but even her punk gear had been a conformation of sorts. She'd decided she hadn't wanted to belong to *any* group, despite how rebellious punk might have looked. Then, in college, she'd figured out who she really was—big, bold and generous in body, mind and spirit—and hadn't looked back.

She cruised the aisles, giving a soft caress here, offering a gentle word there.

She greeted every plant by name.

"You're strange, you know that?"

At the voice behind her, Audrey spun around.

Gray stood in the open doorway of the greenhouse, and her body betrayed her, tingling with the fire he never failed to ignite in her.

None of that. You are not allowed to let this man affect you.

But he did.

Irritated by her susceptibility to him, she demanded, "Close the door," her tone implying, *preferably with you outside.* "The interior is climate-controlled for my plants."

With a hint of a mocking smile that suggested he knew exactly where she wanted him but didn't care, he stepped inside before he shut the door.

Darn. *Go away. Leave me alone.*

This morning was the first time she'd seen him since his return to town. Before that, it had been a number of years.

He looked too good with the morning's sunlight glinting through the greenhouse roof onto his golden hair. Everything about him was perfect, from his straight nose, to the even tone of his tanned skin, to his strong jaw, to his perfect, dazzling teeth.

She'd forgotten how handsome he was, how with a shot of lightning he awakened latent slumberous juices in her and set them flowing like sap running in springtime. As always, she pulled her unruly attraction under control. Gray didn't need her love— yes, she had truly loved the fun, exciting and loyal little friend that he'd been—and she didn't need his not-so-subtle and undeserved derision. Sad that he'd probably never figured out the source of his disdain for her.

She leaned against one of the counters and crossed her arms.

Keep it light. Keep it normal.

"What have you been doing with your life?" she asked, even though she knew everything about him. She'd collected tidbits here and there, and had kept them in the scrapbook of her memory. He was her enemy now, though, so no sense letting him know that she cared.

He stepped farther down the aisle, coming ever closer. "Starting and running a business."

"Successful?" she asked, even though she knew. Oh, how she knew, and how proud she was of him. Her former friend had done well for himself.

"Of course." Funny that he didn't sound arrogant, but rather matter-of-fact and perhaps puzzled that anyone would think an endeavor of his *wouldn't* be successful. Or maybe it was just a casual arrogance.

"What kind of business?"

"Importing computer parts for the government."

With a glance, she checked out his suit. Why on earth was he wearing one at eight in the morning?

A simple pair of jeans and a T-shirt would have sufficed. Did he even own jeans?

His rumpled tie, the unbuttoned collar of his shirt, the hair that sported rills where it looked as though he'd run his fingers through it impatiently, scorned his casual arrogance. Maybe Gray wasn't as together as he'd like her to believe. But if not, why not?

"The business is lucrative, I take it?" she asked. The suit looked like it cost big bucks.

He nodded. Of course. Gray would make a success of anything he touched. Golden boy. His surface confidence nearly unnerved her. Nearly, but not quite. She'd seen him at his worst, naked, both literally and figuratively. She knew he put his pants on one leg at a time, just like any other man. She knew exactly how vulnerable Grayson Turner could be.

He glanced around the greenhouse, his gaze seeming to linger on the timeworn corners of the old place. Humid streaks trailed the inside of the glass walls. So what if it looked bad? She would fix it all when she had money. "So," he asked, "what's so important in here that you locked yourself to the door?"

"My life." She decided she might as well come clean and let him see exactly how kooky she was. "These—" she swept an arm wide to encompass the tables of seedlings and plants she nurtured like vulnerable infants "—are my babies."

He quirked one eyebrow. "Babies?"

Her natural defiance kicked in, and she lifted her chin and nodded.

"This is what you do for a living?" he asked. "I thought you did something with rocks."

"I did. I was a geologist for thirteen years. I decided to come home to open a floral shop."

"Why? Geology would probably pay more than the income from a flower shop in a small town."

"After all these years, there's still a glass ceiling for women in certain industries."

His swift glance down her body spoke of things he wouldn't express overtly. Again, his disdain. "Did you dress like that on the job?"

"I expressed my individuality." She'd been defiant at work, yes, but she'd done a hell of a good job. "I paid a price for it. I worked for thirteen years at something that should only ever have been an avocation. Collecting rocks was a hobby and should have stayed that way, but I made enough to do what I really want to do." At least, barely.

She gestured toward her fledgling plants in this greenhouse, and the two as-yet-unfilled greenhouses beyond the windows. "I earned what I own here. I paid good money for it. I scrimped and saved and nickeled and dimed. For years I did what I *had* to do. Now, I'm doing what I *want* to do. Flowers are my passion."

But for the occasional self-indulgence, like the vintage Chanel suit she wore today, she'd scraped by and had put the rest into savings and investment accounts.

Through the years, she'd even sewn her own clothes. Still did.

She shot him a look, uncertain whether the sound he'd just made was a snort or a clearing of his throat. Either way, she wasn't so naive that she didn't know judgment when she heard it. "There's more to life than the bottom line. Money isn't everything, Gray."

"No? You're a romantic, Audrey. Everyone needs something to live on."

"True, but how much is necessary and how much overkill? Why is it no longer okay for businesses to believe that making millions is enough? Everyone wants to be the next computer geek gazillionaire, at any cost. *People* no longer matter, only more and more money. Insane, unreasonable amounts of money."

"Is that what you see is wrong with the world these days?" She thought she detected a glint of admiration in his eyes. Or maybe not. His mouth had a cynical cast to it. Surprise, surprise. Their philosophies, after all, directly opposed each other.

"One of many things."

She couldn't fix the world, but she could control her small corner of it. "I want to spread joy with my flower arrangements. I want to spend the rest of my life doing something I enjoy. I can make this business work."

He nodded, cataloguing that information, but why?

His fingers drummed against his thighs, as though

gy hummed through his body needing

ne Do you dress like that when you go on

What does that have to do with anything?"

but it was none of his business. She'd had her

boyfriends, most of them good men. She'd

ver considered one a keeper. "My boyfriends

never complained about my clothes."

ay shrugged and looked at the plants. "Tell me

ut them," he demanded.

She watched him and remained silent. The man
had no authority over her.

"Please." He'd softened his tone.

"Okay."

The first row held her myriad weird and wonderful mushrooms.

"What is *that?*" he asked, indicating a hedgehog
of a mushroom.

"Lion's mane," she answered.

"It looks like Cousin Itt," he said, "but with shorter
hair."

The corner of Audrey's mouth kicked up. She'd
often thought so, too.

Gray stepped closer, using his body to make her
uneasy. She was pretty sure his subtle intimidation
was deliberate. Oh, please. As if that was going to
work on her.

She had to be honest with herself. To a certain
extent, it did. Where with every other man on the
planet she was strong, Gray left her vulnerable. The

woman in her liked the man in him too mu[
ing down the barricades erected between
business adversaries.

He unsettled her, the heat from his body p[
ing the careful walls she constructed against h[
smelled clean and crisp and green, like her [
like the forest after a rainfall.

Even though his cologne reminded her of an ea[
forest floor, of evergreens, something else hove[
around him, too. Cigarette smoke. Yuck. She wou[
have sworn the boy she'd known, who'd loved natur[
and impish exploration, could never turn into a man
this cold and be a smoker to boot.

Tall and fit, he loomed over her. Maybe she should
be afraid, but she wasn't. So many years ago, Gray
had been her little buddy. He would never hurt her,
but his heat so close to her right arm, and his sheer
forceful presence, distracted her. Audrey forgot what
she'd been about to say.

This close, she noticed things about him that gave
her hope he might not be stronger than her, cracks in
his perfect veneer, tightness in his jaw and a tension
that radiated from him like static electricity.

He might want the world to believe he was in control, but something was bothering Gray, feeding his
nervous system with darkness. She knew as surely
as she recognized her own heartbeat that he was a
deeply unhappy man.

About to open her mouth to ask, *What happened*

to you, Gray? she felt his withdrawal, as though he sensed she saw too deeply.

He pretended a normalcy whose authenticity she questioned, and asked, "What are those?" He walked to the next row of plants.

She swallowed her concern. If he didn't want to confide in her, there was nothing she could do.

"Rare orchids." She held herself back from naming all of her orchids. Not everyone shared her enthusiasm.

Thelymitra ixioides, with its bright blue flowers that bloomed on warm, sunny days, waited patiently for her attention. She thought of telling him how hard it would be to get it to bloom indoors, but held her tongue, wary of this über-practical man and his motives, of his probable question, *So why do it?*

Whimsy. Pure utter whimsy that he would never understand.

She didn't want to tell this cold stranger too much, didn't want to disclose her hopes and dreams to a man who would use them against her.

"And those?" he asked, pointing to her baby sunflowers.

Despite herself, absurdly pleased that he showed interest, she disclosed the names of both her dwarf and her giant varieties. "Coming along nicely, my dears," she whispered to them.

She showed off the miniature topiaries she was training into the shapes of small animals—a rabbit and two hedgehogs and a squirrel with a bushy tail.

She indicated her *Clematis aureolin.* "I'm growing this for the strange hairy seedpods it will get in the fall. If you thought lion's mane looked like Cousin Itt, these will be little green baby Cousin Itt wannabes."

He didn't return her smile. Where his height and big body had failed to intimidate her, his cold, flat eyes did. If eyes were the windows to the soul, Gray's eponymous ones had the shutters firmly closed against her. Or against everyone?

Where are you, Gray? Where did you retreat to all of those years ago when you left me alone?

The temperature in the room dropped, February in August, and the warmth of the day leached out of her.

This was not her friend, not the boy she'd run wild with over Turner fields when they were barely old enough to be out on their own. They'd trusted each other. They'd looked out for one another.

Audrey shivered. Gray wouldn't watch out for her now. He was her enemy. He wanted to bring her down.

Amused by her discomfort, the corners of his lips twitched. "I don't know much about flowers, but this is all really strange stuff. Peculiar. Not standard fare for a floral shop. Why are you growing it?"

Audrey's glance flew to the poster she'd hung beside the door for inspiration, advertising the Annual Colorado State Floral Competition in Denver on the second Sunday in September. Gray turned to see what had snagged her attention.

He jerked his thumb toward the poster. "What's this?"

She shrugged. She planned to win the trophy. She needed the $25,000 award desperately, and even more, the yearlong contract being offered to the winner to provide all of the arrangements in one of Denver's boutique hotels, as well as the hospital's gift shop. The future clients and prestige the win could bring would be huge for a fledgling business. Gray didn't need to know that, though.

He stared at her and must have seen something on her face. Hope and determination, she guessed. She'd never been a great card player, had lost every hand of poker she'd ever played. He smiled, but not nicely, as though he had a secret, but one he didn't intend to share with her.

She'd always believed that somewhere beneath that crisp, cool exterior the Gray Turner she had known must still exist. Oh, how wrong she'd been.

"You're wrong, Audrey."

Nonplussed, she stared. The man could read her mind?

Tapping a finger against the poster, his grin mocking her belief that, despite her quirkiness, she'd grown up to be a better person than the man he'd become, he said, "Money *is* everything."

He left the greenhouse. Chilled, Audrey rushed down the aisles, touching her plants, drawing hope from their fledgling fight to survive, struggling to drive the chill from her blood.

Gray hadn't returned because he was interested in her work. He'd needed to find where she was vulnerable, and he had.

Knowing his reputation as a hardheaded businessman, she knew he would use it against her, but she didn't have a clue how. While she might be strong enough to fight the attraction she felt toward him and win, she knew she wasn't a fraction of the businessperson he was.

She'd been a business owner for only nine months.

Her rib cage cradled her pounding heart as though it were a baby bird needing protection.

What if—?

Audrey, stop. Just stop. Gray's playing games, messing with your head, but you don't have to let him.

She left the greenhouse and locked it behind her, wishing she could coat the building in steel to protect her babies from the likes of Grayson Turner.

She strode to her car, morning dew moistening her feet through the peekaboo holes in the toes of her shoes. She glanced back over her shoulder. Sunlight glimmered from the many panes of her greenhouses, igniting shimmering golden jewels in the middle of emerald fields—and a fire in her to burst Gray's arrogant bubble.

No, she didn't have to buy into his intimidation tactics. She was strong.

CHAPTER TWO

AUDREY'S HEADY PERFUME followed Gray out the door, trailing him like a scarf that wrapped itself around his shoulders with comforting hands. Nuts.

Nothing about Audrey said *comfort*. Words that came to mind were sexy and strange and disconcerting, but comforting? Never.

The black eyeliner slanting up at the corners of her violet eyes made them exotic. In the middle of her pure, clear-skinned face, the effect was violently erotic.

Unnerved to feel anything good about the woman, he ordered himself to snap out of it.

She had the power to hurt his family, and he wouldn't stand for it.

Babies. Gray laughed. She'd called her plants her "babies." Nutbar. Defeating this woman was going to be a piece of cake.

At least in grilling Audrey, he'd calmed down enough to see his father without confrontation.

Gray drove to his parents' home. At thirty-six, he shouldn't be living with his mom and dad, but they were getting on in age, and he felt better being around in case something happened to one of them.

Set apart from town on its private cul-de-sac, the gray stone house with the white trim and black lacquered front door spoke of well-bred money, of discreet, respectful living.

He'd had a good upbringing. So why was he screwed up these days? Why so neurotic?

The garage door was open and Dad was inside. Good. There were things that needed to be said.

"Dad?" he called.

Dad had his head buried inside a deep box. "Aha!" He stood, triumph and a childlike joy lighting his face. "Here they are."

"We need to talk—"

"Remember these?" He held an old snorkel set of Gray's in his hands, the rubber of the ancient flippers dry and cracked.

"Yes, I remember. I must have been nine or ten when you bought them for me." He didn't have time for this. They had issues to settle. Huge issues.

Dad wore an old cardigan, ratty around the edges from years of use. White hair curled over the collar of the sweater. Disgraceful. Dad used to be particular about his grooming.

"What happened to you, Dad? Something's changed." The words were out of his mouth before good manners could stop them, a sign of how bad Gray's nerves were. Dad's aging, the slow crumbling of a once-powerful man, affected Gray, left him sad and a little lost. Left *him* somehow smaller, at a time when he was already vulnerable with residual grief. Marnie was dead.

Stop. Concentrate on the here and now, on business.

"I turned eighty last year." For all of Gray's recent worries about Dad's state of mind, especially given the shaky business dealings lately, Dad had understood his question perfectly.

Gray waited for more explanation. When it didn't come, he prompted, "And...?"

"And *you* try turning eighty and looking back on your life and realizing how much time you spent indoors in a stuffy old office when you could have been out *doing* things." He pulled out a plastic oar belonging to an old dinghy that had been relegated to the dump years ago. "Look!" His chuckle held a strange glee that Gray had never heard before, not sinister, just, again, childlike.

Gray couldn't get past his surprise. Dad had regrets? "But..."

"But what?"

"But you loved the business."

"Past tense. I'm tired. I want to enjoy what's left of my life. I want peace."

How had Gray missed Dad's transformation from a savvy businessman to a reluctant one? Gray had tried to visit as often as possible, but given that he'd taken after his father with twelve-hour days and a demanding, if loved, girlfriend, it had been hard. Obviously, he hadn't come home often enough.

"You're here now," Dad asserted. "You take care of the business."

Speaking of which...

"Did you sell a piece of land to Audrey Stone in the winter?"

"Jeff Stone's daughter?" Dad looked up from the box he was still rummaging through. A fine fuzz of white stubble dusted his unshaven chin. Dad shaved *every* day. Apparently not today.

The gray eyes that Gray had inherited still seemed sharp, but his glance shifted away from Gray's. What was he hiding? Over and over, Gray had had to find out things about the company from Hilary or the accountant. While Dad seemed to welcome Gray into the business, he also stonewalled him at too many turns. Something strange was up with his father.

He *said* he was tired. He *said* you take care of the business. His actions spoke a different language. Dad couldn't let go of the reins.

"Yes," Dad replied. "I sold land to Audrey. Why?"

"It's in the heart of the land I want to sell to Farm-Green Industries."

"Hmm. Too bad."

Dad had become a master of understatement. Gray gritted his teeth. "Why did you sell?"

"Jeff is sick."

"What does that have to do with the land?"

"His daughter needs to take care of him."

Gray bore the frustration of dealing with Dad like

this, but only barely. Conversation was like pulling freaking teeth out of his head one by one. Without anesthetic. Where was the man who used to be open about everything?

"Dad, what does that have to do with our land?"

"She needed a place to grow plants and flowers for her floral shop. She needs to support herself and help her father. We stopped using those greenhouses years ago. Shame to see them go to waste."

"But we've spent months hammering out this deal with Farm-Green. They aren't going to take it with a huge hunk of land missing from the middle."

"I never wanted to sell to them anyway. When they first started sniffing around two or three years ago, I told you that."

God, give me strength. "We've gone over this a hundred times. You need to look at the big picture. Look outside of Accord. The economy isn't what it used to be. The whole country is suffering. The lumberyard isn't bringing in a fraction of the money it used to. We need that money to pay your employees." Let alone take care of all of the other dubious decisions Dad had made lately.

"So, find a different solution. Something else that will work. If one thing doesn't, find another."

"There won't be another company who'll pay what Farm-Green was willing to so quickly. It could take a year to find someone else who's interested, and then months more of negotiations. I'm turning myself inside out to come up with creative solutions to our problems."

Dad shrugged. "When one door closes, another opens."

One of Dad's empty pronouncements. He thought they were nuggets of wisdom. Not even close. New-age gobbledygook.

"Did you at least get a good price?" Gray wouldn't put it past his father to give the land away for sentiment's sake.

Judging by Dad's annoyed frown, he'd asked the wrong question. "Of course I did. I spent sixty years working as a successful businessman."

Yes, Gray knew that, but Dad had lost his grip on reality. He was eighty years old and changing, reverting to childhood, or something. He should have retired twenty years ago, but what would he have done instead? Retirement would probably have killed him, but in the past months that Gray had been home, he'd finally had to accept that Dad needed to step away from the business altogether before he sent the whole thing down the drain. Dad was still too sharp for this to be Alzheimer's. This wasn't a failing, wasn't even dementia, just a change. But why?

"Isn't Jeff Stone the one you pay a salary to even though he's off work?"

"I pay him a reduced salary. An early retirement."

"Even though he was short of fulfilling his requirements?"

"He's going blind." Gray flinched at Dad's harsh

tone. "Jeff worked for me for twenty-nine years. His macular degeneration precluded him from working his final year."

"He would qualify for disability. Why make the company bear the financial burden of his care?"

"He would make a pittance on disability. He has medical bills. He needs an operation that will cost a fortune. He's middle class, not a millionaire." Dad pulled the second oar out of the box but threw it onto a growing rubbish heap when he discovered it was broken. "Paying Jeff is no burden. He worked hard for me and, by extension, since you enjoyed the secure childhood and higher education the business bought, for *you*. The least we can do is show our appreciation."

Dad was too softhearted to run a successful company in today's environment. Disability was designed for this situation, for people like Jeff.

Gray opened his mouth to argue further, but Dad forestalled him. "Selling those greenhouses to Audrey was the right thing to do. Give it some thought and you'll agree."

Before he said something too harsh, Gray left the garage. For sixty years, his dad had done everything right, but in the past year, it seemed he'd been getting it all wrong. Or maybe longer. The further Gray dug into records and finances, the more he realized that Dad had been making risky investments and dubious decisions for a while.

Also, he'd caught him lying more than once. No,

that wasn't fair. They weren't lies, just convenient half-truths so that Gray had to double-check everything Dad told him to find the truth for himself.

His stomach burned.

Did Mom have antacid tablets in the house? He could use a couple. Or the whole bottle.

Inside, he found her sitting in the living room. Where Dad's grooming was suffering with age, Mom still looked perfect.

Dressed to the nines even this early in the morning, she wore a silk blouse with a soft pastel print and a tweed skirt, her still slim legs encased in stockings and her feet in stylish black heels.

She sat on the sofa reading a romance novel. She had just turned seventy-five, for Pete's sake. He didn't need to catch her holding a book with a photograph of a half-naked man clutching a busty woman on the cover.

Even so, when she peeked at him over the rims of her reading glasses, her once-vivid blue eyes faded now, his heart swelled. A cloud of white hair framed a tiny face. Her welcoming smile warmed him. This amazing woman had given him everything, the absolute best childhood.

"Can I get you anything?" he asked, and he meant *anything.* For his parents, especially Mom, he would do whatever was asked of him. "A cup of tea?" Mom loved her tea.

"I'm fine," she answered. "I've already had four cups this morning."

"Mom," he said, hesitating because he didn't want to offend, but needing to know. "What's happening with Dad?"

She didn't seem surprised by the question. "He's tired. He's had a lot of weight on his shoulders for a long time. He needs to let go and relax."

"He said it started when he turned eighty."

She set her glasses down on top of her book. "Oh, it started well before that. He's been tired for years."

Startled, Gray asked, "Why didn't he tell me? I would have come home sooner."

Those faded blue eyes studied him shrewdly. "Would you have?"

His mind flew to an image of Marnie with her hands on her hips, obstinate in battle with him. "Yes," he said, but he'd taken too long to answer.

"Truly?"

Gray slumped into the armchair. "I don't know. Marnie didn't want to live here. She loved Boston."

"You would have had to have made a choice. Your parents or your fiancée. I understood that, Gray, so I didn't tell you about your dad's state."

Gray leaned forward and rested his elbows on his knees. "Mom, I love you and Dad. I would have worked out something."

"What could you have done? You loved Marnie, too, and Boston is not within commuting distance. Would you have lived six months here and the other half of the year there? Like a child in joint custody?

What kind of life would that have been, especially once you had children?"

"I don't know. I would have come up with a solution."

Mom closed her book and put it on the side table, giving him her full attention. "Why did it take so long for you and Marnie to set a wedding date? You were engaged for five years."

Mom had always been too perceptive. Getting away with anything in his adolescent years had taken real skill and subterfuge on Gray's part. "There were things we couldn't agree on."

"Like where to live?"

A heavy sigh gusted out of him, and he admitted, "Like where to live. That was the biggest obstacle."

"So, even though your father and I tried to protect you, you were caught up in our drama anyway."

"You were aging. There's nothing anyone can do to prevent that. You're my responsibility, Mom."

"Such a shame that we had only one child."

"What else could you have done? I came along so late." He was a surprise for his parents after they had long given up hope of conceiving.

Mom smiled, and her eyes got misty. "Yes. We were lucky to have you."

The conversation had become too maudlin for Gray. He didn't want to think about feeling alone as a child, about how much he missed Marnie, or about how old his parents were.

"What do you know about Audrey Stone?" he asked.

Mother perked up. "She's the most interesting thing to happen to this town in years. I'm so glad she came back home to live. Have you seen her?"

He'd run out on breakfast, so he explained what the emergency had been.

"What was she wearing?" Mother asked, clearly excited.

"Wearing?" She'd thrown him. He'd just told her that Audrey had the means to scuttle a huge deal for the family and Mother wanted to know what the woman was wearing?

He rubbed his hands over his face. As dear as his aging parents were, he didn't have time for their eccentricities.

"Well?" Mom persevered.

Gray pointed to a large illustrated hardcover on the coffee table. In a full-page photo on the cover, Jackie Kennedy wore the pink suit she'd had on the day her husband was assassinated.

"She wore a suit like that, but it was gray with white trim."

His mother caught her breath. "A vintage Chanel? I always knew Audrey had class."

He thought of the full curves shaping the suit. Class? Yes, but also a whole lot more.

"No hat?"

He mentioned the red hat that had matched her lipstick and her nail polish and the glimpse of her toenails he'd seen through her open-toed black suede pumps, which looked as though they'd come straight out of the forties.

"Describe the hat."

When he finished, Mother nodded her approval. "A pillbox. You don't see those anymore. Was she wearing gloves?"

Thinking of those bright red nails, he shook his head.

"Ah, well," she said, "I guess times have changed. Too bad she hadn't really completed the outfit, though, if you know what I mean."

He didn't have a clue.

"Have you thought anymore about what we discussed last night?" she asked.

What they'd discussed many nights since he'd moved back home had been his getting married and having children. His parents wanted to meet their grandchildren before they died. Gray still had to produce those grandchildren. First he needed a partner. It should be the least he could do, but he thought of Marnie and held his breath until the pain passed.

"I'm thinking about it."

Mother smiled. Honestly, he lived to make her happy, but how did a man snap his fingers and, poof, there would be a wife, ready and willing to bear his children?

He headed upstairs to his bedroom. He needed to change his shirt. It wasn't yet nine o'clock in the morning and the day not yet hot, but under his business jacket, he'd been sweating like a linebacker.

Since the car accident, his body had been betraying him in strange ways. A giant rodent gnawed gaping holes in the cool, collected persona he'd cultivated in business, and he didn't have a clue how to boot the offending creature from his body.

He picked up a letter that had arrived yesterday, addressed to his father, but Gray handled all of his parents' correspondence these days. They'd relinquished that responsibility happily, and thank God for that. What if Mother had opened this instead of him?

The thought sent a shiver through him. Mom would have been devastated. He had to protect her at all costs.

He read it yet again with a creepy fascination, as though rubbernecking at a traffic accident.

I have three children to support. Their father is dead. My oldest son has Duchenne muscular dystrophy. I can't pay for his therapy. He needs a wheelchair. I need money. I'm desperate. I'll go to the newspapers.
Shelly Harper

Who was this woman? This Shelly? Was she for real? Were her accusations true? That Dad was her father? He checked the postmark. Denver. Too close to home for comfort's sake, only an hour away.

At heart, Gray was a cynic and took nothing at face value.

And yet, he had an eerie suspicion that everything she'd said was true.

She'd enclosed a birth certificate, hers, with his dad's name on it, along with a photograph of herself that showed a strong likeness to Dad. The final shot, though, of three children, one of whom was the spitting image of himself at around nine or ten, left him shaken.

It all seemed legit. These kids looked like family. The woman bore an eerie resemblance to him.

Nonetheless, after he'd received the letter yesterday, he'd posted one back to her. *I need proof. Give me a DNA sample for testing.*

Let's see if she had the nerve to provide one.

His gut screamed she was telling the truth. In business, he trusted his instincts all the time—they rarely steered him wrong—but how could this be real? Dad couldn't possibly have committed adultery. Could he have? *Dad?*

If the woman's allegations were true, Gray would need quick money to buy her off. It took time to come up with the kind of cash she demanded—four hundred thousand dollars.

Four hundred thousand dollars. Mind-boggling. He started to sweat again.

Yes, his business was successful, but he wasn't a millionaire. He didn't have buckets of cash lying around.

He'd already started things rolling yesterday with

instructions for his CFO to liquidate certain of his own assets, but it wouldn't be nearly enough.

Farm-Green was willing to buy *now*—the ultimate answer to this mess.

The woman's threat filled him with cold dread.

How could Gray ever let Mom find out? How could she survive the betrayal once she knew that her husband had been unfaithful, that she'd been wrong about his character throughout her marriage?

He dropped into his old desk chair. It squeaked under his weight. He wouldn't let Mom be ruined by *this*. He threw the paper on to the desk—not while he had any say in the matter. But what could he do? If this woman was telling the truth—and it sure looked as though she was—she had a real need.

Then again, if what she claimed was true, she was his half sister and only a year older than he.

Man, that floored him. He'd been a happy child, but so alone. For a long time, there'd been an emptiness inside of him, a wish for more, a sense that he'd lost something he couldn't name and couldn't get back.

For years, he'd wanted a sibling.

Was he willing to accept this woman's assertions too easily because of a long-buried wish for a brother or sister? For something to combat being alone in the future after his parents died, and to assuage his current loneliness?

How was her existence even possible? Dad had adored Mom all of his life. Dad, the epitome of ethics and morals, a man whose backbone and strength of character were admired by all, couldn't have had an affair.

Gray, though, was stuck considering the unthinkable, that his dad had fathered an illegitimate child while married to his mom.

Talk to Dad.

Can't. What if I find out it's true?

Suck it up and ask.

It would shatter Gray, make a mockery of his history and his parents' history.

You need to know.

In fresh clothes, he went back out to the garage where Dad still puttered.

This whole thing could be cleared up with one conversation.

When Gray stepped close, Dad looked up and smiled. Gray's heart hammered. He was about to blow Dad's world apart. And his own.

He handed Dad the letter.

"What's this?"

"It came yesterday." Try as he might, he couldn't keep the foreboding from his voice. Was Dad the man he thought he'd known all of his life? Or a stranger like the one he was becoming now?

The man took a pair of wire-rimmed reading glasses out of his sweater pocket and read the letter.

"What is this?" He sounded genuinely confused.

"Have you ever known a woman named Edie

Kent? She was this woman's—" he gestured toward the letter "—mother."

"This woman who says that I'm her father? No. I've never even heard of Edie Kent." He thrust the paper back at Gray. "You don't believe this crap, do you?"

Gray handed him the photo. "Look at her son."

Dad's skin paled. "My God, he looks like you. Like seeing a ghost. That's impossible. Coincidence. Nothing more. They say everyone has a double somewhere on earth."

Now for the crucial question he'd never thought he'd ask his father. "Did you ever have an affair?"

Dad scowled. "How can you even consider that? I adored your mother. Always have since the second I first laid eyes on her, and always will." He slammed the photo against Gray's chest, and Gray barely caught it before it fell to the ground. The man still had some power in him.

Gray's dander rose. He wouldn't have even considered the possibility that Dad would do this, but that photo was damning, and waiting for DNA results would take too long. Plus, his dad was becoming a stranger. He needed to know *now* so he could put his mind to rest on this problem at least. He had too much hanging over his head, too much that needed to be settled, and all of it taken care of instantly. Yesterday.

"Is it possible you could have gotten drunk one

night and slept with this woman's mother without remembering?"

"No. Once I married your mother, I became a homebody." Dad strode out of the garage, and Gray followed. "Besides, when would I have had time? I had a business to grow, and I worked my butt off to do it."

He stalked around to the front door. "Can't believe you even considered that I might have—" He spun back to Gray. "Don't you know me at all?" The anger had left his voice, replaced by hurt. He entered the house and closed the door behind him, as though Gray were no longer welcome in the home he'd grown up in.

Given the changes at work, given Dad's crazy decisions, Gray was left to wonder whether he knew him at all.

He felt as low as low could be. He'd just hurt and alienated his father. But he'd had no choice. He'd had to know.

AT ELEVEN-THIRTY, Gray stood in John Spade's law office tamping down rising nausea, not sure he'd heard the immaculately groomed lawyer clearly.

"Jeez, John, what are you doing these days? Having facials? Mani-pedis? You've primped the daylights out of yourself."

"Stop avoiding the issue," Spade said. "Can you do it?"

The sweating had started again the second the

lawyer had made his crazy suggestion. His absurd, *impossible* suggestion. The fresh shirt Gray had changed into at home was already soaked. Again.

"You mean have my father deemed unsound of mind?" he asked, unable to mask his distaste. "Unfit to run the business he built from the ground up?"

John leaned back in his chair. "For God's sake, Gray, stop pacing and sit down. You're making me nervous just looking at you. This isn't like you."

No, it wasn't. He had a cool head for business, but business problems had never hit so close to home. His father had never been blackmailed before, and Gray had never had problem after problem dumped on him, one on top of the other, until he was drowning in an ocean of anxiety, hanging on to a bit of flotsam by his fingernails.

Was the universe out to get him or something? What had he ever done to deserve all of this?

Oh, quit with the self-pity. Shit happens to everyone. Deal with it and find solutions.

This—what John wanted?—was one hell of an ugly solution.

"The sale of the property was legitimate," John continued. "I'm just giving you an option. A way out. Has your father been incoherent at all lately? Has he had memory loss?"

Gray stalked to the window and stared out on to the town. In the distance, he could see the sign for Turner Lumber. "Of course he's had memory loss. He's eighty. He's not senile, though. He doesn't have

Alzheimer's. It would kill him if I went behind his back and did something like this."

"Don't get emotional. This is business."

Gray knew all about how to run a business, how to separate emotion from whatever had to be done to protect the bottom line, but this was his family they were talking about. "He's my *father*."

"He's also the head of Turner Enterprises, which you're telling me needs a significant influx of cash. Selling that land is the smart thing to do. Audrey Stone is standing in your way. This is a solution to that problem."

"It would devastate my parents."

"It has to be done." John's eyes cooled to the color of wet slate. "I'm good at my job, Gray. This is possible. If I didn't think this could be done, I wouldn't suggest it."

Gray considered himself a tough businessman, but John's expression chilled even him.

"Go home and give the idea some thought." John stood. "*Rational* thought."

Gray left John's office but stopped just inside the front door of the reception area before stepping outside, tasting bile in his throat. Declare Dad unfit? Declare his mind unsound? Insane. This couldn't be happening.

No. There had to be a way around it.

He left the office and stood on Main Street, disoriented, his skin clammy and his breathing shallow.

He recognized the symptoms for what they represented. Shock.

And why wouldn't he be shocked? How could he declare a man he loved and admired unfit, a father who'd done his absolute best for his son?

It would be like stabbing him in the back.

Et tu, Brute?

Like the worst betrayal.

Benches lined the sidewalk, and he sat on one, needing a minute to wrap his head around a difficult decision.

Declare Dad unfit.

Impossible.

What then? Was it better to have Mom learn that her husband had fathered an illegitimate child and then didn't have the honor to admit to the affair or support the child?

But Dad wouldn't do that.

It looked as though he had.

Gray didn't know how much he could trust his father. He'd been hiding things. Was he hiding the truth about this? He'd seemed sincere, though. But that photo...

Circuitous thoughts boggled Gray's mind.

Pain radiated from his hands and up through his arms. He glanced down. He'd been clenching his fists. He stretched tight fingers. His nails had left arched red welts in his palms.

He couldn't betray Dad.

Before he would even consider deep-sixing his

dad's good standing, he needed to try a couple of things—first, attempt to buy back the land. If that didn't work, then second, he had to go to Denver and meet with the woman. Maybe she was lying, and, in person, he'd be able to detect her lies, and the problem would be solved. He could call her bluff. He'd buy himself time to take care of issues at work without this woman's demand.

Four hundred thousand dollars.

Did she think they were made of money? Ridiculous.

Across the street, Audrey's tarted-up floral shop, The Last Dance, stood out like a peacock strutting on white sand. What on earth dancing had to do with flowers was beyond him.

He crossed Main and checked out the window display—a microcosm of who the woman was, quirky, boldly colorful, and even classy as Mom had suggested.

He didn't know why the success of her creativity made him angry, but it did.

She had to sell that land to him, had to save him from betraying the father whose business decisions he might question, but whom he adored.

The sign on the front door said Closed, but he could see Audrey inside. He tested the doorknob. Unlocked. He stepped into a shop that smelled floral and felt cool.

A dog came out from behind the counter and

sidled close to Gray, butting his hand with his head. Instinctively, Gray petted him, and the dog closed his eyes, leaning into the caress.

The lovely trust of this uncomplicated creature moved him, reminded him of his Bernese mountain dog, Sean, who'd died a month after the accident, compounding Gray's already raw grief.

His chest hurt and his throat ached, locked as he was suddenly and inexplicably in that grief again. It happened too often, brought on by nothing and everything.

A movement to his right caught his eye, breaking the spell of pleasure/pain the dog brought out in him. Audrey turned from the flowers she was arranging and watched him silently. Beneath wariness, he could almost detect compassion in her eyes, but why? What was she thinking? What did she see in him?

He looked away from that knowing gaze and down at the long-haired brown-and-white beauty. "What's his name?"

"Jerry."

Gray thought about the dog's name and did a double take. "Isn't he a springer spaniel?"

"Yep." She waited, watched, wondering whether he would get the joke. He got it all right. Jerry Springer Spaniel.

If he weren't so pissed off at the woman, he'd laugh. Her sense of humor was every bit as quirky as her style.

"Yeah?" he asked, feeling the rare hint of a grin tug at the corners of his mouth. "Who are his parents?"

"We don't know the father. We've done DNA tests, though. The results promise to be shocking. We think his mother slept around. It could get ugly."

Audrey leaned her elbow on the counter and rested her chin on her fist. Her other hand sat on her cocked hip. She had good hips—ample and shapely. A smile tipped the corners of her lush red lips, pride in her own joke.

That tiny smile did a number on his equanimity, threatened to turn him soft, to treat her with tenderness when he couldn't afford to. If he had any hope in hell of pulling his family out of the mess they were in, he had to hang tough.

He straightened and removed his hand from the dog's head, denying both himself and the dog pleasure. These days, Gray was more at home with pain.

"Sell me the land."

He'd shocked her. She stepped behind the counter, putting distance between them. "No."

"I can move your plants to other greenhouses. At my cost."

"Moving them at this stage would kill them. Besides, the nearest greenhouses are miles away. I don't even know if there are any available."

Damn. "I can research it."

"No, I won't risk killing my plants by disturbing them. I don't *have* to. I own that land legally."

"How much do you want for it?"

"Nothing. I'm keeping it."

"I can give you far more than the plants you're growing are worth."

"No."

His jaw, where all his tension centered, cramped. "What's your problem? They're only flowers."

"What's *your* problem?" she countered. "Is money all you think about?"

"These days? Yes."

"Money is *not* all that matters in life," she asserted.

It is if it saves my mother, my family, our business and all its employees. He would never say this to her or to anyone else in town. He would never show vulnerability to an opponent or give her ammunition to use against him.

As far as the business went, only Gray and his accountant knew how close to the edge they were. As far as Gray knew, he was the only one who'd received the letter. That could change, though, if the woman didn't get what she wanted. *I'll go to the newspapers.*

The thought of the tawdry truth splashed across newspaper headlines, the thought of his mother finding out about Dad in that way, in any way, left Gray chilled. Desperate.

He thought of how Mom had looked this morning, fragile yet perky, about as classy a woman as he'd ever known.

How could he let this destroy her?

How could he get Audrey to sell? Now? Today?

"Name your price," he demanded, an incredibly stupid move for a smart businessman, but he needed that land.

"I don't have one."

"Everyone does. What's yours?"

"Gray, leave my shop."

"No. Not until you promise to sell to me."

A frown formed between her dark arched eyebrows, and she edged her hand toward the telephone. "Seriously, Gray, go now or I'll call the police."

"No." He couldn't, not until she agreed.

She reached under the counter for…what?…a gun? For mace?

He was frightening her. He might be mad to get the land, and she might be the strangest woman he'd ever met, but scaring her was unconscionable. Intimidation to get her to sell? Yes. Outright frightening her? Dead wrong.

He backed away.

"Think about it," he said, the slightest thread of recklessness seeping into his voice. As a businessman, he was making mistakes left, right and center.

She shook her head, and there was such implacability, such conviction in the movement he knew she would never sell, no matter how high his price.

When he turned and left, desperation wrapped around his throat like a noose. He was going to have to do the unthinkable and have Dad declared unfit.

No. Before he did that, he would drive into Denver and see this woman for himself.

He couldn't wait—for DNA results, for the woman's next move, for another damn day. On the heels of that thought, he swore. He couldn't leave today. He had an appointment with Dad's accountant that couldn't be put off.

Tomorrow then. He'd go to Denver first thing tomorrow.

Time for a showdown.

CHAPTER THREE

Gray sat in his car for ten minutes getting his emotions under control, and then started the drive down Main toward Turner Lumber on the end of town opposite to where his parents lived. He couldn't go home to face them.

Not yet. Not while he *considered,* let alone actually started, the process toward turning against his father.

He noticed a woman he'd gone to school with walking down the sidewalk. She was one of the descendants of the original founding father, Ian Accord. She carried herself with an elegance and grace, with an air of confidence Gray had often witnessed among the rich. Wealth was a language he himself spoke, and being tongue-tied by his current money problems disheartened him.

Down the street, Audrey Stone stepped out of her flower shop and locked the door behind her, then started in his direction, her pigeon-toed stride oddly endearing.

Full curves moved in different directions. She looked clumsy, but those curves, that walk, the slightly askew pillbox hat—those full red lips—were so insanely feminine, he started to smile.

When she stopped in front of a lingerie shop to look at some feminine froth of satin and lace, Gray imagined it cradling her shapely body. His latent smile spread.

When he realized what his foolish mouth was doing, he made himself stop.

Do not even think *about finding this woman attractive. She's your enemy. If she hadn't bought that land from Dad, you wouldn't be in your current predicament.*

With a screech of tires, he drove on.

In the parking lot of the massive lumberyard and hardware store that had been in his family since long before Gray's birth, he threw out the gum he'd been chewing and opened two fresh sticks, chewing hard until his shaking hands calmed and he could breathe easily. Why, for a man who was known as a sharp businessman, did just walking into his father's business leave him feeling so...afraid? Why did everything these days?

His tension filled the car like dark gas.

He forced himself out of the vehicle and into the building, heading past the large shop to the offices that occupied the second floor. Turner Lumber catered to both contractors and the average man. And woman, Gray reminded himself. There were a lot of knowledgable women out there doing their own repairs these days.

The store covered half an acre of land and served all of the towns for miles around. Even in a city the size of Denver, you would be hard-pressed to find a better-stocked, more efficient supplier. They also rented equipment, a part of the business that used to be a going concern. Since the downturn in the economy, there was less construction. As well, homeowners no longer had the money for renovations.

There had been a spurt of construction when a new ski resort had been built outside of town, but Dad had taken his profits and had invested in risky ventures. When Gray had tried to change them to something safer, Dad had vetoed him. For a man who'd been a smart business owner for so many years, Dad's actions these days seemed like a textbook case of how *not* to run a business.

Businesses suffered everywhere, including Turner Lumber. And yet, Dad was giving money away left, right and center. It had to stop. Cauterizing the hemorrhaging of money was Gray's job.

Upstairs, he found the renovations he'd ordered nearly finished. Part of dragging Turner Lumber into the twenty-first century had been modernizing the office. Gone were the separate cubicles of old, replaced by a huge open space filled with desks and office modules. At the moment, they were squeezed into one half of the space while the floors on the other half were being refinished.

The office kept the idle lumberyard workers busy now that traffic had slowed down there. So far, Gray had managed to keep everyone on the payroll. He didn't know how much longer he could hold out.

If he was smart, he'd start slashing now, but sentimentality kept getting in the way. Was this what Dad felt when he walked in here?

Gray stopped to talk to the office manager, Hilary Scott. She, like all the employees, wore a cotton mask over her nose and mouth.

"Here." She handed him a mask. "You should wear it until these guys finish their work." A frown wrinkled her forehead.

"You don't look happy," Gray observed. "What's the problem?"

"The noise."

"That's temporary. It won't last."

"The dust. Look at our desks."

A fine gray film settled over everything.

"I'll have a cleaning crew come in on the weekend."

Hilary sighed. "But what kind of chemicals, or even old mold, have you stirred up with this destruction?"

Gray loved language, loved how he could manipulate it to his advantage in business, but hated how it could be corrupted.

"This isn't destruction, Hilary. This is change."

She didn't answer, just stood her ground like a wiry-haired bantam hen.

"In another week, things will settle down," Gray said.

"Given how hard it is to get work done in *this*—"

she gestured with her chin toward the open space, not the contractors and their work, he noticed "—I fervently hope it gets better."

He barely held himself back from shaking his head. New ideas were always hard to implement. Hilary and her employees had been working with the same systems for years. "These changes should further innovation and fresh thinking." Something Turner Lumber could use, he didn't say aloud.

"The open concept should inspire a more communal sense of the company, and the resultant community should inspire more communication and new ideas."

Hilary nodded but didn't look convinced. "We already enjoy plenty of community here."

"Then you should support an increase in that." He had enough resistance to deal with from his dad. He didn't need to face it here at work, as well.

"Listen, Hilary." He sounded testy. Too bad. He was on edge and tired of facing problems everywhere he turned. "Given that *you* called me home to help, I expected cooperation from you."

"I didn't think you'd be changing everything."

"What did you think I'd do?"

"Make it the way it was before your dad started making dubious choices."

Hilary was as naive as Dad was. There was no salvation for the company without upgrading it, not in the current financial environment, not using strategies that were forty and fifty years old.

He entered the office he'd set up for himself in the corner to catch his breath and to prepare for his meeting with Arnold Haygood, Turner Lumber's accountant. His area had sliding walls that opened to the larger space. Most of the time he left the walls open, keeping himself involved. When he needed to have sensitive conversations or make phone calls that he didn't want overheard, he could slide the walls closed for the best of both worlds.

Still, that feeling of suffocation, the difficulty breathing, had followed him into the office, and had nothing to do with renovation dust or face masks.

He needed to push the deals through on the sale of the land and finish liquidating more of Dad's assets, so Gray never had to step in here again, never again had to experience this cloying panic.

Maybe it was time to sell the company. He'd been fighting the idea, keeping it as a last resort. He shouldn't let emotion get in the way of business, but as much as these were Dad's people, they were also his.

Despite his current anxiety, his memories of running through this place as a child were good. He knew everyone who worked here. What if the new owners mistreated them?

Before leaving Boston, he'd toyed with the idea of selling his company there and moving here to live, not just swooping in to fix whatever was wrong, but to actually stay and run Turner Lumber. Leaving Marnie behind, though, never being able to visit her gravesite, saying goodbye yet again, this time permanently… He couldn't do it.

Then he'd come home and all of this weird behavior had started, the panic attacks and anxiety, the suffocation.

So then he'd thought he would hire a good manager to take over. But now, with the letter from this woman, and more and more demands on limited dollars, he had to consider that maybe it was time to just sell.

Panic clutched at him again. If having Dad declared incompetent made him nauseous, the thought of how disappointed Dad would be if he sold the company rather than keeping it and running it himself as part of his heritage made him positively ill.

"Hilary," he called.

Seconds later she stood in front of his desk. She was nothing if not efficient.

"After the men finish the renovations for the day, have all of the employees gather in the office."

Hilary waited, but Gray didn't explain. He knew he needed to make changes and he knew the staff should be told, but he had to confirm everything with Arnie before he spoke. He and the accountant could hash out details this afternoon.

At lunchtime, Audrey closed her floral shop and walked down Main to the Sweet Temptations Bakery and Café, resolutely avoiding thinking about that disturbing incident with Gray. He'd been strange, almost

unbalanced, but still so handsome, so smoothly...
right.... With those pale gray eyes so striking against
his perfectly tanned skin, it almost hurt to look at
him.

There'd been that brief moment when he'd let his
guard down, when he'd been petting Jerry, his expression tender and almost wistful.

Then he'd turned hard. She disliked that version
of the man with all of her heart.

A movement in the window of Enchanté caught
her attention, Marceline waving and gesturing toward a black teddy with pink polka dots and pink
bows. Oh, so cute. Oh, so sexy.

She couldn't possibly afford it.

Audrey had dresser drawers that overflowed with
basques and silk knickers and corsets. Oh, she loved
lingerie. She'd been diligent in her search for amazing undergarments at excellent prices. With her full
figure, she needed good support and quality material.
So much beautiful French lingerie. So little space,
time and money.

And no one to wear it for. She did wear it, though,
every day, but, oh, it would be lovely to have someone to whom she could show it off.

She shook her head and mimed drying tears from
the corners of her eyes, making Marceline smile, and
walked on. Someday she would share her favorites
with a special someone.

At the café, she ordered a couple of soups and

sandwiches then carried lunch along Main to the Army Surplus.

When she stepped into the store, she breathed deeply of the mothballs and incense that made up her friend's unique scent.

"Noah?" she called.

He came out of the back carrying a pile of boxes, bobbing up onto the balls of his feet in his signature walk that kept him looking young and boyish, one of the things she adored about him.

He bussed her on the cheek. She didn't return the favor. Noah didn't like lipstick. She giggled and thought of doing it anyway, of leaving a big swath of red gloss across his cheek, but suppressed her inner imp.

"What did you bring today?" he asked.

"Tomato garlic soup and pastrami on rye."

"Hot mustard?"

"You got it, cowboy."

Noah smiled, cleared off the counter and pulled up a couple of stools. He retrieved their bamboo reusable cutlery from a drawer and handed it to her while she set out their lunch, the routine comforting. They might as well be a married couple.

And don't think she hadn't wondered many a time whether she should be marrying Noah. He suited her perfectly. She couldn't ask for a better friend. Too bad that she wanted more in a relationship than this easy friendship.

"Want to go to a concert in Denver?" Noah asked.

He named a date in October when a band they both liked would be performing.

"You bet."

It was a pair of young Swedish women with old souls, throwbacks to sixties hippies, and their music resonated with Noah. They were also insanely talented and very young.

"How can they be successful at such an early age?" she mused.

"Adolescence lends itself to creativity. You remember how creative you were back then."

Yes, she did. It had been a magical time.

And so painful.

She'd had no female influence to guide her into womanhood. Mom had already been dead for nearly ten years. Audrey remembered being confused, with a body that was blossoming too quickly, too early. She'd hidden her loneliness under a tough veneer and her burgeoning breasts and hips under big clothes.

Dad hadn't had a clue how to help her.

"Those girls in the band were probably supported by their parents." Noah threw his sandwich wrapper into the recycle bin. "Imagine where you'd be today if your dad had supported your interest in flowers instead of pushing you into geology."

"He only wanted what was best for me."

"I know, but only *you* could decide that. Not him."

They'd been through this argument before, so Audrey said no more. Nothing either of them said would change the fact that she'd worked in an industry she shouldn't have for too long.

She was where she needed to be now, though, and just in the nick of time to take care of Dad.

Noah seemed to understand and changed the subject. "How did the standoff go at the greenhouse this morning?"

"Fine," she answered. "Gray didn't even know his father had sold the land to me."

"Figures. Dude just wants to make money so badly." He pointed his wooden spoon at her. "You watch out for that guy. He's a corporate snake in the grass. I don't doubt he can get down and dirty when he needs to."

"Relax, Noah. The sale was legal."

"I don't trust him."

"Don't worry. I'll be fine."

Audrey smiled, but Noah didn't return it, and that chilled her.

"Listen, Noah, I dealt with plenty of Gray's corporate doppelgängers in my previous job. I can be as tough as I need to be."

"Yeah, but—"

"No 'buts' about it. Seriously. I can take care of myself."

"I know you can." Noah's sentiment sounded hollow. He should be the last person on earth to condescend to her, but she knew their history made it hard for him to think of her as independent.

In high school, when she'd been only fourteen,

and too smart and a year ahead of her peers, and already trying to express her individuality with weird clothes, he'd caught a bunch of kids bullying her. Older Noah had given them hell. Even as a young teenager, Noah's personality had already been set in stone, as though he'd come out of his mother's womb fully formed. No one Audrey knew had better ethics or morals or stronger convictions, and he wasn't afraid to act on them.

When he'd rescued her from the kids making fun of her spiky hair, her big boots and her baggy clothes, when he'd taken her under his brotherly wing, she'd been grateful, but it had been an uphill battle ever since to get him to see her as a grown-up. Maybe that was why they'd stayed friends and nothing more.

Too bad Noah's version of support didn't match what she needed these days. She buried her disappointment and ate her lunch.

When she left, though, Noah called to her, "Audrey."

She turned from the doorway.

"You know I want only what's best for you, right?" He smiled, his lips full in the middle of his red beard, but creases furrowed his forehead.

Oh, Noah. He didn't even begin to get the similarities between her father and him. Hadn't they already established that Dad had always wanted what *he* thought was best for her, too?

"I understand," she said to ease his worried frown and left the shop.

GRAY TOSSED HIS pen on to the desk and took a deep, calming breath. Either that, or he would throttle the closest person. Considering that it was Dad's blameless accountant, that wouldn't be fair.

"I tried to talk Harrison out of this innumerable times," Arnie said. "He wouldn't budge. He wanted to give his people all of these benefits."

"The company can't afford them, though. I understand Dad's urge, his largesse, given how long most of his employees have worked for him, but did he have to give them everything? Massages, for God's sake. Orthodontics. *Orthotics.* Couldn't he have chosen a cheaper benefit package? Just eye glasses and dental? Did he have to opt for the whole kit and caboodle?"

"I used those arguments myself, but he was..." Arnie's glance slid away.

"Go ahead. Say it. Dad was stubborn."

"Yeah, he was. About this, at any rate."

"We have to cancel the contract with the insurance company."

If the situation hadn't been dire, Arnie's look of horror would have been funny.

"What?" Gray asked. "We have to."

"It's one thing to fight with a union or a group of employees about implementing this kind of thing, but once it's done, it just shouldn't be taken away."

Gray took another of his calming breaths. "It's either that or layoffs, right?"

Arnie's mouth became a thin slash in his aging face. "Yes."

"Layoffs are the last resort, so we get rid of the benefits." Gray glanced at his watch. Six o'clock. His head ached. He and Arnie had been hammering away at the budget, making cuts wherever they could, but the benefits package Dad had bought his employees a few years ago was the biggie.

"Come on," he said. "Hilary should have everyone gathered by now."

He stood and slid the walls of his office open. Many of the employees were already there. Turner Lumber employed over fifty people.

Some looked relaxed and others tense. Some expected him to be his dad. Others knew he wasn't.

"The cashiers are just cashing out their tills downstairs, and then they'll be up." Hilary led him to a table she'd set up along the far wall, then took a militant stance. "I put on a pot of coffee and ordered in goodies from the bakery to tide everyone over until dinnertime."

The defiance in her voice bugged him. Honest to God, she didn't get that he wasn't mean or stingy or hard-hearted, but a realist. Certain things had to change to save the company, but they could still afford doughnuts.

He was tired of tension in the company and with Hilary. He'd had to call her to task more than once for her spending of company money without his permission. Worse, she'd actually called Dad a couple of times to make sure that what Gray was doing was okay with him. The woman needed to screw her head on right. She was either for or against him.

In the meantime, she ran the everyday details that Gray didn't want to touch with a ten-foot pole. He needed more responsibility in his life like he needed a lobotomy.

What would the company do without Hilary?

"Thanks," he said, to appease her. "It was good of you to think of it."

Hilary smiled, but reluctantly.

To satisfy her further, even though he didn't have a sweet tooth, he bit into a doughnut. Hilary grinned.

Stifling a sigh, he turned away to socialize, asking about spouses and children.

When the last of the employees had finally dribbled in, Gray called for their attention.

He thanked them for their loyalty over the years and their hard work. Then, with Arnie by his side, he unloaded his bombshell.

"We're canceling the benefits package my dad gave to all of you a few years ago."

The eruption of complaints hit the rafters, the sound level sending the throbbing in Gray's temples into overdrive.

"Cripes," he mumbled to Arnie. "You'd think I was killing a litter of puppies."

"Can I say I told you so? Once you've given something to people, they take ownership. You try to take it back and they don't thank you for having given it to them in the first place. Instead, they think they're being robbed." Arnie shrugged. "Human nature."

Once Gray got the crowd under control again, he got right to the point. "Here's the alternative. Lay-offs."

Again, more grumbling, but this time more subdued. Shock, no doubt.

"I'm fighting tooth and nail to not have that happen. I've kept you all on and plan to continue to do so, but you have to work with me. We need to cut corners like crazy. The economy is bad across the country."

Mumbling all around. The employees' fear smelled metallic, like spilled blood.

"My concern," Gray continued, "is that once I let any of you go, you won't get another job. The retail, hotel and restaurant sectors of Accord are doing well because of tourism, but industry is suffering. We need to fight hard to save Turner Lumber."

He stalked to his office and slapped a hand against the office wall he'd slid open earlier. "This," he said, "will be open all day most days. If any of you have ideas on how to cut costs, how to improve service to the customers so they'll return more often, how to change *anything* that will help this company stay in business, you come to me and I'll listen."

Tired to the bone, he all but mumbled, "I'm heading out now. I'm sure you all have a lot you want to discuss without the boss hovering, so stay as long as you need to. Everyone still has jobs for now. See you tomorrow morning."

He left the office. Where minutes ago, it had been full of noise, now it was silent. Perhaps they finally understood the situation. Despite how he'd tried to make changes recently, they had resisted and hadn't understood fully how bad things were.

But Gray had. Maybe now they did, too.

CHAPTER FOUR

"AUDREY!" THE PANIC in Dad's voice had Audrey dropping the dress she was sewing and running downstairs. It was seven in the morning, and she'd been up since six.

After her run-in with Gray yesterday at the greenhouses, she'd planned to wear something bold today to bolster her morale. The red dress with the huge white polka dots that she was hemming would have been perfect, but she would opt for something else.

She rushed into the living room. Dad sat in his favorite recliner rubbing his shins.

"What happened?"

"Walked into the coffee table. Why did you move it?"

She hadn't. His eyesight was failing rapidly if he couldn't see the monstrosity in front of the sofa that could house a small village.

"You have to remember to turn your head when you move. Learn to use your peripheral vision." Macular degeneration caused vision loss in the center of the field of vision. Dad could no longer see and recognize faces, not even his own daughter's. Or his own, for that matter. Good thing. It was probably a godsend that when he looked into a mirror, he wouldn't see how much he'd aged in the past year.

"It's hard walking forward while turning your head sideways," he said, voice ripe with frustration. "I try."

"I know you do. It's a huge adjustment."

She sat on the table and lifted his pant legs. "You'll be sporting some impressive bruises tomorrow."

She glanced up at his impassive face, his vibrancy drained by his affliction.

"The skin isn't broken. I'm sorry, Dad. There's nothing I can do." She rubbed his shin gently to soften that news, then stood and walked to the hall. "I'm going back up to my sewing."

"Don't."

She stopped in the doorway and watched him expectantly. Stress had ravaged his once handsome face. Deep creases bracketed his sullen mouth. *Oh, Dad.*

"Read to me," he said, sounding so much like a little boy asking for a bedtime story she almost smiled. She had wanted to work in the greenhouses before heading into Denver today.

But Dad needed her.

The more and more trouble he had with his eyesight, the more childlike he became in his demands. An avid, lifelong reader, Dad could no longer read to himself. He resisted listening to the audio books she got for him from the library. She knew it was more than stubbornness. It was fear. If he started using them, it would be an open admission of how much he had lost in his life.

And he had more worry hanging over his head. Dry macular degeneration had already caused a blind spot in the center of his vision. If his condition changed to *wet* macular degeneration, blood vessels could grow under his retinas, leaking blood and fluid, and distorting what was left of the little vision he still had.

The doctors couldn't predict whether it was a given.

Poor Dad.

It would be arrogant of Audrey to believe she understood how taxing Dad's life must be these days. Her eyesight and her health were perfect.

"Dad, I have to get to work. I can read to you this evening."

"You call that work? That shop? Mucking about with flowers?"

Audrey braced herself, heartily sick of this old argument. "The shop allows me to live in Accord with you."

"I don't need you to live with me. You didn't have to come home."

Oh, Daddy. Of course she did. She'd returned to town as soon as Dad had been diagnosed a year ago. How could she not have come home? Dad might be stubborn and unrealistic in his views that he could live alone, but she loved him. They belonged together, especially in his time of need. She was all he had left.

"I can get around this house just fine," he insisted.

"And town? Do you get around town fine?" Dad sucked in a breath. She wasn't being cruel. Just realistic. "You refuse to leave the house. How would you get your groceries?"

"I'd have them delivered. Or hire a kid to pick them up."

But they wouldn't be Audrey. They wouldn't read to him because he could no longer read to himself. They wouldn't cook him the meals he loved. Or force him to eat the healthy stuff he hated. Or spend time with him in the evenings.

Audrey held her tongue and picked up the print book from the end table. It tied into Dad's fascination with World War II. Audrey didn't get how Dad could listen to talk of war when his own son had been killed in Afghanistan.

She opened to the section on the Berlin Airlift.

Please, please, please, let me read something uplifting.

When she started reading, though, Dad said, "Not that stuff. Turn to the Invasion of Normandy. All the good stuff, all the turning points happened in the battles."

"But the good stuff for me is the wonder of the airlift and human interest stories like Uncle Wiggly Wings."

The stern set of Dad's mouth eased. "You've always been too soft."

"It's not just the human interest aspect. I love the politics. The airlift was significant, huge, the beginning of the Cold War."

"I know, but read about Normandy." His tone softened. "Please."

It destroyed Audrey to read about lives lost. They were more than numbers to her. They were all young men like Billy. She missed her brother and his goofy sense of humor. She wished like hell that he'd never joined the army. There wasn't a man on earth less suited to it than Bill.

Dad had his own way of dealing with his grief. Hearing about war, about the logistics of it, as though he could control it in some odd way by understanding it, seemed to be his way of dealing with the loss of his son.

So, she read to him about battles and casualties.

After retrieving Jerry from his kennel out back, Audrey left the house. Jerry could no longer live indoors with Dad. He'd tripped him one time too many. Not on purpose, but simply because Dad couldn't see the dog sleeping on the living room floor.

To save everyone's nerves, she'd started keeping him outside. She didn't know what she would do once the weather turned cold in the fall.

Jerry sat in the passenger seat, and Audrey rubbed his ears before dropping him off with Noah for the day. She was late getting to the greenhouses and watering her plants, and even later still getting on the road to Denver

The reason for her trip to the city was twofold. She'd set up interviews with three occupational therapists to take on Dad as a client in September after she'd won the floral competition and that monetary award. It would make a couple of months of in-house occupational therapy affordable. The year's contract would mean she could finally contribute to the household.

A therapist could teach Dad how to take care of himself, how to cook despite the darkness and the blurriness. How to do his laundry. How to get out of the house. Maybe a stranger could have luck where Audrey hadn't in persuading Dad to use a white cane. Or not. Audrey could only try. The alternative was to give up, and that was out of the question.

Dad wouldn't even go outside to walk down the street he'd lived on for nearly forty years.

Eventually, hoping for improvement in his eyesight, they would have an operation to pay for, if only Dad would give in and try it. It would take a miracle to convince him. She was taking a break for a while. Eventually, she would have to broach the subject again.

Audrey had a lot riding on getting that award. Too much. She couldn't afford to consider that she might not win.

She'd sunk all of her savings into buying the greenhouses, stocking her shop and paying rent on the store. She had yet to make much of a profit. She needed to cast her net wider than just Accord to make enough money to be comfortable.

A win in the competition would sure make that easier.

The second purpose of the trip was to take a look at the area in which she would set up her booth in the competition. She had the dimensions, but it was hard to judge without actually seeing what she had and how to use it to the best effect. She had an appointment with the woman organizing the show.

JEFF HEARD AUDREY drive away, and leaned over the far side of his armchair to pick up the breakfast he'd hidden there. Audrey fed him healthy pansy food. Egg-white omelets with spinach in them. Yuk. He wanted real food. Bacon and whole eggs.

Careful to avoid the coffee table, he walked toward the hallway with small steps, like a toddler just learning to walk and afraid of falling down. At least a toddler would have excitement mixed in with the fear, the joy of getting up off the floor and really moving.

Jeff was going backward, not gaining but losing—everything—with nothing to look forward to but more darkness and less mobility.

Crap, shit, goddamn. For a man who didn't like profanity, he sure was using a lot of it lately. He'd never let his children swear when they were growing up, but now he cursed all the time. He had a pansyassed way of doing it, though. He couldn't even say them out loud.

He swore a silent blue streak now because it was the only thing that relieved this damn frustration. Momentarily.

Feeling his way along the wall, noticing where the seams of the wallpaper he'd put up well over thirty years ago pulled away from the plaster, he wondered who was going to fix it. Who was going to take care of the things that could go wrong in an old house? Who was going to maintain what he'd spent a lifetime treasuring?

Audrey?

Between the shop, the greenhouses, sewing, cooking...and taking care of him, when would she have time? The girl was already stretched to the limit.

His fingers traced the flocked roses on the walls. Irene had chosen the paper. Too old-fashioned now. Had been even back then, but his wife had been that kind of girl. A romantic.

Like Audrey.

After Irene had died, he'd preferred his son's humor, his devil-may-care, full-speed-ahead brand of life.

Oh, the laughs they'd had.

Billy.

Jeff shook his head violently. Tears weren't allowed. They weakened a man.

Billy had understood that. He'd joined the marines. Billy had been a man to admire.

In the kitchen, Jeff dumped the omelet into the garbage and eased his way around the cupboards until he found a frying pan. He was going to make scrambled eggs, and he was going to use the yolks.

He managed to locate the container of margarine in the fridge. Margarine! What the heck was wrong with good old butter? His parents had eaten butter all of their lives and had lived into their eighties.

He cocked his head sideways to use what little peripheral vision he had. Made doing everything hard. He found the eggs, managed to break four of them into a bowl and beat them. He felt them slosh over the edge onto his hand. Careful.

After a fruitless search for the salt, he gave up. What had Audrey done with it? He didn't recognize his own cupboards, his own groceries anymore.

He placed the pan onto the large front burner. The control knob was the one on the bottom. Right?

He turned it to low.

Opening the margarine, patting his way around the counter because he was a bloody blind man, he scooped a pat of it out with a knife and scraped it on the side of the pan. He heard it sizzle. Good, he'd gotten it inside instead of on the burner.

Resting the bowl on the edge of the pan, he poured the eggs in. They bubbled and spat, and immediately the room filled with the scent of burning eggs and acrid smoke.

What the—?

He grasped the handle of the pan, smoke smothering his nose like a hot blanket, and tossed it into the sink. Only years of living and working in this room made his aim true.

By feel, he turned the burner knob until he thought it was off. He must have turned it on to high instead of to low.

Bugger, his mind screamed. Shit.

He wasn't a man anymore. If he couldn't get around, couldn't even cook his own meals, he was barely half a man.

How many ways was he a failure these days? Too many to count.

GRAY DRUMMED HIS fingers on the steering wheel of his Dad's old Volvo and cursed the vehicle from here to eternity.

It had broken down halfway between Accord and Denver. For twenty minutes, he'd been waiting for the tow truck he'd called. Time was passing, and it didn't look as if he'd make it into Denver today, leaving another day without this blackmail issue settled one way or the other.

Sure, he could wait for the DNA results, but for how long? Since he didn't trust the woman, he planned to stop at a lab in Denver to pick up a test kit on his way to her home and have her do it in front of him. How she could cheat was beyond him, but he wasn't taking chances. And, today, he could see her, test her with questions, judge her responses. Maybe denounce her outright and put the issue to bed, so he could move ahead with the other problems in his life.

"Action," he stated aloud. Life was about action. Business was all about making incisive timely decisions, and here he was sitting on the side of the highway, stymied.

When he noticed his fingers doing their neurotic dance, he grasped the steering wheel to stop them. He couldn't sit still these days. Ants crawled under his flesh.

Where had his cool, calm manner gone? Where had *he* gone?

A vehicle pulled to a stop on the shoulder of the highway in front of him. Not a tow truck. A hot-pink Mini.

A woman got out.

Audrey.

Of course, it had to be Audrey. It couldn't have been someone he liked, or at the very least, someone with whom he wasn't fighting.

She ran along the shoulder, careful, he noted, to approach on the passenger side away from traffic, calling, "Harrison?" In response to the concern on her face, he immediately rolled down the window. When she saw that it was he who was stranded and not his father, her expression eased.

"Get in," he said.

She climbed in slowly, as though reluctant to join him.

"What happened?" she asked as she sat next to him, bringing with her a cloud of her gorgeous heady perfume.

A momentary shame, a memory of how he'd left her yesterday, flooded him. In her shop, he'd scared her, and it showed now on her face. Untrusting, she crowded the door.

"I'm sorry," he said.

At her puzzled frown, he continued, "For frightening you yesterday. I did, didn't I?"

"Yes, you did. I hadn't thought you were that kind of person."

That shame burned a hot spot in his chest, and he said, "I'm not. I'm under a lot of pressure these days." He glanced at her and then quickly away. "But that's no excuse. Sorry."

"Okay."

He could feel the lovely heat of her full body warming his right arm even though she was a couple of feet away from him. Her face, though? That was pure, innocent. Did she understand what she did to men? Did she get how sexy that contrast was?

He looked out his window toward the cars streaming past them, counting them, doing anything to distract himself from her as a woman. And God, she was a woman.

"Where are you going?" he asked.

"Denver."

Denver. Exactly where he needed to be today.

"For the day or overnight?" he asked.

"Just for a couple of hours. I'm interviewing occupational therapists for my dad."

"Dad says Jeff's got macular degeneration."

"Yes. He has trouble doing anything on his own, and I need someone to come in to train him to take care of himself. I'm trying to build up my business. I'm away from the house hours on end every day."

Must have been tough to deal with. Gray still had his reservations about paying Jeff a retirement rather than making the man go on disability. He planned to pay Jeff a visit one day soon to determine how severe his vision problem was. No need to share that with Audrey, though. No sense in giving them a warning that he was coming. He needed to know exactly how bad or how good Jeff was. Was the retirement really necessary?

Audrey was going to be in Denver for only a couple of hours, but that was all he would need to determine whether the woman blackmailing Dad was a fake.

If he asked to hitch a ride with Audrey, would she ask what he was doing in Denver? Did it matter? He could always lie.

Despite plotting behind her back to check out her father, he asked, "How would you feel about having company for the drive?"

"You?" He heard the glint of humor in her voice.

She had a beautiful smile that lit up the interior of the car. "I don't mind, but on one condition."

Gray tensed. "What?"

"No talk about my selling the land. No pressure. No mention of it at all."

He glanced at her and noted signs of tension around her mouth and eyes, despite the humor. She had issues, too. Worry about her dad, he guessed. If it was more than that, he didn't want to know. They were on opposite sides of a business battle, and that precluded any and all intimacy, including simple curiosity about her life. Enough said. He ignored the tension on her face.

"No talk of selling." He'd pushed her yesterday. She'd said no. If the blackmailing woman he talked to today was a fake, some of the pressure would be off. He could take his time persuading Audrey to sell for the future benefit of his parents and Turner Lumber.

"I'm waiting for a tow truck. Are you in a rush?"

"I have an appointment, but I have a little ti—"

At that moment, they heard the truck pull up behind them.

Gray got out to talk to the driver, who popped the Volvo's hood and looked at the engine.

He tested the battery and it was fine.

"Not sure what your problem is," he said. "Maybe the alternator."

"My parents need a newer car."

"Hey," the guy responded. "These things happen to all cars. This one's in good shape. You should see some of the junk I've picked up off the roads. This car's been cherished."

Yes, Gray knew that. His dad took care of his vehicles, and they lasted forever. Too bad it had to break down today, though.

"Do you want it towed to Denver?" the tow truck driver asked. "My buddy's got a shop. He does great work."

I'll just bet he does and you get a kickback. The thought was uncharitable—Gray's frustration working overtime—but probably accurate. The guy was just trying to make a living.

"No," Gray replied. "Take it to Accord." He named the mechanic his dad had used for years and gave directions.

Audrey moved her car forward so the driver could pull up and hook up the Volvo.

Gray paid using a credit card, retrieved his briefcase from the Volvo and then folded himself like an accordion into Audrey's passenger seat.

"Cripes," he said, "I need a can opener to get in here."

She stared at his body while he climbed in. Even though it was surreptitiously done, Gray caught the admiration. She found him attractive? Well, well. Interesting.

Would he consider using it against her? You bet. Anything to help his cause.

He stared around the interior, suspicious. "You said you scrimped and saved to buy that land, and yet you're driving a Mini. They aren't cheap. And how can you possibly run a florist shop and greenhouses with something so impractical to drive?"

"It was one of my few splurges. This, and the vintage Chanel suit."

"The one you were wearing yesterday with that ridiculous hat?"

Audrey laughed. "You have something against pillbox hats?" She sobered. "I didn't know Dad was having vision problems when I bought this. He hid them for a long time. Had I known, I would have used the money differently."

"I imagine, especially given the business you now run."

"When I have to make deliveries, I use Dad's pickup truck." Her smile dimmed. "It was his pride and joy. It's got enough chrome on it to sink a ship."

Was? "What's wrong?"

"With his macular degeneration, he'll never drive it again."

That bad? The sadness throbbing in her voice had Gray looking at Audrey differently. She put on a good front.

"What are you doing away from the store today? Shouldn't you be in town drumming up business?"

"I'm closed on Mondays and Tuesdays. My big days are on the weekend."

"Why were you in the shop yesterday when I stopped in?"

"Just because the store isn't open doesn't mean I don't have work to do."

She broke the ensuing silence. "Big business in Denver today?"

"What do you mean?" There was no way in hell he was telling why he was heading into the city.

"Are you conducting a big business deal in Denver? Do you need a lot of time?"

To either find out the blackmailer was lying and rip her to shreds, or determine that she might, *might,* be telling the truth? "Nope. An hour should be more than plenty."

Considering that Gray had broken down more than halfway to Denver, and the drive total was an hour long, they traveled for a good fifteen minutes in silence, because Gray found it hard to concentrate on conversation when Audrey's scent and heat and sheer feminine presence filled the cramped interior like thick humidity from a summer storm.

Gray had a fondness for making love in the summer, loved the slip and slide of sweaty bodies during sex.

For the rest of the drive, he tucked his hands under his thighs and gratefully counted telephone poles to kill the temptation to reach for the curves that would make sweaty summer sex sublime.

Sex with Audrey would be nuclear. How could he be so sure of that? He just knew. With her sense of drama and his pure lust, between the two of them they could conjure up one hell of a summer storm.

Thunder, lightning, a tornado or two. The whole nine yards.

Once in downtown Denver, he asked to stop at the lab where he needed to get the test kit.

"I'm sorry to ask, but can you wait?" It was too far to walk from the lab in this industrial and commercial development to the woman's house. Man, he hated being dependent on people.

"How long will this take?" she asked.

"Five minutes."

She relaxed. "I have time. Go ahead. I'll wait and then drive you to your other address."

He almost stumbled getting out of the car, to escape those hot images that had driven the temperature in the small vehicle into the stratosphere, despite the air conditioning going full blast.

In the lab, he bought a DNA test kit, then returned to the car.

Ten minutes later, Audrey dropped him off in front of a coffee shop. They arranged a pick-up location, then she drove away.

Paranoid creature that he was, Gray had purposely asked her to leave him a couple of blocks from the woman's address. He didn't want anyone from Accord knowing about her, least of all someone who might somehow use it against him in their battle about the land.

He walked the rest of the way, his outrage growing with each step.

Even if, *if,* this woman was for real, she had no

right to blackmail his father. She was no better than an opportunist taking advantage of an old man, trying to stir up trouble in a stable, respected family.

He felt better with each step.

Action.

First, he'd take her by surprise by showing up. She wouldn't expect him. If she expected anyone, it would be Dad, an old man past his prime. Possibly, she thought she could manipulate him. She wouldn't expect Gray, though.

Next, if the kid was home, he'd get a good look at him. Photographs lied, could be interpreted wrongly.

Third, he'd get that DNA test. He was sweating again, the shirt he'd put on fresh this morning already drenched.

Fourth, he'd find out why she needed so much money. Four hundred thousand dollars. Mom and Dad were well-off and Gray was a successful businessman, but that amount staggered him. *Floored* him. His pace picked up.

And last, he had to figure out the worst-case scenario. What if she did take her photos and birth certificate to the papers? Who outside of Accord would care? Mom and Dad had often attended fund-raisers in Denver and had been part of an active community. Were they still? How many of their peers were still alive? *Would* it matter if this got out?

This morning, Mom had been so excited about the latest book she'd bought about Jackie Kennedy. She'd sat in the living room in her gracious and graceful glory with her cup of tea, a civilized woman who'd raised a civilized son. But, at this moment, he wanted to do serious damage to a woman who threatened his family.

When it came right down to it, what people thought didn't matter, neither those in Accord, nor Mom and Dad's acquaintances in Denver. What mattered was Mom and what this would do to her.

If it were true.

He stopped in front of an old, run-down house, breathless because he'd been practically running in his need to settle this.

Gray double-checked the address on the slip of paper on which he'd jotted it. Yep, right place.

A rusty bike lay on its side on the front lawn, but otherwise, the house was tidy, the grass trimmed.

Everything needed a coat of paint, but both the walkway and the veranda had been swept recently.

Acid churned in Gray's belly. He knocked on the front door. Despite his resolve to get rid of this woman and the anger that ate at him, his pulse beat erratically in his throat.

What if it was true? What if he was about to meet his sibling?

A moment later, a young boy stood in the open doorway and Gray's breath caught. The photo hadn't lied, had been an accurate portrayal of the tow-headed boy in front of him, a miniature version of Gray himself.

No, no, no. He did not want this to be true, *hated* that Dad could have betrayed Mom.

"How old are you?" he blurted.

"Nine. Who are you?"

"Tell your mother Grayson Turner is here."

A woman entered the hallway behind the boy and stared at Gray, eyes wide and filled with a certain amount of fear.

Good. She should be afraid. Even if she was Dad's daughter, blackmail was evil.

In her mid-thirties, she could be pretty with the right haircut and good clothes. She'd pulled her blond hair into a ponytail, and though trim in a white T-shirt and faded jeans, she looked tired. Gray wasn't sure what he'd expected—maybe trailer trash. He'd always loathed the term, had thought it unduly harsh, but he'd been so rattled and angered by Shelly's attempt at blackmail he'd used it in his mind as an invective when thinking of her.

"I expected someone older." Her voice trembled. "I'm Shelly Harper. Are you his son? I didn't think anyone would come here."

"May I come in?" If his tone was cold, hard, too bad. This woman had the power to ruin his family. And, yeah, she could be his sister. There was an unsettling family resemblance in the cut of her cheekbones, in the lips and strong chin.

She nudged the boy to go down the hallway and stepped aside for Gray to enter. The boy looked between the two of them, sensed the aggression in Gray and shook his head. His little lips thinned. "I'm staying with you, Mom."

Kid had balls.

The smile his mother gave him, though tremulous, was sweet. "No, Sam. I'm fine. I need you to go to the kitchen and make peanut butter sandwiches. Take care of Tiffany and eat your lunch. Can you do that for me?"

"Are you sure, Mom?"

"Yes. I need to talk to Mr. Turner alone."

Sam glared at Gray before he turned to leave, a very grown-up warning in his childish eyes. *Don't hurt my mom.*

Gray had to admire the boy's defiance, but he *would* destroy the kid's mother if he had to.

The woman stared at Gray, her face alive with curiosity, but also hunger. Why? It didn't look like greed—more like need.

"You do know that blackmail is illegal?" he asked. "A federal offense?"

Her eyes looked haunted. "I know," she whispered. "Come into the living room. Please. We need to talk."

She went through a doorway and Gray followed.

A sound, a near moan, caught his attention. Propped among pillows on the sofa, his body twisting forward on itself, his head leaning to one side, a boy stared out through the front window.

Shelly adjusted the pillows to support him better. The boy turned and smiled at Gray.

"This is my son Joe," she said.

Gray didn't know how to ask the question without being rude. "Is he…?" *Mentally whole?*

Shelly guessed his concern. "He's completely cognizant. Very aware. It's just his *body* that doesn't work the way it should."

Gray flushed. It must be a common question, but he was ashamed he'd almost asked it anyway.

"He needs a wheelchair to prevent a spinal curvature that would interfere with his breathing," Shelly said quietly, and he could tell that the effort it took to admit to her needs, to her own failure to provide as a parent, cost her in pride. If pride were a currency, this woman's bank account was overdrawn. "He needs support for his scoliosis."

A high-pitched squeal erupted from the kitchen, and then the patter of tiny feet sounded down the hallway. A whirlwind of blond, pink outrage burst into the room.

"Mommy, Sammy won't let me have juice." A tiny girl flew against her mother. Shelly picked her up and wiped the tears from her cheeks. Gray wasn't sure he'd ever seen a prettier little girl. He guessed she was about four years old.

Like the toys scattered about the room, her sundress was old, most likely bought used, but it was clean and ironed. Her feet were bare.

"You can have juice only once a day, sweetie. You know that."

"Want some more." The girl hiccupped.

"I know." A flash of pain crossed Shelly's face.

"Have water instead. Tomorrow morning you can have more juice."

The kid could only have juice once a day? Maybe Shelly was afraid of cavities. A woman without money wouldn't be able to afford dental bills.

"Hey, midget," Sam called from the kitchen. "We don't have the money. Get back here and eat your sandwich. I poured you some water."

When Shelly set her daughter onto her feet on the floor, she didn't meet his eyes. Ah. The issue *was* money, but not about future dental bills. They couldn't afford juice more than once a day.

Gray thought back to his own childhood, when anything and everything had been available to him. The thought of restricting a child's intake, not because it was bad for them or because it might rot their teeth, but only because you couldn't afford to give them more, horrified Gray.

Was Shelly even able to provide real juice? Or was it colored sugar water?

No wonder the woman was all out of pride.

It made Gray's heart melt, just a little, to see such need.

"Can you smile for Mommy?" Shelly asked.

"'Kay." The girl did.

Gray stared around the living room. She had needs. Desperate needs.

So what? Why should it matter to him? She wasn't his responsibility.

"Go eat your sandwich." Shelly turned the child in the direction of the hallway.

The girl started to leave the room, but noticed Gray for the first time and stopped, her tiny mouth open.

She might be his niece, this tiny piece of extraordinary delicacy and beauty. She had his gray eyes. They might be related.

She opened one little fist and, with her other hand, picked out a piece of a crumbled saltine and handed it to him.

He hesitated, but she said, "You can have some."

He took it from her, and she smiled and, in that moment, Gray lost his heart.

"Eat," she said.

Gray put it into his mouth, but he was awash in nerves, and his mouth was so dry he had trouble swallowing the bit of cracker.

"Go on now, Tiffany," Shelly urged.

Tiffany ran from the room.

Shelly watched her daughter leave and then said, "She has a fifty percent chance of being a carrier."

"A carrier? What do you mean?"

She tilted her head toward Joe, and Gray understood. She might carry Duchenne and give it to her own child.

"She will have to be tested someday."

Gray swallowed, unnerved that a tiny perfect creature like Tiffany could carry something so harmful.

And Shelly was dealing with all of this on her own. "How long ago did your husband die?"

"Eight months. We've been getting by, but he had no insurance, and I've run through our savings. I can't work because of the children."

Joe alone would be a full-time job, Gray guessed.

"I've never done anything like this before in my life. I've never begged for money before, but my children..."

"Why so much money?"

"I need to get through the next ten years until Tiffany can take care of herself. I can live frugally, but Joe will cost me money for his treatments."

She mouthed something, so Joe wouldn't see, and it looked like, "He'll get worse."

Gray knew people, had learned in his business dealings to judge quickly and accurately, and Shelly wasn't lying.

Any and all actions this woman performed were for her kids. Desperation drove her. Gray was sorry that he'd come. It was easier to consider destroying her when she wasn't a real person, when he couldn't tell from a letter that what drove her was a consuming love for her children.

"Sell the house," he ordered. "Invest the profit and then rent."

"We don't own this house." She shrugged, a simple gesture of defeat.

Why hadn't her husband had life insurance? Why hadn't he considered this possibility and prepared his family financially? It was a man's responsibility to provide for his family, for God's sake.

"What kind of work did your husband do?"

"He was a security guard. He worked nights. On weekends, he drove a delivery truck." Shelly glared at Gray. "I can see what you're thinking. He wasn't a deadbeat. He loved his kids and he loved me, and he tried to provide for us as best he could."

She stepped closer.

"I don't have next month's rent money." She'd lowered her voice so Joe wouldn't hear. "The kids and I will be on the street or in a shelter. I don't know what I'll do with Joe. He needs occupational and physical therapy that I just can't afford."

Like a bad nightmare, the woman's tenuous situation got worse and worse.

"That's why I wrote the letter." She went to the sofa, took a hankie out of her pocket, and wiped the spittle slowly drizzling from Joe's mouth. "Your father never gave my mom a cent to help raise me. I guess I'm asking for all the child support he never paid."

"I can't believe my dad never gave your mother support. He's a good man. He takes care of his responsibilities."

"That's not the impression my mom got. She said he seemed to treat everything in life like a game. When he ran away after she told him she was pregnant, she figured she'd never contact the SOB again." She realized she was talking about Gray's father and said, "Sorry, that's just the impression my mom got of him. She worked hard to raise me without taking a dime from my father. She had a lot of pride."

Gray raised one brow. "And you don't?"

For a long moment she said nothing while her throat worked. "I used to. I can't afford it anymore."

She sighed. "It's easier for me to think of this as support my mom was owed all along rather than to call it blackmail. I'm good with money. I can make what I asked for last years. You don't have to worry. I won't ever come back for more."

She stared at him with that hunger again, cataloging every detail about him. "Are there more of you?"

"What do you mean?"

"I mean you're my half brother. Do I have more? A sister, maybe?"

She looked so hopeful he hated to disabuse her. "No," he said a little sadly. "There's only me." And he'd always felt his solitude keenly.

Her tentative smile warmed him. "That's one more sibling than I had before you walked in that door."

His mind couldn't fathom that this woman might be his sister, couldn't let go of the feeling that he'd wanted something like this for a long time, and that it might finally be true.

Damn illusions, though. He couldn't live with illusions.

He took the test he'd picked up from the lab and held it up.

She watched him curiously.

"Let's find out what's real and what isn't," he said.

He opened the kit and took out a cotton swab on a long stick. "Open up."

Her face flattened, and whether it was embarrassment or outrage, it didn't matter to Gray. He was getting this done. No way was he handing nearly half a million dollars to a stranger based on a kid's face and a woman's smile that might be the same as his own, and a family similarity that could simply be coincidence.

"I can do it myself," she said. "Give me the test and I'll go to the bathroom."

"No. We do it here. Now."

He watched her swallow her self-respect. She stepped closer and opened her mouth. He swabbed the inside of her cheek, making sure the cotton was soaked with her saliva.

Her chest rose and fell too quickly, and her cheeks turned red.

His own breathing grew unsteady. He'd been raised better than this, with old-fashioned values, to never invade a person's space and their privacy. He'd been taught to treat others with respect, but this *had* to be done.

Hardening his emotions, he pulled a couple of hairs from her head to add to the kit. Shelly had brought this on herself. He was merely protecting his family.

He sealed the kit in front of her, then put it away in his briefcase where another envelope sat, contain-

ing hairs Gray had taken from his father's brush that morning. It looked as if one of them had the root still attached. With a little luck, it would be enough.

Turning to leave, his guilt not assuaged despite ordering himself to stop caring about these people, his gaze fell on Joe.

Could Gray walk away? Could he reasonably leave these people to fend for themselves when their hardship was so dire? Whether or not they were related? Gray had never lacked a darned thing in his life.

He pulled his checkbook out of his briefcase, ignoring the papers he'd had drawn up for Shelly to sign, relinquishing all claims to his father and his money. Intuitively, he knew she wouldn't. She believed every word she'd said. Gray understood what Shelly probably didn't, that her mother could have lied to her about who her father was.

He wrote a check to cover the rent, plus a couple of hundred extra for groceries.

If it turned out that this was all a scam, then it would be the first time Gray had ever been taken for a ride. Somehow, he knew...his chest hurt...he knew...his pen slipped in his fingers...she could be, might be, was likely family.

Dad. Who are you really?

He handed the check to her and said, "I'll get more to you when I can."

Torn into two men, on the one side a savvy businessman and on the other just a lonely guy, he rushed from the house.

Because his emotions were too close to the surface, and he hated that, and because Shelly looked as though she might cry, he walked down the street without looking back. He had no choice but to help this woman, which meant he needed to get his hands on all of that money she'd asked for her.

Awash in disappointment that his task hadn't turned out the way he'd hoped, that he couldn't write Shelly off as a phony, or an opportunist, he nearly missed seeing a convenience store on the corner.

He'd given her money for groceries but wanted to do more. In fact, he wanted to give Tiffany juice. He wanted her to be able to go to her older brother and not only ask for a glass whenever she wanted it, but to actually be given one.

Once inside the store, he cursed himself. "Sentimental fool," he whispered.

Even so, he bought two big jugs of orange juice and a couple gallons of milk. Sam was too thin, so he also picked up half a dozen packages of sliced meats and cheeses, as well as whole wheat bread, containers of potato and macaroni salad, along with ice cream and four chocolate bars, one for each of them, including the mother. Somehow, he doubted she would eat hers, would probably hide it away to share among the kids another day.

Then, because he wondered about what that chocolate and the extra juice might do to a kid's teeth, he bought three new toothbrushes and a tube of toothpaste—one with a good, cavity-fighting record.

On impulse, he picked up a tiny pair of pink flip-flops decorated with turquoise glass beads. They almost fit in the palm of his hand.

Fool. He didn't care.

Leaving the bags on the veranda, he rang the doorbell and strode away hard and fast. He didn't want to be caught, as though giving, charity, were an action of which he should be ashamed.

Halfway down the street, he leaned against a tree, out of sight, and watched.

Sam opened the door, stared at the bags of groceries, then yelled for his mom.

All but the boy on the sofa crowded onto the veranda.

Tiffany squealed and pulled a jug of juice from a bag and barely missed dropping it on her toes before Sam snagged it.

"Juice, Sammy. *Pease.*"

Sam went back inside.

Shelly turned away and surreptitiously wiped her cheeks. She peered up and down the street, but Gray hid behind the tree. When he peeked back out, she had stopped searching for him and was going through the bags.

In danger of becoming maudlin, Gray turned to leave but heard Tiffany squeal again. Was it a normal part of her speech? He'd heard it three times within the past half hour.

Tiffany had discovered the cheap sandals and sat on the top step to put them on. Shelly disappeared inside the house with the groceries, leaving Tiffany alone on the veranda admiring her pink-and-turquoise-clad feet.

Was she safe? Gray studied the street. There was no one else around.

A moment later, Sam ran outside with a pink plastic cup in one hand and a fistful of cold cuts in the other.

He handed Tiffany her juice and a slice of cheese and said, "See ya later, Tiff. Tell Mom I'll be at Brian's playing."

Jumping on to the rusty bike, he took off down the street, shoving meat into his mouth while he steered with the other hand.

Gray shook his head. No helmet. Too dangerous. His immediate burst of anger at the kid's mom dissipated. If he had to choose between food for his children and buying a bike helmet, the decision would be a no-brainer.

The front window curtain fluttered, and Gray realized that Shelly was watching her daughter while she sat on the step and drank her juice and ate her cheese, chattering to herself. And stared at those silly, cheap sandals.

Like a sap, he strode away fast because tears threatened.

Whew. Too much emotion flooded him—satisfaction that he'd helped a needy family, bittersweet happiness that he had a sister, regret that Dad hadn't done more for his illegitimate child and last, anger at the father he loved so much.

Also, he felt a surge of hope. He had a family. Lately, he'd been aware of his parents' ages. Any day now, Gray could be on his own. Completely.

Suddenly, here and today, he had a family. An emptiness that had started in the middle of his childhood was slowly filling up. He had a family, he thought, wonder filling him until he felt light-headed.

He walked away, another amorphous feeling in his chest taking shape and developing a name. Pride. In himself. He'd done something good. Really good.

His heart swelled and filled with the milk of human kindness, something he'd always blasted in his cynical way.

If his colleagues could only see him now, they wouldn't believe what he'd just done. Rather than annihilating an opponent, he'd actually helped one out.

He couldn't stop here. He needed the rest of the money that Shelly was demanding. If he were in her shoes, he wouldn't let up the pressure until he got it.

Gray had bought them a few weeks with his check, but Shelly would be back. In her situation, he wouldn't stop until he had everything he'd asked for. He wouldn't trust nebulous promises about more money to come in the future. He'd want it all in the bank now.

His fingers gripped the handle of his briefcase. He wasn't a complete fool. The DNA test would go back to the lab, even though he suspected the result was a foregone conclusion.

He needed Audrey to sell. Torn between elation and despair, hands tied, he understood that the decision had been taken out of his hands.

He was going to have to betray Dad.

CHAPTER FIVE

AUDREY HAD INTERVIEWED three therapists in a local coffee shop, separately. One she hadn't liked at all, one was okay, and the third was wonderful. She felt like Goldilocks choosing a chair or a bed to sleep in, but the one who felt "just right," Teresa Grady, had backbone. She could handle Dad. She also had compassion, which Dad sorely needed.

Teresa would be happy to come to Accord in September. Audrey had booked her for two full months.

Now, Audrey was here in the huge conference center, striding toward the back with a sinking heart. She'd come to check out exactly where her booth would be. She'd been sent measurements, but they'd seemed so small, she couldn't believe they were accurate. She wanted to see it in person, so she could judge exactly how she would design the space. She hadn't expected to be in the back of the room.

Janeen Walken led her to the far end of the sterile space. "Here you are."

Audrey's booth would be backed into a corner as far from the front doors as possible. They might as well have buried her in concrete. "You've got to be kidding. Why am I stuck back here where no one will see me?"

"Lot selection was done by lottery."

Not being a cynical person by nature, and not sure why she was suspicious, she didn't believe that a twist of fate had put her back here. "Where will Bolton Florists be displayed?" Bolton was the largest floral franchise in the west.

When Janeen hesitated, Audrey knew she'd hit on something.

"Answer my question," she demanded.

Janeen took her to a spot across from the front door where everyone would see Bolton the second they walked into the show.

Lottery, my patootie.

The show would be juried, but also, a portion of the winning vote would be determined by show attendees. In other words, the paying public, who would be influenced by how easy the displays were to locate, would be voting on what they saw. They would be voting for their favorites, but how could a booth become their favorite if they couldn't find it?

They had to be able to see them to vote fairly.

"This is a prime spot," Audrey said. *"The* best spot. You expect me to believe that Bolton *happened* to win this by lottery?"

Janeen's gaze slid away. "Yes."

"Give me a break. You and your peers are frauds. You've been bought."

Janeen's expression hardened. "How dare you?"

"Seriously? Do you really think that everyone is so stupid that they won't see the truth?" Her voice echoed in the empty cavernous chamber. "The largest floral franchise in the west is up front while the new kid on the block is in the back corner."

Janeen shrugged but didn't respond.

"Someone must consider me serious competition." Audrey stepped forward and poked her finger toward the woman's chest, careful that she made no actual contact, no matter how provoked. "I'm going to win this contest. Unlike Bolton and whoever else is your pet, I'm going to win fairly."

"Are you threatening a member of my board?" The deep voice came from behind Audrey. She spun around.

Walter Reed stood a few feet away. He'd been a friend of Harry Bolton's for years. The floral industry in the state was surprisingly small. Everyone knew everyone else's business. As soon as she'd opened her shop, she'd found out everything she could about her competition.

Bolton was huge, had been in business for years and produced the same arrangements they'd been designing for most of those years.

Audrey wanted to breathe fresh creative energy into the industry. People were ready for innovation. She was sure of it.

The contract with the hospital that was being offered as part of the prize was currently held by Bolton.

Harry would fight tooth and nail to keep it, including getting down and dirty about it. Pun intended.

How on earth it had slipped out of Harry's hands and into this year's prize package was a mystery. Audrey had heard rumors, though, that people *were* tired of white carnations and red roses. They wanted something new.

And Audrey could, and would, deliver when she won this competition. *Take that, Harry Bolton and all of your old cronies, and stuff it where the sun don't shine.*

"You can't threaten Janeen." For a big man, Walter Reed moved as soundlessly as a sly cat. She hadn't heard him approach. "Do you want to end up in court?" he asked.

"Where was there a threat in what I just said?" Her blood boiled, but she could deal with this guy. "I made a promise. I'm going to win. How is that a threat? Be careful what you accuse me of, Walter, unless *you* want to end up in court.

"As I just said to Janeen, I plan to win *fairly*. Unlike others in this competition."

She stalked from the building, her pulse beating like a maraca. This was bad. So bad. She'd need a plan, a strategy to bring customers to the back of the vast room. With nothing in it, it felt like an airplane hangar. Full of participants with large floral displays, Audrey would be buried. Insignificant.

She'd just booked Teresa for September and, without the win, she would have to go into debt to pay her. As well, both she and Dad lived on his retirement package from Turner Lumber.

If Audrey couldn't bring in more money from the business, she would have to continue to live on his earnings. He'd worked hard all of his life. That money was his. She was a grown woman. She should be supporting herself.

Ten minutes later, still panicking despite how confident she'd sounded with Janeen and Walter, she picked up Gray in front of the coffee shop as per their arrangement.

When he got into the car, though, she sensed that something about him had changed, shifted.

"Can we stop at the lab again?" he asked.

"Sure." She waited for more, but he was staring out the window. "Are you okay?"

"Hmm?" He turned to her, and she was surprised that his regard, hazed by distraction, wasn't razor-sharp, wasn't ready to skewer her because she was an enemy. "Oh. Yeah. I'm good."

When his glance landed on her face, his gaze did sharpen. "*You* don't look okay. What's happened?"

Should she tell him? He would probably laugh. It would so work to his advantage. She could imagine him rubbing his hands together like a cartoon villain.

He did look different, though. There was a softness about him that hadn't been there on their way into Denver. She didn't know what kind of meeting he'd just had, but it must have been a good one.

Not that she would trust him completely. She wasn't *that* naive.

"I just checked out my booth placement for the show. It's in the back of the building, in the far corner, while Bolton Florists will be front and center. They had the nerve to tell me it had been done fairly by lottery selection. Fairly! Ha!" Gray watched her with a bemused frown. "Can you believe it? I told them I was going to win, and I will."

She'd suffered a setback, sure, but damned if she'd let it kill her.

She explained about how the voting would work. "If no one sees my entry, how can they vote for it?"

"Do you have a plan?" Gray asked.

"I'll drag people to the back if I have to. I'll dress up like a clown to get their attention. I'll do whatever it takes."

"You really want to win this, don't you? Why? Why is it so important to you?"

"You mean apart from the monetary award?"

"Let's start with that."

"It's $25,000, which is significant. Also, though, there's a one-year contract involved that would have me delivering arrangements weekly to a boutique hotel in Denver and—" she lifted one finger because this was significant "—*all* of the flowers and arrangements in the hospital gift shop."

Gray whistled and nodded. "Good one."

She smiled. As a business owner, he got it.

"What do you plan to do with the cash award?" he asked. "Expand your business?"

She stopped at a red light. "Pay for the occupational therapist I need to hire for my father. Just for a couple of months. He can't do much for himself. He's slipping into depression."

She tried to keep her own blues from her voice, but every day, no matter how hard she tried to remain positive, a low-grade sadness plagued her.

Most of the time she managed to either bury it or rise above it, but sometimes when it felt as if the whole world conspired against her, she could no longer hold it at bay.

"How does macular degeneration manifest?" Gray asked.

"Dad can't see in the center of his vision. He can't read. He used to devour books."

"Is there anything that can be done?"

"Some people have luck with surgery. We don't have the money for that."

"Why not use the money to get him surgery rather than hiring a therapist?"

"Two reasons. One, there are no guarantees that it will work. And two, convincing Dad he should risk surgery is like trying to fly a kite in a hurricane. He's terrified of anyone cutting into any part of him. I mean, really terrified."

"Why? Bad experience when he was young?"

"Worse. Bad experience with my mom. She went into the hospital to have her appendix removed and never came out alive. It ruptured while they were prepping her and they couldn't save her."

"That's not an unsuccessful surgery. That's nature, the body failing."

"Tell that to my dad. He thinks they botched the surgery and killed her."

"That's not a reasonable reaction."

"No, it isn't, but he was crazy with grief after Mom died, and nothing and no one could console him. He's been afraid of anything to do with illness or surgery ever since."

"So...you'll live with his decision and hire a therapist."

"Yes. I think if there were someone in the house all day with him, he would have a distraction. He would eat properly while I'm at work. The therapist could take him out, could convince him to become involved in the community again. Would teach him *how* to become involved again."

They'd arrived at the lab.

"Okay, makes sense," Gray said, an uncharacteristic understanding in his voice. "Hold that thought. I want to know more, but I need to drop off something."

Again, he was gone for all of five minutes then they headed out of the city.

Gray picked up the thread of their conversation. "Is the money the only reason why you want to win so badly? I mean, for me it would be." He grinned. "I'm guessing for you, there's more."

With a rueful tip of her lips, she said, "You're right. It isn't the only consideration. While I need the money and the win would be good for business, would in fact be huge, it's also an emotional thing for me. It's a whole lot more than the award. It would be a validation that I made the right choice in giving up one career for another."

After a moment's hesitation, she said, "It was my mom who gave me my love of gardening. I can barely remember her, but I do know that she loved roses and dahlias, and her gardens were a blaze of color. It's—" She shifted uneasily in her seat, afraid to trust Gray with too much.

"What?" His voice sounded new, different, compassionate.

A brief glimpse of his expression confirmed she hadn't imagined the sympathy.

"When I'm gardening, I feel close to her. I sometimes feel her presence."

He didn't scoff, and she could have kissed him for that.

His brows rose, as though he'd just had a thought.

"So, if you loved it so much, why didn't you just do that instead of studying geology?"

"My dad."

"He wanted you to study geology? Why?"

"He wanted me to *not* garden."

From the corner of her eye, she saw him nod.

"I'd want my children to go into something that made more money, too."

"It wasn't that. I look too much like my mom. My love of gardening reminds him too much of her."

"That's why your dad doesn't want you to own a floral shop. It keeps reminding him of her."

"Bingo." His insight impressed her. "It pains him to see me have anything to do with flowers and gardening. All of these years later, he should be over the loss, but—" she shrugged "—he isn't."

"I guess we heal at our own pace."

"It's been thirty years. When I first came home last year, I did put a garden in around the house, but I caught him staring at me through the window when I was planting. I couldn't stand the sorrow on his face. I had to stop right away and never went back to it."

"His grief didn't stop you from opening your shop."

"Dad doesn't have to actually see me doing that. It's away from the house."

"Hey, a thought. If your dad stopped you from gardening after your mom died, how did you keep the interest alive?"

She smiled, because the memories were so bittersweet. "I made myself a little patch in the woods. I begged, borrowed and stole seeds, and grew flowers in the wild. It kept Mom alive for me. And, of course, y—"

Oh, dear God, she'd almost blurted the truth. She had almost said, "Your mother gave me a piece of her garden." It was one of the things she was certain he wouldn't remember, and one of those things she knew Abigail wouldn't want her to share with Gray, wouldn't *want* him remembering.

Gray asked, "There was what?"

"I was just going to say that I had my ways. I gardened with my aunt until she died."

When he looked as if he might pursue it further, she ended with, "It's my vocation. What I desire to do more than anything else on earth."

Gray nodded, then stared out the window at the passing scenery.

"What about you, Gray?"

He turned back, expression surprised and alert. "What about me?"

"Is the business your vocation? Is it what you were meant to be doing?"

She felt him stare at her profile for a long time, but she had the sense he wasn't seeing her.

He didn't answer the question. Whatever he was thinking or feeling was firmly locked away from her.

ON WEDNESDAY MORNING, Audrey thought she'd made it out of the house without Dad stopping her, but then heard a "Hmph" from the living room. It was only seven, and she was heading out to put in a couple of hours in the greenhouses before opening the shop.

After yesterday's trip to Denver, she really couldn't afford the time to read to him this morning.

She peeked around the doorway.

"Dad, how are you feeling today?"

"Not great. Rotten." He looked haggard. Bags darkened the skin beneath his eyes.

"Did you sleep at all last night?"

"No."

"I'll fix you an omelet and fruit salad before I go." She'd found yesterday's egg-white omelet in the garbage can and the burned frying pan in the sink. She'd made him toast this morning, but maybe that wasn't enough.

"I don't want a bowl of fruit."

Audrey suppressed a laugh. He made *fruit* sound like a dirty word. "I'll have the omelet, though. Use real eggs."

"I always use real eggs."

"You just use the whites. There's no flavor in those."

Audrey sighed. "They're healthy, Dad. I want to keep *you* healthy." She'd lost her mother and her brother. Would anyone blame her for trying to keep her father healthy? She had no one else.

For all they knew, his macular degeneration had been brought on by his unhealthy, cholesterol-laden food choices. Or it could have been the thirty years of smoking. Thank goodness he'd managed to quit. The doctors said that either one could have caused the problem.

"I don't care about being healthy," he said, sounding peevish. "What's the point?"

Had he meant to stab her in the heart? To imply that he didn't matter to her? That she didn't matter to him? Didn't he understand that she had no one else but him?

"What's the *point?* Mom's dead—" he flinched "—and Billy's dead—" another flinch "—but *I'm* still here."

Dad's face tightened, and he seemed to stop breathing.

She fought to bring herself under control. She didn't hurt people like this, but damn it, he was all she had left. Why didn't he get that?

"Dad." Her voice wavered. "Don't I matter to you?" Pathetic question. *She* was pathetic, always chasing his love and respect. For Dad, it had always been about Billy. Wasn't it dumb that she was so jealous of her dead brother?

He softened, his chest folding gently and his shoulders easing. "You matter," he said, barely above a whisper.

The breath she'd been holding whistled out of her. "If that's true, if you won't take care of yourself for *you,* do it for *me.*"

He covered his face with one hand. "It's hard."

She was on her knees on the floor in front of him in a flash. "I know. Oh, Dad, I do know. I can see how hard it is." A tear slipped down her cheek, and she brushed it away.

"I don't want to lose you." She stood abruptly. "Here's the deal. I'll make you an omelet with whole eggs and two slices of bacon—"

"Only two?" A grin tugged at the corner of his mouth. He liked negotiating.

"Two," she said, her tone emphatic. "I'm already compromising on the egg yolks. In return for my beneficence, you have to eat a bowl of fruit."

He scowled, but it had no heat behind it. Her anger must have frightened him. Or maybe it was her question. *Don't I matter to you?*

"Okay," he said grudgingly, as though he were giving her a huge concession, when, really, she was the one who'd given in, wasn't she?

She went to the kitchen to speed her way through making an omelet with whole eggs.

She spread toast with margarine instead of butter, but added the raspberry jam he liked. When she set the tray on his lap, she kissed his forehead and touched his shoulder. Almost all of the brawn and muscle were gone. Dad used to be so strong.

"I'll see you at dinnertime," she said. "I'll barbecue steaks and corn on the cob." His favorites.

"Okay, good." He sounded mollified.

She stepped out of the room and around the corner so he wouldn't see when she rested her hand over her heart. They'd had their arguments over the years, always about what she should do with her life, and there'd been some real doozies, but, oh, she couldn't stand what the macular degeneration was doing to him.

Worse, she couldn't stand that he wouldn't fight. This anger that churned inside of her scared her. She rarely lost her cool. But being angry with Dad at this time seemed wholly inappropriate. Guilt flared. He needed patience, not her judgment.

Until a month ago, she'd come home from the shop every day to fix him his lunch, but he'd stopped eating it. All he wanted to do was sleep.

She let him, but she knew depression when she saw it.

Dad was wasting away in every way.

Now, Audrey paid one of their neighbors to bring him lunch, but as often as not it went uneaten. The bottom line was that Dad needed to learn to do for himself, to be independent, to try to become again the active man he'd always been. He needed to get back his pride.

Having someone in to *do* things for him was not the answer. Having someone teach *him* to do was.

He needed to get out of the house and to be distracted from his depression.

She hung her head, giving in to the inevitable. Dad needed a therapist now, not in September. She would have to call Teresa to see when she could start. She would have to go into debt to pay Teresa's salary and then pay it off once she won the contest, the win being an arrogant assumption. She had no choice. She had to believe she would succeed.

She stepped back into the living room and broached the subject gently. "Dad, I've been thinking that I need some help around here."

He stopped chewing and looked at her blankly. "Help? You mean like a maid? Can we afford one?"

"No. I don't mean a maid. I mean an occupational therapist."

The sound of Dad's cutlery hitting his plate rang discordantly in the room. "I don't need a babysitter." The jut of his jaw became mulish. Underneath the anger, the stubbornness, she saw desperation.

"I don't mean a babysitter," she assured him. "I mean someone to teach you how to do things for yourself." Audrey knelt in front of him again, knowing that her face would be nothing but a blur, but needing to be close. "If I win the competition, I'll have the award money and I'll have that regular money coming from the hospital contract."

She took one of his hands in hers, but judging by the rigidity of his fist, he wasn't going to listen to reason. Still, she had to try. "I need to be able to focus on work. A therapist would be here every day to make sure you learn how to cook and eat properly and to get you out if you need to go."

Dad didn't respond. Audrey tried to put herself in his place. If she were him, she would miss the loss of her independence keenly.

"This will work out for the best." Still, Dad said nothing. She stood. There wasn't much more she could do to convince him that this would work.

She left the room and had just opened the front door when she heard Dad's breakfast tray and all of the dishes and cutlery on it hit the living room wall.

Her stomach turned over. She couldn't go back in to face him, not when her own anger boiled too hot, when she might say something she couldn't take back, that would hurt him too much. She'd have to clean up later. She fled the house. She *had* to get away from it and all of its attendant darkness.

JEFF HELD HIMSELF still until he heard the front door close and Audrey's car leave the driveway.

Then…he crumpled.

Even more than Audrey wanting to bring a stranger into his home, her question had shocked him.

Don't I matter to you?

What had he ever done to lead his daughter to believe he didn't care? How could she think that? He loved her dearly.

All that time he'd spent with Billy? It was easier. Billy was easy. Jeff would take him out back and toss the football around, or grab a baseball and a couple of gloves and toss the ball back and forth for hours. No questions that Jeff didn't know how to answer. No heavy conversations about emotion and grief.

What did he know about little girls?

He'd been happy to have Abigail and Harrison Turner take her on outings. Abigail could relate to Audrey. Jeff couldn't, but he'd never meant to make her feel unloved.

Lordy, how was he supposed to make this right? He wasn't a man who just blurted *I love you* to those around him.

He'd behaved like a child. He could at least clean up. He scooted forward in the armchair and dropped on to his knees on the floor. Weaving his way through the furniture, he found the tray, then felt around for cutlery, dipping his fingers into the omelet by mistake. He tossed it on to the tray.

He couldn't make Audrey come home to this. He hadn't heard the plate break, so he assumed he wouldn't get a nasty surprise like a chip of broken china in his finger or palm.

Working as best he could, he picked up what he could find, put it on the tray and carried it to the kitchen, yet again exasperated that a trip that should take thirty seconds took him five minutes.

Once there, he managed to fill the sink with water and dish detergent—too much, judging by how high the suds were—and washed the plate and cutlery and tray, along with the cooled frying pan.

He carried a damp sponge to the living room to clean the wall but had no idea how much jam he got and how much he left behind.

He sighed, long and hard. He never used to be peevish or childish. He used to be a strong man, admired and respected. Where had his strength gone?

He didn't want a stranger in here teaching him how to cook and dress and brush his teeth. He didn't want a stranger touching Irene's things or changing things. Changing *anything*.

He didn't want a therapist. He didn't want change.

He couldn't stop it.

He ran his palm over the wall, but couldn't tell what was clean and what wasn't.

He'd have to ask his neighbor, Essie, to help him when she brought in his lunch.

GRAY JOGGED ALONG the edge of the highway, ran as if his life depended on his sweating every drop of moisture out of his body, willing the sweat to leach his toxic grief and anger out of him.

The questions that had bothered him yesterday persisted. Had Dad been unfaithful to Mom? Was he capable of cheating? Was Shelly Gray's sister?

The warm fuzzies that had filled him after giving the money and food to the family had dissipated once he'd returned to reality in Accord.

He ran hard, his feet slapping the damp pavement like fish on water, and waited for the endorphins to kick in.

He'd been a runner since college. It had proven to be a guaranteed stress reliever.

Not today.

Slap, slap, slap.

He hadn't slept last night. Hadn't eaten breakfast this morning. Hadn't been able to think coherently about the issues at work, or anything else.

His head hurt. His stomach churned. Those red crescents in his palms, made by his fingernails when he clenched his fists, seemed to be permanent.

He'd become what he'd always feared—a rational man who'd lost control of his life. And yet, wasn't he busting his butt to find solutions? He could. He could make this all come out right one way or another.

He ran and ran. Slap. Slap. Slap. Still, those elusive endorphins refused to show.

Normally an athletic man, today he felt awkward and flat-footed. His lungs burned.

He didn't need a therapist to understand he was trying to outrun his demons, to outpace a decision that was making him ill. He needed money fast.

He ran until his legs turned to jelly, until he thought it might be possible to walk into his parents' home and look them in the eye, rather than avoiding them as he'd done since returning from Denver yesterday. But he could never be the same son he'd always been.

He couldn't look his father in the eye because he had doubts about him, and no longer had confidence that he really knew him. He couldn't look his mother in the eye because he knew something that she didn't. Something awful.

He turned down his parents' street, and his heart sank.

Audrey's pink Mini sat in the driveway.

He hardened every soft emotion he'd developed yesterday during their drive home together, every ounce of compassion for her father, every speck of admiration for her fortitude, every sweaty particle of lust, until he could walk into his parents' house without being affected by her.

Because…to save his family, he had no choice but to destroy Audrey.

AUDREY HADN'T GONE to the greenhouses.

Dad's worsening state and his violence, this morning's confrontation, rattled her. She'd needed uplifting companionship and blessedly normal interaction with another woman, anything that would take her mind off Dad.

She had driven straight to the Turner house on its private cul-de-sac, absurdly happy to find that Gray wasn't at home.

He might have seemed more…human…on their drive home from Denver yesterday, but she still didn't trust him.

Harrison had answered the door.

"Hi, Mr. Turner."

His expression had brightened and he'd smiled. "Hi, Audrey. We were just talking about you recently."

They had been? "Do you mind if I come in to visit Abigail?"

"Of course not. She's in the living room."

Audrey had found Abigail ensconced in a cozy armchair sipping tea from a china cup. An infinitesimal, brief rush of commingled guilt and regret in Abigail's eyes had been replaced quickly by longing and pleasure.

Audrey understood the guilt and wished she could throw her arms around Abigail to reassure her there were no hard feelings. All of those years ago, the woman had merely done what she'd had to do as a good, caring mother to protect her son.

Audrey remembered as a child sitting quietly, the calm eye of the storm, while the adults swirled around her in a frenzy of caring, nurturing and fear. And intense panic. What to do about Gray? What to do *for* Gray?

When Abigail struggled to rise, Audrey said, "Please sit. I just wondered whether I could visit for a few minutes before I open the store."

Abigail clapped her hands together once, and said, "I would love it more than anything. Harrison, can you get another cup? The tea is fresh."

Audrey sat on the sofa, and Abigail did get up to join her. When she settled close to Audrey, she sniffed. "Oh, your perfume is heavenly! Let me guess. Chanel. A classic."

Audrey waited, proud of Abigail for guessing correctly, but would she get the rest?

"Not Number 5. Chanel Number 19. I always preferred it to Number 5. Such a rich scent. It has more body. More romance."

Audrey smiled. "It's my favorite."

Abigail responded with a wide grin of her own. There wasn't another person on earth with whom Audrey felt more in simpatico.

Harrison returned with another cup and poured

tea for Audrey, then settled into an armchair with the newspaper.

"I have a new book," Abigail crooned, as though she'd won a lottery. She pulled a hardcover from the coffee table, a photo collection of Jackie Kennedy's wardrobe while she lived in the White House.

"Ooooh," Audrey said. "This looks wonderful."

"First tell me what you've created lately." She fingered the fabric of Audrey's skirt. "Did you make this? It's beautiful on you."

Last night before hitting the sack, she had hemmed the red sundress with the big white polka dots she'd been working on yesterday morning when she'd ended up reading to Dad instead. It had a fitted halter bodice and a flared skirt with a half crinoline to give it body.

"I heard you were wearing a Chanel suit the other day. Real? Or did you sew a replica?"

"Vintage." She pointed to the pink suit Jackie Kennedy wore in the book cover photo. "Very like this, but also different."

"That's because Jackie's suit wasn't a Chanel."

"That's what I heard. It wasn't a knockoff, though."

Abigail frowned. "The First Lady did not wear knockoffs. The fabric was sent to her by Coco, but the suit was designed and made by a New York dress salon, Chez Ninon. It was much, much cheaper than a custom-made Chanel and made by Americans."

"Pretty smart move for a president's wife to make."

"I thought so." Abigail stared at the photo of Jackie

Kennedy in the suit that was later covered with JFK's blood. "Such a shame. On November 22, 1963, I was thirty years old. I remember watching the assassination on television and crying for all that had been lost, and thinking, this is history in the making. I don't care about conspiracy theories or who shot him for certain, but I do know that this woman—" she tapped her finger on Jackie Kennedy's photo "—suffered because of his death. No matter that he was a philanderer."

Audrey reached for her hand and held it.

Shaking herself out of the moment, Abigail said, "Let's not talk of sadness. Wait until you see some of Jackie's other clothes. Look at her magnificent wedding dress."

An hour later, Audrey and Abigail were still involved in the book and chattering about clothing, and Audrey's mood had risen from the depression into which Dad's health had plunged her. Thank God. She could open the store without a black funk hanging over her.

She glanced at her watch. She would rush over to water her plants first and be only a few minutes late opening the shop.

Feeling someone watching her, she glanced up. Gray had come home and stood in the living room doorway in gym clothes, with sweat sheening his face, staring at her and his mother, his expression guarded.

She'd stayed too long. She hadn't wanted to see

him. Or so she'd thought. Her pitter-patter heartbeat put the lie to that.

He frowned at Audrey. She wished, so badly, that he would smile like he used to do when he saw her, but he'd been only seven. They'd been so young the last time they'd been friends.

A devastating discomfort rattled her. He didn't want her here. That was obvious. Yesterday's warmth was gone. She didn't know what had happened between then and now.

Too bad. Even so, she was glad she had decided to come. She'd been missing Abigail.

She kissed Abigail's cheek and said, "Thank you for allowing me to visit. You were exactly what I needed this morning."

"No, thank *you*. Anytime, Audrey. Come next week. I've ordered a book about Coco Chanel. You would love it. It should be in by then."

Audrey turned to leave, but Abigail wrapped her arms around her, clung to her and whispered, "I'm sorry. I would do things differently now."

She heard tears in Abigail's voice. Oh, no. No, no. "It's okay," she rushed to reassure, her voice pitched low so Gray wouldn't hear. "Really. Please, Abigail, it's truly all right. In your shoes, I would have done the same thing."

She pulled back, and Abigail looked for the truth in Audrey's eyes. What she read there was the forgiveness that Audrey had granted freely a long, long time ago. She released her hold on Audrey's shoulders.

Audrey brushed past Gray. He smelled of green forests and fresh sweat, but no cigarette smoke. Thank goodness. She felt the heat of his body like a brushstroke on the canvas of her skin.

His glance, though, froze her blood.

GRAY WATCHED AUDREY leave the house and drive away, a voluptuous Audrey Hepburn, her expression innocent, pure, and yet deeply sensual. Knowing. He wasn't sure that made sense, but it was the only way he could describe it to himself.

The woman was color, life, vivacity.

On a visceral level, she rattled him, made him wish for youth, innocence, oblivion. Relief from too many problems.

He wasn't a man who caved in to his needs. He was strong. Or had been. He needed that strength back.

He couldn't let the easy understanding of yesterday's drive together get in the way of protecting his family's security.

"What did Audrey want?" he asked his mother. At Gray's sharp tone, Dad put down his newspaper and stared.

Startled, Abigail asked, "Want?"

"Why was she here?"

"To visit. Remember? I told you. She used to visit regularly until you came home. I'm glad she dropped by today. I've missed her."

"What was she wearing?"

"A dress she designed and made." His mother smiled proudly, as though she'd made the dress herself. "Didn't it look wonderful on her?"

"It looked old-fashioned."

"It was meant to."

"Anyway, I didn't mean the dress. I meant, what is that perfume she wears?"

"Chanel Number 19. Lovely, isn't it?"

"It's okay." It was heavenly.

A look that he couldn't interpret passed between his parents. Mom handed him the teapot. "Would you make a fresh pot before you leave for work, dear? This one's ice-cold."

He left the room and filled the kettle, but tiptoed back down the hallway while he waited for it to come to a boil. His mother was up to something. He stood just out of sight beside the living room doorway.

"We handled it all wrong and look what it led to, Harrison."

"It's water under the bridge," Dad said. "It happened a long time ago. It has nothing to do with now."

What happened a long time ago?

"The repercussions carry on to this day. I'm going to fix it."

Fix *what?*

"Abigail, don't meddle." Dad used his best *I'm-the-boss* voice.

Mom ignored it, as usual. "I'm not meddling. I love that girl and I always have, ever since she was little, and I realized I would never have a daughter of my own. She used to feel like part of my family."

She did?

"I want to feel that again. I want to have her over for dinner, exactly as any normal family would do with a friend."

What did she mean "normal?" They were normal. Weren't they?

"Please, Abigail, don't do this." The plea in Dad's voice shocked Gray.

"I won't be dissuaded, Harrison. I listened to you all of those years ago instead of to my heart. We handled it badly." If Dad sounded emotional, Mom was determined. "I'm fixing this situation if it kills us all."

"It just might," Dad murmured.

A long silence followed, and Gray realized he'd heard as much as he was going to. What had they meant? What were they talking about? He returned to the kitchen and made Mom's fresh tea, pondering what he'd heard. He never would have thought his parents kept secrets from him. He'd been wrong.

First, Dad's infidelity had rocked him. *Alleged* infidelity. Now what? What was Mom talking about?

Carrying the pot, he entered the living room.

Mom glanced up and said, "I'm inviting Audrey to dinner on Friday night."

"Okay." He kept his tone reasonable. "It's your home, Mom. You can invite whoever you want. I'll head into town for supper."

Mom picked up a magazine from the coffee table and snapped it open. "You will not. You will eat dinner here with your father and me *and* Audrey."

His soft, pliable mother had just issued an order. "Okay," Gray replied meekly, but as he walked upstairs to shower and dress for work, he wondered what the heck was going on.

AN HOUR LATER, Gray strode into Turner Lumber, burying those troubling images and feelings of suffocation as best he could.

Hilary met him with a frown. "We have a situation." She looked nervous.

He led her to his office and pulled the walls closed. "What is it?"

"Yesterday, while you were gone to Denver?"

He nodded.

"One of the employees must have called your dad and told him that you'd gotten rid of the benefits he gave. While you were gone, he reinstated them."

"What? But how? Arnie was going to take care of it in the morning."

Hilary nodded. "He did. Your dad came in in the afternoon. When I wouldn't place the call, he did. The benefits are back on the table."

Gray swore a blue streak. Harrison had gone behind his back, just like with the banked sick days.

Déjà damn vu all over again.

One of the first things Gray had done was to abolish the banking of sick days. Dad had already paid out thousands and thousands of dollars to longtime employees who'd taken five and six months off work before retirement. That money brought in nothing. No productivity. No profit. Just money whirling down an insatiable drain.

When Harrison had found out what Gray had done, he'd reinstated the policy. And now he'd done the same with the benefits.

Dear Christ. How was Gray supposed to save this place if Dad scuttled every decision he made?

"Those benefits are going to bankrupt the company," he said, anger barely contained. "Maybe five, ten years ago it would have been okay, but not now."

Oh, God, Dad was operating behind his back, undoing the very things that would save the company. Gray was going to have to do it. He was going to have to talk to John Spade.

First, he flew home to persuade his father to rescind his decisions, but got more of the same sliding glances, the same half-truths, the same new age so-called wisdom.

He left home with no more sense of satisfaction than when he'd arrived. He couldn't let Dad continue to destroy Gray's efforts to save the company. The world had changed. The economy had changed. Dad didn't get it. *He just didn't get it.*

When Gray had threatened to cancel the benefits again, Dad had said, "You can try, but every time you do, I'll reinstate them. This is my company, Gray. I will always have the final say."

That's what scared Gray. They were going to lose the company, but nothing Gray could say would convince Dad of that.

What was going on with him? If he was as tired as Mom said, why wasn't he leaving all of the decisions to Gray?

Determined now, decision made, Gray drove to Spade's law office all the while thinking, *God help me, I don't want to do this.* John granted five minutes of his time. It took Gray all of two to get the procedure started.

"How does this work?"

"We'll petition family court for guardianship for you over your dad. He'll become a dependent adult. We'll petition for guardianship of his property in probate court."

Gray moaned. "Jeez. That's bad. We're treating him like a child."

"We'll seek a psychological evaluation. I'll hire a professional to conduct it."

Gray loosened his tie and undid the top button of his shirt. He couldn't breathe. "What if Dad won't agree to the evaluation?"

"We can have the court order it."

Sick to his stomach, he asked, "They would force him?"

John nodded. "He's been making decisions that are killing the company."

When Gray didn't respond, John assessed him with a thoughtful gaze. "Okay, listen, Gray, this is how it's going to go down. You're emotionally involved. Understandably so."

John stood and rounded his desk. "From now on, I take care of this. You do nothing. Go about your normal life. Take care of your dad's business, but leave this to me. *All* of it. I'll get this done for you, but you don't ask questions to which you don't want to hear answers."

He ushered Gray to the outer door. "Are we clear?" Judging by Spade's expression, he would be as ruthless as necessary.

Stomach churning, Gray strode to his parked car before he could change his mind. Who knew guilt could be physical, could leave a man feeling like either losing his breakfast or smashing his fist through the windshield?

Once back at work, he pulled three sticks of gum out of a package he'd bought earlier, crammed them all into his mouth and chewed furiously.

If he did this, would Dad ever forgive him? How long could Gray live with the guilt? But then, how much longer would Dad live? Even hinting about Dad's death cut off air to his lungs. Besides, the guilt wouldn't end on Dad dying.

Gray would still have to live with Mom's hurt, with her sense of betrayal. She would no longer trust Gray, wondering when he would turn on her. Thoughts of Mom brought to mind the contents of that letter and the despair on Shelly's face.

If he went back on the promise he'd made to

her yesterday that he would deliver the money she needed, he didn't doubt that Shelly had the backbone and the extreme motivation to take her story to the papers.

It would kill Mom to learn that Dad had been unfaithful, but particularly if she read of it in a public forum.

Declaring Dad unfit would corrode their family unit. Gray would never be welcome in his parents' home again. Talk about being between a rock and a hard place.

Gray had no choice. Like any good businessman, he could do whatever needed to be done. And he just had.

CHAPTER SIX

ON FRIDAY MORNING, Gray had picked up a mile-long list of ingredients for Mom's dinner tonight. Now, he stood in The Last Dance, waiting for a flower arrangement she had ordered from Audrey.

Waiting being the significant word.

Audrey was with another customer, a woman he recognized. Laura Cameron. Every boy in high school, including himself, had had the hots for Laura. She had a stunning figure, beautiful eyes and lush chestnut hair. She also had a baby in her arms. Must have gotten married. Or maybe not, these days. It just showed that he was still out of touch with a lot of the townspeople.

Audrey oohed and aahed over the baby, chucking her under the chin and making her giggle, rather than dealing with a customer. Him.

"I just love her outfit," Laura said. "Thank you so much for making it, Audrey."

"Thanks for bringing Pearl in so I could see it on her." She reached under the counter and pulled out a small camera. "Let me get a shot."

She hadn't even acknowledged Gray. Even if she was pissed at him because he'd been so cold to her on Wednesday morning when she'd visited his mom, this was no way to run a business.

Jerry came from the back, spotted him and ambled over, pressing his wet nose into Gray's hand. Gray couldn't resist the soft insistence of his attention, the quiet assumption of Gray's affection.

While he rubbed Jerry's ears, he watched Audrey, because it seemed that, as long as he was in the same room with her, he could do nothing else.

Today, she wore an emerald-green dress with white stripes. He thought the style was called a halter dress. He wasn't sure how the engineering, the mechanics, worked, but that must be strong material. Those straps around her neck were holding up a lot of…stuff.

She took a photo of Pearl and then put the camera on the counter. "Let me hold her."

Gray rolled his eyes. Seriously? She was keeping a paying customer waiting?

Pearl went into her arms easily and nuzzled her neck, rooting until her mouth came close to one of Audrey's breasts, and Gray's temperature shot through the roof.

He'd wanted children. Marnie had wanted children. If they could have only agreed on where they would live after the wedding, they would have already been married and had a couple of kids when she died. Gray would already be a father. Harrison and Abigail would already be grandparents.

Losing his fiancée had shattered him. Not already having a family to replace the parents who would die someday soon from old age killed him. On top of that, he was about to lose his dad because of a business decision that had to be made.

He wanted…he wanted…life to be full and whole and good, and for all of this bad stuff to stop happening. As hard as he tried to steer his life forward, as hard as he pressed on the accelerator to get ahead, the car kept stalling. When he did move, roadblocks hovered every few feet.

He wanted a normal life with a loving woman on one arm and his baby on the other.

Audrey giggled because Pearl was still trying to get to her breast.

"I have to feed her after I leave here," Laura said, laughing, too.

Pearl looked as though she belonged in Audrey's arms. The rightness of Audrey holding a baby sapped Gray of all sense.

An image, puissant and fierce, of her opening her dress and putting a babe to her full breast, shocked him. His fingers clenched in Jerry's fur, and the dog whimpered. He eased his grip. So what if she looked good, wholly feminine and maternal holding a child? What did that have to do with him?

He'd seen a lot of women with babies, *tons* of them, so why was he suddenly brain-dead stupid just because Audrey Stone was holding one?

Gray forced himself to erase the image of Audrey breastfeeding, as breath-robbing as it was, from his mind.

He turned away until he'd collected himself. One day he would have a family. He just had a few obstacles to overcome first.

The idea of wanting Audrey at all, craving all of the lush sexiness of her body and the generosity of her spirit, was terrifying enough without images of her holding not just any baby, but *his*.

Why she intimidated him—no, that word was too mild; he'd been right the first time in that she terrified him—both puzzled and confused him. He'd never had trouble with women before. So, what was it about her that scared him? She was a woman, nothing more.

When Laura finally left, she nodded to him, and he smiled, but when he approached Audrey about his mom's flowers, his smile slipped.

"This is no way to run a business. You don't keep a customer waiting while you fall apart over a baby."

The joy on Audrey's face dried up, and Gray felt as if he'd killed a baby rabbit. The sun had just gone behind a bank of storm clouds. He couldn't seem to stop himself and plowed on.

"You'll never be a success if you treat customers so shabbily."

She didn't say a word, just reached for a wrapped

package, as though she couldn't get him out of her shop fast enough.

"Here's Abigail's arrangement." She named the price, and he paid with his credit card.

About to leave, she stopped him with a quiet, "Gray."

He looked over his shoulder.

"This is a small town. The way business is run here is by being friendly, open, communicative. By being part of the community. If you don't recognize that, *you'll* run into trouble here."

She was right. He'd overreacted with his impatience and his big-city get-it-done-yesterday mind-set.

After that image of her holding the baby, after those revelations of how deeply his longings went, he realized how much he needed to keep this woman at a distance. At a long, far, miles-away distance.

She couldn't be his friend. She couldn't be his lover. He was about to betray his dad. He couldn't get close to Audrey and then betray her. Because he would. Betray her. She was going to lose those greenhouses to him, and he was going to save both his mother from disappointment and disgrace, and Turner Lumber from bankruptcy.

How could he avoid Audrey, though? She was coming to dinner tonight. He would have to ignore her. Not look at her. Acknowledge her as little as possible. Put a bag over his head. Bury his head in his mother's garden.

He hoped she showed up in a paper sack.

FOR AN HOUR, since Audrey had arrived and while they'd eaten dinner, Gray had been watching one strap of her dress slip from her left shoulder. She would smooth it up, but five minutes later it would complete its inevitable slide down her white skin.

He'd never seen such unblemished skin.

She hadn't shown up in a paper bag, but a white dress with black Eiffel towers tilting at jaunty angles all over the fabric. The dress hugged her curves to a drop waist, then flared out from her hips.

An upside-down arch of fabric swooped from the top of her bodice up over her shoulders. She must have been wearing one hell of a strapless bra because the collar of the dress was too wide to allow for bra straps. Whatever the undergarment, it must have been a real feat of engineering to hold up all of that lovely flesh.

He glanced at Audrey's face. She'd caught him staring at her chest. His face flamed, but maybe not as much as hers did.

"Do you two remember when—" Mom began, but Dad cut her off.

"Abigail," Dad said, his tone as stern as Gray had ever heard it, his rudeness out of character. "Don't go there, sweetheart."

Dad had tried to instill in Gray flawless manners. For the most part, it had worked, until lately, when Gray seemed to be impatient with everything and everyone, but no wonder. His life had been hit by too many hard events in the past year.

For once, Mom heeded Dad.

Audrey's wide violet gaze flew between the two of them, and Gray again had the sense that everyone in the room knew what was going on but him. *What?*

Why would there be things in his family left unsaid? Why would Audrey know about them? She wasn't part of his family. He'd never been friends with her. He'd spent some time with her father because Harrison and Jeff had been friends, but not with Audrey.

That strap fell from her shoulder again, snagging his attention. His mother popped up from the table and left the room to return a minute later with a small wicker basket from which she pulled a pincushion.

"Let's fix that for you, dear. These boat collars are so attractive, but they have to fit just right."

"I made it a little too wide," Audrey said, "but didn't have time to fix it before I left home."

"Of course not, with your father requiring so much care."

"I don't see why he couldn't have come over with you," Dad said. "I count your dad a good friend."

"I couldn't persuade him to come," Audrey said, distress in her voice. "He never leaves the house."

He only half listened because he couldn't stop staring at Audrey's shoulder. He'd seen hundreds of shoulders. He'd had a healthy appetite as a teenager. He'd sneaked plenty of issues of *Playboy* into the house.

He'd had plenty of girlfriends, had seen beautiful—no, *gorgeous*—shoulders, so, what was it about Audrey? The retro clothes? The fact that she did nothing to flaunt her sex appeal? The fact that she just *was* sexy without even trying?

He didn't even need to touch her, simply look. Men were visual creatures, and for Gray looking was an aphrodisiac. Foreplay. Imagining how soft her skin must be was pure pleasure.

He'd never known he could be satisfied just glimpsing skin, that even knowing he would never touch it could be a joy.

When Mom cinched the strap tightly and started to pin it, Gray yelled, "No!"

Three heads swung his way, all with wide eyes and mouths agape.

"What, dear?" his mother asked.

What indeed? There were so many *whats*. What was wrong with him? What had gotten into him?

What could he say? Don't cover her alabaster skin? I want to ogle our guest for the rest of the night? I want to see how far that strap will slip? I want to know what she's wearing underneath that's keeping all of that amazing flesh in place? To see whether it's practical or whimsical? Industrial or sexy? God forbid it should be sexy. It might kill him. Cardiac arrest guaranteed.

On the other hand, on Audrey, maybe even industrial looked sexy.

Where had today's vow made in The Last Dance to keep his distance gone? Was his resolve so weak where Audrey was concerned that he turned to jelly just because of an ill-fitting dress strap?

She nibbled on her bottom lip. All of her lipstick had been worn away while she'd eaten, and her mouth was every bit as pretty without artifice as it was when painted.

He didn't want to want Audrey. He didn't need this flash flood of desire tumbling through him.

"Nothing," he mumbled. "I meant nothing."

They continued on with dinner, and Gray settled into a better, calmer place.

This was how he had always imagined it could be with Marnie. He'd tried to get her here many times, but had managed it only once.

The visit had been fine, but Marnie had been too formal, too aware that this was small-town America and she didn't fit in.

She'd tried, he'd give her that, but she'd never wanted to visit again. And living here? Even knowing that his parents were so old and wouldn't be around forever, and that he wanted to spend their last few years with them? Off the table.

Despite her quirkiness, Audrey fit in, not only into town, but also into this family. Into Gray's home.

He picked up plates and carried them to the kitchen where he rinsed them, then loaded them into the dishwasher.

Straight-armed, he leaned against the counter, the edge biting into his palms, trying to figure out what was wrong with him, why a woman who was so far from his ideal could fry his brain so thoroughly.

He returned to the dining room with the pot of coffee and filled cups.

"Thank you, dear," Mom said. "I know this seems rude, but does anyone mind if we take our desserts into the living room? I'd like to watch *Say Yes to the Dress.*"

Audrey popped up like a jack-in-the-box. "Yes! I'd love to."

Abigail laughed, took Audrey's hand and all but dragged her to the front room.

Gray followed slowly and asked, "Dad, are we really going to watch TV while we have a guest?"

"Are you kidding? Your mother is addicted to *Say Yes to the Dress.* She told me earlier that Audrey is, too."

"Dare I ask what *Say Yes to the Dress* is?"

Dad grimaced. "It's a reality show about women shopping for wedding dresses."

Just before they joined the women in the living room, Gray said, "Shoot me now."

Three hours of torture later, Mom asked him to walk Audrey to her car. How was watching women shop for wedding and bridesmaids' dresses supposed to be fun? Maybe if you liked shoving bamboo stakes under your fingernails.

Despite that, his mood mellowed and his mind eased more than it had in months, and it was because of Audrey.

The happiness she'd given his mother by enjoying the show, the pleasure she'd taken from it, made Gray want to do foolish things, like taste her full lips and lick her high cheekbones.

She walked beside him, her confidence in herself, her supreme belief that she was okay exactly as she was, part of the calmness that settled over him.

He'd never met a woman more comfortable in her own skin, less affected by fashion's supposed ideal image, by society's pressures to look a certain way.

Audrey, the woman who was supposed to be his enemy and who, for some nameless, faceless reason, terrified him, was a surprise.

She'd thrown him for a loop.

She sighed, and it sounded like contentment, as though all were right with the world. He knew it wasn't. She had her father to deal with and him to fight about the land, but he'd noticed this thing about Audrey, this amazing ability to live in the moment. She took each second as it came and derived whatever joy she could from it.

"Your parents are the best people," she said. "I love your mom."

Me, too. "Thank you."

She glanced at him, skin pale and hair jet-black in the gathering night. "For what?"

"For making her happy tonight."

They'd reached the car, and only the most meager light drifted this far from the porch, so he couldn't be certain, but he thought her smile might have been shy.

It enchanted him.

Before thought, before sanity, came an impulse so strong Gray couldn't resist—to hold on to this lovely normal evening with both hands, because one day soon his world would explode.

He reached for Audrey. With one hand behind her head and his other across the back of her waist, he hauled her against him, fast and hard, her curves full and giving against his body.

There was nothing gentle about what he wanted— to drown in Audrey, in her generosity, and in her weird wisdom when she looked at him, and in her quirky, bright spirit—to eradicate what he'd done this week, to give himself the gift of oblivion.

His mouth came down on the lush lips that had tempted him all evening. She stiffened and then gave, her arms wrapping around him like the sexiest freaking security blanket on earth, offering sanctuary.

She tasted as good as she looked, and felt like heaven, like dreams come true, like time standing still. She gave to him so completely, she melted the iceberg of his heart, pouring a single-minded devotion over him.

What—? How—?

He stopped questioning and gave in to her tenderness, the surface heat scorching, but the underlying affection real and true.

Audrey cared for him?

He drank her in, inhaled the perfume that drugged common sense out of him and left him reeling.

Slowly, she pulled away and licked her damp bottom lip. He stroked his tongue down her soft neck to the shoulder that had tempted him all evening.

"Gray, stop," she whispered, placing her hands against his chest and setting him away from her, as though he were a naughty boy.

"No," she said and opened her car door. "We aren't doing this." She leaned one hand on her hip, a gesture he was beginning to recognize—she did it when she was shaken and trying to force a confidence she didn't feel.

"Don't ever kiss me again. Ever." Her trembling voice betrayed her calm stance.

Afraid that his voice would betray his own shakiness, he forced himself to be cocky.

"Why not? You enjoyed it as much as I did. I felt your excitement."

"My body responded, yes, but my mind and my heart don't want you."

"Why not?"

"I don't like you."

The simple conviction, the unnerving sentiment, shattered him.

What about the tenderness he'd felt from her? The affection? Had he imagined it? Did he miss Marnie so much, was he so starved for love, that he was making things up? Imagining warmth where it didn't exist?

Had he become that deranged since the accident?

Audrey Stone didn't like him.

It shouldn't hurt. It did.

Brazen it out. "What does *like* have to do with anything?"

"I have to like a man to be involved with him."

"Why don't you like me?"

"You aren't the person I've always thought you were. You used to be a good person, a person worth liking."

"When?"

"A long, long time ago." She got into her car and drove off without a glance at him.

How did she know he used to be a good person, and how long ago was a long, long time ago? Certainly, not in his memory. He'd never had enough exposure to Audrey for her to pass judgment on him, for her to know whether he was good, bad or indifferent.

How did she know he was no longer a person worth liking? Just because he was trying to boot her off the land? It was business. Surely she could see that. Emotion had nothing to do with a sound business decision.

GRAY PARKED IN Jeff's driveway and got out of the car, a bottle of Chivas Regal in his hand. He would have chosen something different for himself, Laphroaig or Aberlour, but Dad had said Jeff liked Chivas.

Time to find out how bad Jeff's eyesight really was, or if he was faking it to get money out of Dad.

Despite how bad Audrey and Harrison said Jeff's

situation was, maybe it called for an objective observer, someone who wasn't emotionally involved.

It was Saturday afternoon. Audrey would be at her shop. She'd said that Jeff didn't go out. Gray stood a good chance of catching Jeff alone.

It seemed that Gray's job since he'd returned home was to separate the honest lot from the cheaters, the expenses that were justified from those that weren't.

He hadn't seen Jeff in maybe six or seven years and didn't know what to expect.

Gray knocked three times. Finally, he heard slow shuffling. The door opened. Jeff, looking decades older than the last time their paths had crossed, squinted against the sunlight.

"Who is it?" he asked, while looking straight at Gray. How could he not recognize Gray? He'd worked for Dad for so many years.

"It's Gray Turner, Mr. Stone."

Jeff cocked his head this way and that like a curious bird, then sighed. "I'll have to take your word for it. Can't see worth a damn."

"I heard you didn't get out much and thought you'd like a visitor. I brought Scotch."

Jeff grinned. "You always were a good one for bringing the right gifts. Come on in." He shuffled into the living room at a snail's pace, his hand never leaving the wall, his gait unsure, hesitant.

So, was he putting on a show? How much was real? Was Dad just an easy target these days? Was Jeff in trouble or getting away with murder?

Jeff gestured vaguely toward a sofa. "Sit."

Vertical lines bracketed his mouth. Permanent unhappiness.

Gray remembered Jeff used to be happy all of the time, but that had been years ago when Gray had been a teenager and still lived in town, still spent time at Turner Lumber and saw Jeff regularly. When had Jeff changed? After Billy's death in Afghanistan?

Dad had called Gray about it, devastated that his friend's son had died. Gray thought about how much he had wanted a family with Marnie, about how much he'd been affected when watching Audrey hold a baby, and wondered how awful it would be to lose a child. Overwhelming. He suspected it might even be worse than losing a fiancée. And that had been godawful.

"I'll get us some glasses." Jeff walked straight into the mammoth coffee table. "Holy Hannah Mother of God!" Jeff's anger was real. No playacting here. He had a strange way of expressing anger, though.

A vague thought metamorphosed into a memory. Gray had been about fifteen or sixteen and working in the lumberyard because Dad had insisted that he learn every aspect of the business. He had cursed about something, dropping a board on his foot. Whatever. Jeff had been right there reading him the riot act.

"If you can't find a good way to express your anger outside of profanity, then don't say anything." Hilary, who had come down from the office to handle some paperwork, had stood nearby. Jeff had tilted his head toward her. "Especially in front of women."

It had seemed unrealistic at the time, but there'd been no doubting Jeff's passion.

Gray steered the man to an armchair. "Sit. I'll get the glasses. Where are they?"

"In the kitchen. You remember where that is. You used to run wild in here with Audrey."

That pulled Gray up short. He did? No way. *Audrey?* He had no memory of playing with Audrey here or anywhere else.

Somehow, though, he did know where the kitchen was. Duh. It was down the hallway at the back of the house, where most any kitchen would be in a house this old. Simple logic, that was all.

He opened a cupboard and retrieved a couple glasses, but stopped at the doorway, shivers running up his back. How had he known the correct door to open? There hadn't been a speck of hesitation. He'd gone straight to the right cupboard.

No way did it mean anything. Coincidence. Nothing more. He forced the question from his mind.

In the living room, he poured them each a shot of Chivas.

"Cheers," Jeff said, holding out his glass in Gray's general direction. Gray reached over and clinked his glass against Jeff's.

Jeff brought the drink to his mouth slowly and sipped. Gray wondered how a lack of eye-hand coordination affected eating and drinking. Jeff sighed. "That's good. Thank you." He relaxed a little.

Gray was still arrested by the changes in Jeff, by the rapid aging. Maybe…maybe everything was true. Maybe Dad was doing the right thing by Jeff.

Staring at his father's friend, memories formed, images of flying, feelings of joy. Gray grinned. "Whenever I visited the store you used to pick me up and swing me high into the air. Then you'd pretend you were going to drop me."

"When you were little, yeah." Jeff's smile emphasized the grooves in his face, but eased the unhappiness. "You used to giggle like a girl." He said it fondly without criticism. Jeff had been twenty years younger than Dad and physically strong, and somehow Gray had sensed that he loved children.

Gray remembered that weightlessness, that pure and utter exhilaration, the complete trust he'd had in Jeff. He'd forgotten it over the years. What else had he forgotten?

"You mentioned that I used to visit here. How old was I?"

"Real little. You started coming when you were only three or so. You and Audrey were real pals."

They were? He had no memory of that. No *way*.

"I used to take Audrey to work after her mother died, and the two of you would run around the back fields like a pair of puppies. That is, until—" Jeff closed his mouth, compressed his lips, as though he'd said something wrong.

"Until?" Gray asked, but Jeff shook his head. The well of that conversation had run dry. Jeff wasn't giving out any more information. What the heck?

He poured them more Scotch.

Jeff changed to the topic of the Turner business, asking how things were. Gray expressed concerns, and Jeff offered input. He'd worked there for so many years, he knew the business through and through. His insights were sound. Smart. Gray casually introduced the topic of the huge benefits package to Jeff.

"I told Harrison it was a mistake to give people too much," Jeff said. "I worked at Turner Lumber for nearly thirty years. Harrison was a generous guy. A good employer. Best ever. But honest to God, you don't give the company away in chunks like that."

"Yes!" The word exploded out of Gray. "I've been trying to tell him that. The concessions he's given are nuts. Banking sick days. How stupid is that?" The drink had loosened his tongue, and he couldn't seem to stop. "Paying out thousands of dollars to employees at retirement because they *weren't* sick. Some guy said he shouldn't be penalized for being healthy. That's damn— Sorry, that's insane. Sick days are *insurance* against illness, not a *guarantee* of easy money for doing nothing. It's one of the things bankrupting the company, but Dad won't budge on the issue."

"Buddy, I hear you and I understand." Jeff held out his glass for a refill, and Gray obliged, so damned gratified to hear an *employee* express reservations about those swollen benefits. The man had a good head on his shoulders.

Jeff sipped his drink. "There are benefits people do need, though. Ever taken a pair of kids to the dentist? Costs a fortune just to fill a tooth. Hard on a workingman's salary." He leaned forward. "Do you have any idea how much it costs to give birth to a baby in a hospital?"

Gray shook his head.

When Jeff mentioned an amount so high it shocked Gray, he choked on the sip of Scotch he'd just taken.

"Are you serious?" he asked.

Jeff nodded.

Gray shifted. Should he have contracted a cheaper package, rather than throwing out the whole thing?

He studied Jeff. He'd forgotten what a good man he was, how loyal he'd been to Harrison, not only as an employer, but also as a friend.

Jeff's pleasure in seeing Gray seemed sincere. Wouldn't a guy who was pulling a fast one have hesitated to let Gray in the door? His problem with his eyesight seemed real.

"Do you want to come into the office one day?" Gray asked.

"Don't get out," Jeff said gruffly. "Can't drive anymore."

"I can pick you up and drive you home later."

Jeff made a noncommittal sound.

"I'd like you to see the changes I've made." Gray cursed to himself. *See.* Unfortunate choice of words.

Again, they changed to another topic.

Gray was glad Jeff couldn't see his face because a sudden rush of shame sent heat to his chest. He'd come here with bad intentions, with distrust, to investigate a man who had only ever treated him and his family well.

He'd been away from this town too long, had worked in a city where employees could be a transient lot, where one didn't enter a company at twenty-five and stay until retirement. Where there were dwindling supplies of loyalty. Where *me* in both employers and employees was the order of the day.

Humbled, Gray sat back in his armchair prepared to give Jeff however much time he needed to feel wanted, to feel cared for, to feel vital.

Two hours later, when he and Jeff were well along in finishing the bottle, and feeling in harmony with each other and the world, Gray heard the door open. Then Audrey entered the room, but stopped when she saw Gray.

"What are you doing here?" Her glance shifted between him and her dad.

He wondered whether she was remembering that kiss. He was. He stared at her mouth. For endless moments, she stared at his.

The silence was broken by Jeff. "Look who came to visit. Haven't seen Gray in years."

Audrey's eyebrows rose, and Gray didn't know whether it was because Jeff was slurring his words or because he sounded so animated.

"You guys are drunk." Her accusatory tone was mitigated by a soft smile. She mouthed *thank you* to Gray silently.

For getting her father drunk?

"I'm glad you had a good visit."

Oh. For bringing social congress into her dad's life. Gray's belly warmed, and it wasn't the Scotch. It felt similar to when he'd bought Tiffany those cheap flip-flops. Guilt tried to crowd out the warmth, because his motives hadn't been pure when he'd come here today.

They were now, though. He'd missed seeing Jeff over the years. He remembered so much, the best of which was how well Jeff used to treat him.

Today, this weekend, might be all of the warmth Gray would feel in his life for a long, long time if that thing with his dad went through.

Desperate, as though a giant ax loomed over his neck, Gray blurted, "Jeff, remember when you used to take me fishing?"

"Sure do. Your dad and I were great fishing buddies."

"Want to go again? I could take you and Dad out to Pine Lake tomorrow."

Jeff rubbed his hands along the tops of his thighs. "I don't know how I could."

"I can be your eyes. What is there to do? You put a lure on a hook and you toss it into the water."

An expression of such wistfulness crossed Jeff's face that Gray pressed the issue. "I won't take no for an answer. I'll pick you up at five o'clock. You aren't afraid of getting up early, are you?"

Jeff snorted. "Been getting up early for work since I was sixteen. I can outwork and outfish you any day, city boy."

A load of stress eased from Gray's shoulders. Why? It was just a fishing trip. He turned to Audrey. "We need to work out the logistics of getting my car home." He grinned. "I've had too much to drink."

An hour later, after car jockeying with Audrey and his dad, both Gray and the Volvo were home.

"Come on," he said to his father, leading him to the garage, giddy like a little girl getting her first Barbie doll. Tickled pink. God, what a dumb expression. True, though. He was happy. He was drunk and feeling like a million bucks, and he was going fishing. *Fishing.*

"Let's get the canoe onto the car tonight."

Dad followed, his excitement about going fishing putting a new spring in his step.

CHAPTER SEVEN

GRAY WOKE WITH a weight on his chest. It took him a moment to figure out that it was dread, the ax looming. Then he remembered why his alarm had gone off at this ungodly hour, and a smile spread across his face.

He was taking his dad and Jeff Stone fishing.

After he showered the residual effects of yesterday's Scotch from his system and dressed, he went downstairs to find Dad already eating breakfast. Mom turned from the counter.

"Good morning, dear."

"Mom! What are you doing up?"

She smiled. "Making this." She handed him a cup of coffee already doctored the way he liked it.

"You're an angel." He wrapped her in his arms and squeezed, emotions, good and bad, clogging his throat. This might be the last hug he would ever share with his mom.

"Hey, hey, sweetheart," she said, her voice muffled against his chest. "You're only going to Pine Lake, not the Antarctic."

Gray pulled away, then sat at the table where a full plate waited for him, bacon and eggs and toast.

Mom picked up a thermal bag from the counter. "I've packed the three of you a lunch. I'll put it beside the front door." She left the room.

"You didn't have to get Mom up so early to do all of this."

Dad harrumphed. "I'd like to see you try to stop her."

It took another twenty minutes before they were ready to leave. Then Harrison kissed Abigail and said, "Go back to bed."

She yawned. "I probably will. You have a good day. Bring home some trout for dinner."

It was still dark when they stopped to pick up Jeff, who stood on the front porch waiting for them.

Audrey stood beside him, a red flannel robe cinched at her waist. Puffy white slippers encased her feet like furry rabbits.

She didn't wear a stitch of makeup, and her clean skin, her fresh complexion, made her look younger. Her hair formed a messy nimbus around her fine features. The dawn darkened the violet of her eyes.

Gray thought of that kiss again. How could he not when she looked at him with gratitude for what he was doing for her father? Did she like him now? Was he redeeming himself? He didn't know why it should matter, whether he had or not, but it did.

With a hand on her father's elbow, she directed him as though he were a treasure, mutely trusting Gray to keep him safe. She retreated into the house.

Gray wished she were coming with them, envisioned her in rubber boots and jeans and a flannel shirt tied at her waist, her face as fresh as it was now without eyeliner, mascara and lipstick.

She would be a vision sitting in a canoe in the sunshine. Had she ever fished with them when Gray was young? No, he remembered no time that she had ever joined them. Billy had when he'd been really young, but that had stopped when he became a teenager and started to run around with a crowd older than Gray's. Why hadn't Audrey also come? Maybe it was as simple as not being interested. Maybe those were the times she'd gone off to garden with her aunt.

Reluctantly, he turned away. Something else bothered him…why, if Gray had spent so much time with Jeff, had he never been friends with Audrey? Jeff had said they were, but Gray didn't believe it. He would remember.

Had Jeff just naturally spent more time with Billy and sometimes with Gray, because they were boys and he could relate to them? With a little more thought, he realized that so much of his relationship with Jeff had been based around the lumberyard. Of course, Audrey wouldn't have been part of that.

He guided Jeff to the car. Looking hesitant, not wholly believing that today could work, Jeff settled in. They sipped coffee from thermal mugs while Gray drove them to the spot where they used to fish when he was young.

At the lake, the sun peeked over the horizon, shaking the sleep from the world and setting the surface of the water on fire.

As he unpacked the car, took the canoe from the roof and settled Jeff into the middle seat, got out life jackets and loaded Mom's lunch, Gray thought of old traditions. He'd turned away from them for ages, sometimes in those early years away at school coming home at Christmastime reluctantly, resenting the time away from new friends and city attractions.

In a matter of days, what he had treated so callously could be torn away from him, and he missed it already.

No, he wouldn't think about that today, wouldn't waste time on the future. He would cherish these moments in the here and now with two men he'd respected all of his life.

Gray helped Dad into the front, Dad's hand frail and his step unsteady, and seated himself in the rear.

Dipping the paddle into the lake and steering them out onto still, crystal water in the quiet hush of dawn felt almost religious, sacred, the silence hallowed.

Soon, they had lures in the water and were talking, memories of the town and the business flowing from his father's and Jeff's lips like manna from heaven.

"Jeff, do you remember the time..." Dad paused in what he'd been about to say to include Gray. "Gray, you were there. You were already a teenager by then. We'd rented one of those small cottages on the far side of the lake."

"I remember," Gray said. "It was a boys' weekend. I think I was about twelve and Billy about fourteen."

"Yes. Do you remember what happened that night?"

Jeff was already laughing. "Gray, your dad and I were on the dock smoking cigars and talking. Must've been about two in the morning. You boys were inside in bed asleep."

"We'd been drinking these godawful Black Russians," Harrison said. "Vodka and Kahlúa. What the hell were we thinking, Jeff?"

"Your dad was wearing this straw fedora he loved. It was ancient—"

"Belonged to my father."

"It was disreputable. Holes in it everywhere. Looked like a mouse had been chewing it." Jeff cast his lure into still water.

"I loved that hat."

"Anyway," Jeff continued, "a gust of wind took it off your dad's head and sent it into the water. Your dad got up to retrieve it."

Dad was laughing. "We'd been out in the canoe earlier and had gotten water in it, so it was up on the dock turned facedown to drain and dry out."

"Your dad had to reach across it to lean into the water to fish out his hat. He put his hand on it, the thing tipped on to its side, and your dad went head over teakettle into the water. Fully clothed."

When they finally stopped laughing, Harrison said, "A lot of help you were. My clothes and shoes were waterlogged, and you didn't do a thing to help me out of the water."

"How could I? I was laughing too hard."

"Hey," Gray interjected. "I remember something."

He'd been laughing with them, thinking that this was only their memory. "When I got up in the morning, Dad's wallet was on the fireplace hearth and all of his ID was spread out. His driver's license was curled up at the edges, and his money was wrinkled."

"He'd put it all there before we went to bed to dry in front of the fire's embers."

"Boy, we were hungover that morning, weren't we, Jeff? We never drank Black Russians again."

Gray smiled while Dad and Jeff ran through story after story, often about a lot of people Gray knew.

Gray had lost more than he'd known when he'd turned his back on Accord, on the people.

Hours later, with six fish between them, Gray dropped his father off at home. Then he took Jeff to his house, where they scaled Jeff's two fish together, Gray guiding Jeff's hand and the two of them laughing when Jeff got the angle wrong and scales flew into their faces.

They left the fish for Audrey to cook when she came home, and sat in the living room to toast a good day with the meager remains of the bottle of Chivas.

All in all, it had been a good day. The best.

AUDREY FINISHED HAULING the last bags of yesterday's soil delivery into the back of the store. She'd been too busy yesterday and today with customers to unload the shipment. Just as well that she trusted the townspeople to not steal her product. It had been sitting out back on skids all Saturday night.

She didn't mind being busy. Busy was good. It meant money in the cash register. It also meant her feet were killing her. She'd had next to no time to sit.

"Come on, Jerry. Let's blow this pop stand." He followed her out the door and waited patiently while she locked up. By the time she got home and put Jerry in his kennel with a bowl of food and fresh water, she was dead tired.

Dad sat in the armchair waiting for her.

"Well?" she said. "Did you catch any fish?"

Dad's face split with a grin bigger than anything she'd seen in years. It took her breath away. Dad was happy.

Thank you, Gray.

"Go look in the kitchen," he said.

She did and then came back.

"Two fat, gorgeous fish. Well done." On impulse, she kissed his forehead and hugged him, then pulled back. "You smell like you've been fishing all day."

She helped him up the stairs to the bathroom. "Shower while I make supper. Frozen fries okay with you? I'm too pooped to make mashed."

"Frozen are good. Do we have any corn?"

"Only tinned. Will that work?"

"Yep." He didn't complain when she chose his clean clothes for him, a sign of just how improved his mood was. She hated how sometimes he mixed a plaid shirt with a patterned sweater.

You're anal, woman.

So what? I like fashion.

She skipped downstairs to fry fish and cook vegetables. Even though she'd told Gray she didn't like him, if he were here at this moment, she would kiss the daylights out of him for putting a smile on her father's face.

ON MONDAY MORNING, bolstered by the good time he'd had fishing the day before, Jeff decided he'd tackle those basement stairs that had intimidated him since his eyesight had begun to falter. He planned to visit the basement.

Billy used to live down there. Jeff hadn't gone down since his eyesight had first faded.

Somehow, today, he felt a need to connect with his son. When Billy was a child, they had gone on so many fishing trips together.

Yesterday, Jeff had been happy, but he'd also thought of Billy. Billy should have been in the canoe with them.

The story about Harrison falling over the canoe on the dock into the water had brought back good memories. It had been a father-son weekend, and Billy had been happy.

He hadn't returned after that year, though. He'd become a teenager and had been out with his friends. He'd grown up and away from his father. A couple of years later, he'd gotten a girlfriend, Monica Accord, who had later become his wife.

Jeff could no longer see his son, but he needed to connect with him somehow, to feel Billy's spirit. In the basement, Jeff could sit in his place, among his things, and maybe feel close to him there.

Audrey had left for work, so Jeff had the day for himself and it stretched too long ahead of him. Days used to be measured in hours—how much work could he get done before lunch, how much before going home for the day? Now? It was marked off in the excruciating slowness of minutes and the ticking of a clock on a mantel.

Why Audrey had to work when the store was closed puzzled him. She'd said she had to water and weed and trim and prune her plants at the greenhouse.

Fair enough, he guessed. Funny that the thought of her working with her flowers didn't make him as angry today—maybe because yesterday had been such a good day.

Feeling his way along the wall, he arrived at the basement stairs.

Billy's domain.

Jeff used to be angry that Billy had gone off and gotten himself killed. Underneath Jeff's puzzlement when Billy had enlisted—he'd always been a lover, not a fighter—had been fear. He hadn't wanted to lose his boy. Jeff used to be furious with Billy's best friend, Gabe Jordan, for taking Billy away.

Jordan had set him straight on that. Last year, Gabe had confessed that he hadn't persuaded Billy to go to war; in fact, he'd tried to dissuade Billy from going. But Billy had gone anyway—a sign of courage. His son had been strong. A hero. Like all of those boys who died in World War II. Heroes every one.

Jeff opened the basement door and felt for the light switch. Darned blurriness. Where was the first step? He shuffled. Moved his foot forward. Too far. Felt himself slipping.

He grabbed the handrail. His foot skidded off the stair. Pain in his shoulder. He couldn't hold on. His weight carried him forward. He went down, and down and down, rolling and banging his way to the bottom.

He hit the floor hard, landing on his left hip, pain a harsh reminder of helplessness. *You can't do for yourself anymore. You aren't a whole man anymore.*

He panted and waited for the pain to pass, then checked out his hip. It wasn't broken, but he'd be black and blue tomorrow.

In more than sixty years of living an active life, he'd never had as many bruises as he'd gotten in the past year.

With the fingers of his right hand, he felt the face of his watch, the one Audrey had given him with the raised numbers. Ten to ten.

Audrey probably wouldn't be home for hours.

He couldn't lie here all day.

Leveraging himself onto his uninjured hip, he pulled himself up.

He was weak. He used to be strong. He'd let himself go. How could he not? He wouldn't go to the gym, wouldn't entertain the crowd with the spectacle of the blind guy trying to pump up.

His attempt to step onto the first step failed. His hip was too sore. He needed to sit for a while.

He tested it. He could walk. He just couldn't climb. Shuffling, he found the sofa by bumping into it.

In adolescence, Billy had turned the basement into a hangout for himself and his friends. Jeff hadn't touched a thing.

In his mind, his son still lived down here, in the things Jeff could no longer see clearly but could feel, in the old sofa and armchair, in the posters on the wall of whatever movie stars and models had been hot at the time, in Billy's football awards on the shelf under the small basement window.

Gabe used to run in and out of this house.

Jeff had thought he was Billy's friend. Why hadn't he protected Billy from that IED? Why had it been Billy who had been killed and Gabe only wounded?

Jeff rubbed the side of his head where it had hit the railing on the way down. *Calm down. War is capricious. Only fate decides who lives and who dies. Not you. Not the soldiers themselves.*

His hand smoothed the worn fabric of the sofa. Billy used to sit here with his friends to watch football games on the old TV.

Jeff's palm touched the remote. Still here from the last time Billy had used it? If only he could feel Billy's heat still radiating from it. He picked it up and turned on the TV. A talk show came on. He'd go nuts if he watched daytime junk until Audrey got home. *Watched* being a weird word choice. All he did these days was listen.

He dozed until his empty belly woke him. *Jerry Springer* was on.

No. He couldn't listen to this drama, to the foul language. What kind of low humans thought it was okay, even desirable, to air their dirty linen in public?

These people lived while a good man like Billy was gone.

Jeff flipped channels. Nothing better. Crap and more crap. By feel, he hit the button on the VCR. Maybe Billy had been watching a movie when he had last sat here. He could share that with Billy, as though his son were sitting here beside him.

He closed his eyes. Silence. Nothing in the machine.

And then...Billy's voice.

Jeff's eyes shot open. "Billy?"

It wasn't his son alive. It wasn't a ghost. It was a voice from the past in an old football video.

Billy and Gabe used to have their friends shoot their games with Jeff's video camera, and then they'd come down here and do endless replays and analyses of how games had been won or lost, as though they were budding coaches as well as players.

"Gabe!" Jeff heard his son yell. "Pass it here."

Billy must have fumbled the ball, because he swore and then laughed. Jeff tsked. He'd taught his son it was bad to swear, but he smiled because of the fun in Billy's voice.

The sound of that laugh, the life-affirming joy in it, brought tears to Jeff's eyes, and he swiped them away.

Real men didn't cry.

He felt his way around the remote until he found the button that let him replay that laugh, once, twice, eighteen, thirty times. He listened with his eyes shut, because even the blurry light at the edges of his vision was a distraction from the purity of Billy's laugh.

With shaking fingers, Jeff wiped his eyes again.

Real men didn't cry.

AUDREY WORKED IN the greenhouse for six hours before quitting for the day. She'd labored right through lunch and was starving.

On her way home, she picked up groceries. Dad had been in a good mood this morning. Maybe he would be open to something healthy like a quinoa salad for dinner.

Her laughter filled the car. Nah. Not a chance would Dad eat quinoa in any shape or form. She settled for pork chops.

Balancing the bags in her arms, she unlocked the front door.

"Dad? I'm home."

No answer.

"Dad?"

He wasn't in the living room. Maybe he was upstairs taking a nap.

She put down the bags and scooted to the second floor. He wasn't there. Strange. Was he in the kitchen, maybe? But he would have heard her call. Worry started to hum through her.

Downstairs, she picked up the bags to take them to the kitchen, but stopped, halted by distant sound coming from the basement.

She approached the door. The hairs on her arms stood up. Billy. Laughing.

Oh. Dad had gone downstairs and had put in one of Billy's videos. What had prompted this?

She hurried down. She really wished he hadn't chanced these stairs alone. They were so steep.

The sight of Dad on the sofa, eyes closed, tears on his cheeks, stopped the words that were about to spew out, the chastisement for coming down here by himself.

How could she possibly give him heck? He'd just wanted to be near his son.

"Dad?" she whispered.

Slowly, as though waking from a dream, he opened his eyes.

She approached the sofa. "Are you okay?"

"Hurt myself."

She noticed his pallor, and her heart stuttered. "What? How?"

His mouth twisted. "You can go ahead and tell me I told you so. I fell down the stairs."

She snatched the remote from his hand to stop that disconcerting, disorienting blast from the past of Billy's voice.

While her pulse pounded, she touched his shoulder. "What did you hurt?"

"My hip."

Oh, Dad. "Broken?"

"Bruised. I'm tired. Help me up the stairs."

He stood and wobbled. She put his arm around her waist, but he hissed in a breath.

"What is it?"

"I wrenched my shoulder trying to stop the fall. Come around to the other side."

She did and gave him her support.

The second they reached the stairs, though, she knew it wouldn't work. Dad's hip might not be broken, but climbing the stairs hurt too much. It was likely swollen. She was a strong woman, but the stairs were steep, and she didn't want to risk both of them falling backward to the bottom.

"When did this happen?" She helped him to the sofa.

"About fifteen, twenty minutes after you left."

"What? Why didn't you call me?"

"I left the phone upstairs. I wasn't thinking."

"You've been sitting here swelling up for six hours

or more." She thought through her options. "I have to go upstairs for a minute. Don't move, Dad."

His lips white at the edges, he tried to smile. "Can't go anywhere."

Who should she call? An ambulance would terrify Dad. Once upstairs, she called Gray. He would help her. She was sure of it. Hadn't yesterday's fishing trip been a truce of sorts?

He wasn't her friend, but he would be decent enough to help, wouldn't he?

She called Turner Lumber and was put through by Hilary.

The second Gray answered, Audrey said, "I need help. It's Dad. He fell down the basement stairs."

"I'm on my way."

Then, silence. Just like that. Agreement.

Audrey unlocked the front door and left it wide-open, then went back downstairs to keep Dad company.

Not ten minutes later, Gray entered the house.

Audrey had been independent since she'd left home at nineteen to attend college. She'd depended on herself, not others, in life, and certainly not on a man, but she nearly crumpled with relief when she heard his rapid footsteps above and then on the stairs coming down.

Thank God. Now they could get Dad upstairs. Put him to bed. Make him comfortable.

"Heard you had an accident, Jeff." Gray stood in front of Dad and bent forward to peer into his face.

A lock of blond hair fell across his forehead. Audrey studied his straight profile, certain that he could handle anything that needed to be handled. He glanced at her and nodded to let her know he'd registered the pain Jeff was in. "How bad are things?"

"Hip's banged up but not broken. I can't make it up the stairs alone."

"That's why I'm here." Audrey wasn't sure she'd ever heard Gray sound so compassionate. Had aliens come and snatched Gray from his body, leaving this warm man in his place?

"Come on."

Jeff stood, and Audrey directed Gray to Dad's right side. Gray managed to get him upstairs, but Dad's skin was gray by the time they reached the living room.

"Maybe we should take you to the hospital for X-rays," Gray said, and Audrey made a slashing motion across her throat.

"No!" Dad said. "No hospitals."

With a puzzled frown, Gray asked, "Are you certain it isn't broken?"

"Positive. I couldn't have come upstairs otherwise, even with your help."

"May I ask for another favor?" Audrey edged Gray out into the hallway. "Would you mind going to the pharmacy to pick up painkillers? We don't usually keep that stuff in the house."

"Sure. Is there a reason why Jeff won't go to the hospital to make sure his injuries aren't serious?"

"Same reason as for not having the operation. My mom's death."

"I figured as much. Just checking. I'll be back soon."

After he left, Audrey wrapped tea towels around two freezer packs and took them to her dad.

"Here. Put this one on your hip. The other is for your shoulder."

She made sure they were placed properly.

"Ten or twelve minutes max, Dad, okay? Time it while I make you a cup of tea."

"I'd rather have a glass of Gray's Scotch."

"Are you kidding? As soon as Gray gets back, you're taking a bunch of painkillers. No alcohol. Besides—" she smiled even though he couldn't see it "—you guys finished it off."

By the time she'd made a pot of tea and had carried it to the living room, Gray had returned.

He got a glass of water from the kitchen and shook a couple of tablets into Jeff's hand. "I asked the pharmacist for the strongest nonprescription painkillers. He recommended these."

Gray got into Jeff's face. "He also strongly urged me to take you to the hospital."

"Won't go," Dad said.

Gray chuffed out a grim laugh. "Yeah. He knows you. That's what he said you'd say."

Audrey sweetened Dad's tea and made sure he drank the full cup before doctoring a second one.

"Stay with him while I make some food? He hasn't eaten all day."

Gray nodded, and Audrey left the room.

In the kitchen, she tried to make an early dinner, but her hands shook. What if Dad had really broken that hip? What if he'd gone into shock and she hadn't come home for another three hours? If the store had been open today, if she had been there instead of at the greenhouse, she would have gotten here a lot later than she had.

Ignoring how clumsy her fingers were, she managed to punch Teresa Grady's number into her phone. She should have done it earlier in the week when she'd threatened to. She'd been busy. No excuse.

Five minutes later, she'd made arrangements to drive into Denver tomorrow to pick up the therapist. Thank God, she was available.

Audrey leaned her forehead against the cool refrigerator. She felt a hand on her shoulder and straightened.

"You okay?"

She turned to find Gray, expression concerned.

"I just arranged to have an occupational therapist come live with Dad for the next two months. I'm picking her up tomorrow."

"And?"

"And?"

"Why does that make you look like the world is coming to an end?"

"Because," she said, "the shit will hit the fan the second the woman steps inside this house."

"Ah."

"Yes. Ah. An enormous ah."

He put his hands on her shoulders and, even though the gesture was brotherly, Audrey felt the heat of his touch to the soles of her feet. Who knew a man's touch could be so comforting and so disconcerting at the same time?

"You go sit with your father while I make dinner for the two of you."

"You can cook?"

He spotted the pork chops on the counter. "I can fry a pork chop. What else were you planning?"

"Asparagus and frozen fries."

"I can do that." He turned her toward the kitchen doorway. "Go."

"Will you stay and have dinner with us? Especially if you're cooking it?"

"Yes. And I'll help you get Jeff upstairs to bed."

Audrey closed her eyes and folded her hands as though in prayer. "Thank you," she breathed.

In the living room, the anger that fear had kept at bay kicked in and overwhelmed her. Dad could have died. He could have broken his neck.

"Don't ever do that again."

Dad's eyebrows nearly hit his hairline. "Come here," he said, voice rough.

When she approached, he held out his hand. She took it in hers.

"I'll never go down there alone again. Okay?" he asked, his chuckle weighted with suppressed emotion. He sobered quickly. "I scared myself, Audrey. I'm not ready to die. Even with these useless eyes, I'm not ready to go yet."

Mollified but still shaken, she hooked her foot around the leg of a footstool and pulled it close. Enough said. Her anger might be appeased, but residual fear and shock hummed through her body. She opened the book about World War II.

"Invasion of Normandy?" she asked, surprised that she sounded so calm.

"Yes."

While Gray cooked, Audrey read to her father in an eerie facsimile of a domestic scene.

Audrey had enjoyed her drive home from Denver with Teresa Grady. It had given her a chance to get to know the woman better. Audrey didn't doubt for a moment that Teresa would be able to hold her own against Dad.

When she turned onto her street, she noticed a Turner Lumber pickup truck parked in front of the house. Gray?

As soon as she stepped into the house, she recognized his voice. Had he come to keep Dad company? Or to ease the tension when Audrey brought the therapist home? Either way, she was glad he was here.

She entered the living room. "Hello, Gray," Audrey said. "Hi, Dad."

Dad had been laughing about something, but stopped. She had tried to sound normal, but maybe her voice had been too bright. Or maybe Dad had just grown sensitive in the past year to nuances and shifting patterns in the people around him.

"There's someone else here," he said. "A shadow beside you, Audrey. Who is it?"

"This is Teresa Grady, your new occupational therapist."

Her father became rigid, his face turned red, and Audrey felt an instant's fear. Could something like this cause a heart attack? A stroke?

He said nothing, anger pouring from him in waves.

"I interviewed a lot of people and hired the best." Audrey stepped farther into the room. "Her credentials are excellent. She's got a great sense of humor. She's willing to put up with you."

Her joke fell flat. She introduced Teresa to Gray. Dad still hadn't said anything.

"Dad, manners," Audrey warned. "Please say hello."

He didn't.

Ooooh. Obstinate man.

Audrey made a sound of impatience. Teresa touched her arm. "It's okay, Audrey. I've dealt with difficult clients before."

"I'm not difficult," Dad barked, sounding difficult.

"We'll see." Teresa motioned for Audrey to leave. "Why don't you start on dinner? I'll do better without you here," she whispered. "Trial by fire."

Gray turned to leave. When Gray said goodbye, Dad grunted.

Audrey stepped into the hallway to thank him for visiting again, but the words stuck in her throat. She clasped her hands over her belly.

How on earth was this ever going to work? And if it didn't, what was her next step?

She knew she should be eavesdropping to find out how things were going between Teresa and Dad, but she just didn't have the strength.

Gray took her hands, pried her fingers open and chafed them between his palms. They warmed. Thank goodness.

She opened her eyes. Here in the darkening foyer, his eyes were calm, the gray deep and unfathomable.

"Hey," he said. "Things will work out."

While the sentiment might have been lame, she appreciated that he was trying to cheer her.

She shrugged, her optimism, her joie de vivre, temporarily spent.

He opened his arms, and, without hesitation, she stepped into them, needing warm human contact too badly to question taking it from Gray. He ran his hands down her back, and she calmed, breathing in his forest-green essence and taking from it the same sense of rightness she got from her land. The same sense of belonging.

She didn't realize she was crying until the fabric of Gray's shirt beneath her cheek became wet. She'd kept this at bay, had maintained her good spirits by the sheer force of her willpower, but God! It felt good to just let *go*.

Gray gentled his touch, and she leaned into him.

When she stopped crying, she pulled away. Gray kissed her, a sweet touch of his lips to hers, and then he was gone.

It was a good thing because, despite what she'd said the other night about never wanting him to kiss her again, had he pushed it at this moment, she would have been all over him.

Had he sensed that? Had he left because he respected her and wouldn't take advantage of her vulnerability? She hoped so. She chose to believe so.

Teresa stepped into the hallway.

Audrey swiped the backs of her hands across her cheeks and straightened away from the wall, forcing her backbone into taking-care-of-business mode.

"Let's get you settled into your bedroom."

"Bedroom?" Dad called. "You mean she'll be *living* here?"

Teresa rolled her eyes to tell Audrey not to worry, that things would work out. Audrey took comfort in her confidence. She picked up Teresa's bag and carried it upstairs for her.

CHAPTER EIGHT

THAT WOMAN STOOD in front of Jeff. He saw her shadowy outline. He'd hoped that he'd been so rude last night she would decide to leave.

No such luck.

He heard Audrey leave the kitchen and walk down the hallway.

"I'm off to get a couple of hours in at the greenhouse before I open the shop. You two have a good day."

"What about my breakfast?" Jeff asked.

"Teresa's going to get it for you."

"Correction," Teresa answered. "I'm going to teach Jeff how to do it himself."

Jeff heard Audrey leave the house.

"You have a lovely daughter," the woman said.

Jeff grunted, but otherwise refused to acknowledge her presence. Why should he? He didn't ask to have a stranger *living* in his house.

"You should hear the way she talks about you. She really loves you."

He wished he could see the woman. "She couldn't love me too much or she'd stay here to take care of me."

"She has to earn a living. As far as I can tell from

the conversation we had in the car yesterday, she's working hard to make her business a success. Just because she works, never doubt her love."

Jeff grunted again. "What now?"

"Now, we go to the kitchen, and I'll teach you how to make an omelet."

"I raised my children as a single parent and cooked for them all of their lives. I know how to make an omelet, woman."

She was silent for so long he might have thought she'd left the room but for that blurry image of her in front of him. "I have a name. It's Teresa. My friends call me Tess. Please use it rather than grunting like an animal or calling me *woman*."

Jeff felt two feet small. He never treated women with such little respect, but *he didn't want her here*. Why couldn't Audrey and this woman, this Teresa, understand that?

"If that's too informal for you, you can call me Mrs. Grady."

After her reprimand, he'd hung his head, but now it shot up. "You're married? Why are you here taking care of me instead of your husband?"

"I need to earn a living. My husband died a long time ago and left me with nothing. I went back to school to learn a trade. I take care of myself. *And* I can take care of you. What do you want for breakfast besides the omelet?"

"No omelet. Eight slices of bacon, well done, and

two eggs sunny-side up fried in butter, with toast and jam on the side."

She laughed, and it rang like music through the room. "Dream on, Jeff."

Her laughter affected him deeply, in places where he hadn't felt anything for a long time. He fought back, because he didn't want those spaces filled, didn't want memories of loving Irene replaced with new ones. "Is this how you conduct business? Making fun of your clients?"

"When they're behaving like two-year-olds, yes."

He could sense her moving closer.

"Listen, Jeff, this is the way it's going to work with me. I understand that you are in a difficult place right now. I am probably the most empathetic person you'll ever meet, but I'm also tough. I don't take shit."

Jeff scowled. "It's not right for you to swear. I don't like it."

"Okay. It was unprofessional. I apologize." She sounded sincere. "Let me rephrase. I won't allow you to treat me with disrespect. I will at all times respect you. If you find that I don't, speak up, as you just did, and I will adjust my behavior."

He wasn't sure, but he thought she might have a finger up in the air. What was she doing?

"Secondly…"

Oh. Counting off points.

"You will try everything I ask you to do. If you don't succeed, I won't get angry. I won't express impatience. Instead, I'll teach you again. Together, we will try and try and try until you learn to adjust to your new situation."

"Situation? Is that what you call it?" he roared. "I'm going *blind.* How about if we skip the euphemisms and call a spade a spade."

"Okay, let's deal with that. Do you want to talk about your feelings?"

"What are you? A psychiatrist?"

"No, but I have a pair of ready and willing ears."

"I don't want to talk." He slammed his fist onto the arm of the chair.

"Fine. Then let's cook."

He remembered last week's humiliation, when he couldn't even make himself scrambled eggs without nearly setting the house on fire.

"I don't want to cook."

"Your choice. But this is the way it will work. I'm going to make *my* breakfast. Not yours. I'm not a maid or a caretaker or a caregiver. I'm a therapist. I don't do *for.* I teach, with the goal of helping you to become independent."

"You would let me starve?"

"If that's what it took to break through your mulish attitude, yes."

She left the room, and he heard her in the kitchen, taking things out of the fridge, setting a pan on the stove, running water.

His stomach grumbled.

He sensed, no *knew,* she wouldn't give in. She would make herself breakfast and sit out there and eat it without feeding him, practicing tough love on him, as though he was a rebellious teenager.

He heard her cooking, and the house filled with good scents and his stomach rumbled again. Then, nothing, and he knew she was eating.

Heck.

He stood and shuffled down the hallway. When he finally stood in the kitchen doorway, he sensed a shape stand up from the kitchen table.

The woman, Teresa, said, "Okay, we'll start with something more basic than an omelet."

He was listening for triumph in her voice, for any trace of I-told-you-so, but there was none. What he did hear was practicality. Quiet acceptance.

She taught him how to make the scrambled eggs that he'd messed up the day before, using tricks to help him adjust to not being able to see.

She wouldn't let him eat from a tray in the living room like Audrey had. She made him sit at the table.

It was possible....

Cooking for himself was possible....

AUDREY MANAGED TO hold herself back from calling home until lunchtime.

Wednesdays weren't usually a hotbed of business with customers, so she used them to catch up on accounts, to place orders for depleted stock and to check out the work of artisans in Colorado who made interesting pottery or garden-themed artwork that she could sell in the shop to augment flower sales.

Today, she was also designing her platform to hold the plants and flowers for the show. Her spot was small. If she couldn't spread out, she would have to build up. She'd already drawn a plan she was happy with and had ordered lumber from Turner's. Later tonight, she would raid Dad's workshop for tools and start building in the alley behind her shop this week, weather permitting.

Rather than defeating her, the challenge of working in so small a space fired her up, gave her creative spirit juice.

She couldn't wait to start.

Overshadowing her fighting spirit was a deep regret. If only Dad could help her build the structure. It really would have been something—to have been able to have shared the creation of it with him. He would have loved helping her.

Thinking of Dad and his restrictions, she finally gave in to the temptation to find out how Teresa was doing.

When she phoned home, she didn't know what to expect. World War III, maybe?

Teresa answered the phone. "Stone residence. Teresa speaking. How may I help you?"

"Oooh," Audrey joked. "You sound like my dad's personal secretary." She'd learned in the car yesterday that Teresa had a lively sense of humor.

She chuckled now. "I try to sound professional whenever possible. Checking in?"

"Yes."

"I'm impressed you waited so long. On the first day, family usually calls within the first hour, expecting fireworks, I guess. Especially when dealing with difficult clients."

In the distance, Audrey heard, "I can hear you talking about me, you know."

Teresa laughed again. "Your point being?"

Dad mumbled something that Audrey didn't catch.

"We made scrambled eggs for breakfast." Teresa's voice, which had sounded as if her mouth was turned away from the phone, was stronger as she spoke directly to Audrey again.

"We? Dad helped?"

"Yes. He did very well. He said he cooked for you when you were a child."

"All the time. Mom died when my brother and I were young. Dad did a really good job taking care of us."

"That's good because it means I don't have to teach him how to cook from scratch, only how to do it with restrictions."

This might work! This just might work. Audrey's sense of jubilation was cut short as Teresa continued, "I'm getting him out of the house this afternoon."

"Oh, jumping jelly beans, good luck with that."

"I'll do it. I always succeed." Rather than sounding rash or overconfident, Audrey heard a smile in Teresa's voice.

Good. Audrey was free to work without worry for the afternoon. Or maybe not.

She heard Dad yell, "I'm not going out!"

TERESA TAUGHT HIM how to make a tuna salad sandwich for lunch. He was so proud of himself, he made a second one.

"Tomorrow we'll make a salad to go with the sandwich."

"I don't eat salad."

"There are all kinds of salads out there."

"I'm not a rabbit. I don't eat lettuce."

"Do you eat cabbage?"

He loved it. "It's okay. I eat it."

"Fine. Then we'll make coleslaw. If you don't want to grate or slice a head of cabbage, we can buy a bag of precut and make a homemade dressing."

"Nothing creamy," he muttered. "I like it vinegary."

"Jeff, don't you get it? I'm here to help you learn to do the things *you* like the way *you* like them. To make the things you want to eat. I can go online and find any recipe you want."

"You'll have to use Audrey's computer. I don't have one." He finished his sandwich and carried his plate and empty glass to the sink. Ornery woman probably wouldn't do it for him.

"Okay. I'll ask her whether I can use it. I'll also ask her to pick up the ingredients on her way home from work. Unless you'd rather come out with me to get them."

"No." No way. Have the townspeople laugh at him while he struggled to do the things they took for granted?

"How often do you go out?" Teresa asked.

Jeff leaned against the counter and crossed his arms over his chest. "Never. I already told you I'm not going out."

"We're changing that today."

"No."

"No arguments, Mr. Stone. You need to get out." She stood up from the table and rinsed the dishes. "Tomorrow you can start to do the dishes with me, but you've done enough in the kitchen today. You did really well."

He shouldn't be so happy with the compliment. Teresa was no one to him. Her opinion meant nothing. Nothing.

"Audrey said you used to work out a lot." She closed a cupboard door after putting something away. "Do you still have your membership at the gym?"

He nodded, but tensed. She couldn't possibly mean to take him there.

"Good," she said. "We'll leave in about half an hour."

"No way. Don't ask me to do this."

"Why not?"

"Why do you think? I'm going blind."

"I mean, let's go deeper. What do you think will

go wrong if you go out? That you'll have an accident? That you'll get hurt somehow? I won't let that happen. I'll be with you the whole time."

"It's not that." How could she possibly understand? She was whole.

"What is it then? Help me to comprehend."

"Everyone will see me," he mumbled.

"So?"

"So they'll see me make a fool of myself. They'll laugh."

"Is that what the people of this town are like?"

He couldn't see her expression. He'd learned to listen. She sounded genuinely interested. Concerned.

"They aren't mean."

"Good, because Audrey led me to believe you're respected in this town."

"I used to be. That doesn't mean people will still respect me now."

"Has your basic character changed?"

He understood where she was going with this. "No, but they always knew me as an active man. I did stuff for people. Chopped their wood. Fixed their homes if they needed help."

"My guess would be they wouldn't make fun of you. That they would still treat you with as much respect as they ever did."

"I don't know."

"Face it, Jeff. We're going to the gym. Audrey told me you fell down the stairs on Monday. We need to keep your body strong so when things like this happen, you can better withstand the impact. Let me put on some lipstick."

"You're vain?"

Teresa laughed, but it didn't sound light and musical as it had earlier. He could swear it sounded a little sad. He'd gotten used to hearing what he couldn't see.

"If you saw me, you wouldn't think so," she said. "To put it bluntly, I'm homely. I like to wear lipstick, though. It gives me the illusion that I have something worth gussying up."

Jeff frowned but didn't respond.

"Go pack your gym bag," Teresa said.

"How are we going to get there? I can't drive."

"I can. Audrey said you have a pickup truck. We'll take it."

"You want to drive my truck?" He couldn't keep the dread out of his voice. It was bad enough that Audrey had to use it for her business, let alone this stranger taking it over.

Half an hour later, Teresa led Jeff out to the driveway, steering him with a hand to his elbow.

"I feel like a darned toddler," he snapped. "I'm being led around like a baby."

"Okay, let's try something different." She let go of his elbow and took his hand in hers, threading her fingers through his. She had a strong hand and a warm palm. "Now we look like we're holding hands. You've got some vision. Use it to see where to step. If you stumble, I have a firm grip on your hand. You won't fall."

The truth was that *he* had a hard grip on *her* hand. He didn't want to fall. He hadn't liked that loss of control, that stomach-clenching sense of having nothing beneath his feet when he'd tumbled down the stairs.

She got him into the truck. She started it, and he sensed her turning her head to check for cars and pedestrians, and then put her foot on the gas to back out of the driveway. The truck shot out.

"Wow!" she whooped. "This thing's got power."

"You bet." Jeff smiled because her laugh was infectious, and bubbly like ginger ale, as if she were a bottle that had been shaken and the contents overflowed onto his hands after he'd opened it.

He wanted to catch those bubbles in his palms and put them to his lips.

While they drove to the gym, Jeff enumerated the truck's features. He loved his vehicle. It had been his treat two years ago for his sixtieth birthday.

When he paused, Teresa said, "I heard you went fishing on the weekend. Are you an avid fisherman?"

"Used to be."

"You just got lucky, mister."

He tilted his head her way. "What do you mean?"

"I adore fishing. I can take you out."

"Are you telling the truth or just trying to get me out of the house again?"

"Both. I won't ever lie to you, Jeff. When I say I adore fishing, I mean it. You've got some amazing scenery around here. I'm betting there's stellar fishing in the lakes and rivers nearby."

"You bet." Some of the gruffness had left his voice.

GRAY HADN'T LIFTED weights since he'd left Boston. He felt the need, especially after the morning he'd just had at the office.

He'd relaxed on the weekend with Jeff and Dad. He'd let down his guard and had temporarily forgotten how things were at work and in his life. He'd been able to forget, until he'd gone into work.

Now his gut was churning again, and he was popping antacids instead of chewing gum. He was counting telephone poles and footsteps and the number of times he washed his hands each hour.

He hated it.

On Monday and Tuesday, he'd ignored the grumbling and had supervised the cleanup after the renovations were completed, but a man could only take so much negativity from people.

Some were smug because they knew that Dad had reinstated the benefits and, earlier, the banking of sick days, and all were angry that Gray had tried to take them away.

Some, though, were worried. They remembered what Gray had said about layoffs. Where Turner Lumber had once been a great place to work, now there was tension, debate, a lack of confidence in the company—all of it bad for business.

A man could deal with only so much tension at work and contain only so much guilt at home—knowing what he'd started with John Spade, what he'd *had* to start, with a break from his parents hanging over his head like Damocles's sword—before he had to find an outlet.

Rather than punch out a wall at work or slit his wrists at home, he came to the gym.

The running wasn't enough. If he couldn't outrun what was bothering him, maybe he could work himself to exhaustion here.

After paying for a month-to-month membership at the front desk of the gym, he was handed a thick towel and shown to the men's change rooms.

Teresa Grady leaned against the wall opposite the men's room door and looked relieved to see him. Odd, considering that she'd met him for all of three minutes last night.

"What's up?" he asked.

"Jeff's been in that change room for fifteen minutes. I'm worried."

"I'll check on him."

He entered the locker room. "Jeff? It's Gray."

"Here." An angry, defiant voice came from the rear of the room.

Gray found Jeff seated in the far corner.

"What are you doing back here?"

Jeff's jaw worked. "Don't want anyone to see me."

"Why not? You don't look strange. You look normal. Like yourself." Except so much older. And frail.

"I have trouble doing for myself. Got myself back here and now can't find the door."

"Give me a sec to get into my workout clothes and I'll take you out to the workout room." Gray opened a locker nearby and changed into his sweats. "What are you doing today? The treadmill?"

"I used to lift weights, but don't know if I can now. Blasted woman made me come here." Gray wasn't fooled by the anger. He heard the wistfulness that Jeff probably had no idea leaked through. Jeff wanted a normal life. He wanted to lift weights as he used to be able to do as a matter of course.

"Today's your lucky day, Jeff."

The man snorted. "Yeah? People keep telling me that." A healthy dose of sarcasm threaded through the anger. "How so?"

"I'm lifting weights today. We can do the circuit together."

"I'll slow you down. Don't you have to get to work?"

"Seriously, Jeff? With Hilary running the place?" Jeff barked out a laugh that sounded rusty. "True. The business would be lost without her."

"Ain't that the truth? The woman's formidable. Let's go."

With a light touch on Jeff's arm, Gray directed him out the door.

Teresa's frown lifted when she saw them.

"I'm going to guide Jeff through his workout," Gray told her. "What'll it take, Jeff? An hour?"

"Used to be an hour and a quarter or more. I've lost it all, Gray. Don't know how long it'll take now."

"When was the last time you worked out?"

"A year ago."

"You'd better take it easy your first time out," Gray cautioned. "How stiff are you from that fall the other day?"

"Pretty stiff. My hip and my left shoulder are the hot spots."

"Start with gentle stretches."

Gray turned to Teresa. "Do you want to go somewhere for a coffee for an hour?"

"Nope. I'm lifting weights, too. The boy at the desk said I could as Jeff's guest today."

Gray nodded. "Let's go." He lifted his eyebrow when Teresa laced her fingers through Jeff's and led the way to the weight room.

"I already found out where it is. I sometimes have clients who need to be lifted and can't do much on their own," she confessed. "I have to stay in shape."

Gray checked her out. She wasn't a big woman, but looked solid in her sweats.

When they entered the room, Gray said, "Go work out, Teresa. I'll take care of Jeff." He turned to him. "What did you used to do?"

Jeff outlined his routine, and Gray said, "Okay, let's start with free weights and then move on. Let's modify your old routine radically. Take it real easy."

They ended up in the gym for well over an hour and a half, slowly deciding how much muscle tone

Jeff had lost and what he could reasonably do at the beginning.

By the end of the workout, the man seemed different, more relaxed. He'd even spent twenty minutes of slow cycling on a stationary bike.

"Let's head back to the change room," Gray said. "I need a shower before I go to the office."

Jeff followed slowly, but more confidently. Gray didn't need to take his arm.

"May I make a suggestion?"

"Sure."

"Maybe you should go home in your workout clothes and shower where your bathroom is familiar to you."

Jeff nodded. "Good idea."

"How often do you plan to come here?"

"I don't know. Teresa made me come, but now I want to lift regularly again, like I used to."

"I'll plan to be here three to four times a week. Do you want to coordinate visits?"

Jeff relaxed. "Yeah. I'd like that."

After he got Jeff safely back to Teresa, Gray took his own shower, dressed and then drove to Turner Lumber, back to the lion's den where he felt as if he fought for his life every day.

When Gray entered the office, he stepped into a jungle, with the surprising delight of watching Audrey's backside as she set a couple of plants on the floor at the top of the stairs. Gray cleared his throat.

She straightened and turned around.

They stared too long, and he knew he needed to get them past the budding intimacy, the understanding and shared compassion for Jeff that was forming between them, because it couldn't last.

With a jut of his chin toward the plants, he asked, "What is all of this and what's it doing in my office?" There must have been a couple of dozen of them, some small, but a couple about six feet tall.

"Hilary called and ordered them. This is all the stock I have, so if you want more, I'll have to get them from Denver."

"Why did she order them?"

She settled her hands on her hips, pleased with herself. "They're air purifiers. Spider plants, peace lilies, English ivy, dracaena, a couple of areca palms and one stunning Boston fern."

Air purifiers?

"Do you want me to arrange them?" she asked.

"No. I can take care of that." They wouldn't be staying. He opened his mouth to call for Hilary, but she appeared beside his elbow, Radar O'Reilly–like in her silent efficiency.

"Yes, boss?" She refused to call him Mr. Turner, because that denoted his father, but she also refused to call him Gray. Because it was too informal? Because he hadn't yet earned her respect as a boss? He didn't have a clue. He was angry with her, though. She'd had no right to order these behind his back.

"It looks like a rain forest in here. Why did you order these?"

His tone angered her. He could see it in the way she stiffened. Too bad. She'd angered him with her presumption that it was okay to spend this money without consulting him.

"They're here to clean the air," she said. "And to add warmth to the room."

"Let me rephrase. Why did you order these without running the cost by me first?"

"Your dad gave me control of the office. If I wanted to order something, he let me."

"Haven't I made it clear that we have to conserve? Buying pastries for the employees is one thing, but ordering a forest is another. It's frivolous and unnecessary."

"But they'll make the place healthier. A *lot* healthier."

"People have worked here for years without health complaints."

"But that was before you stirred up who knows what with the renovations." Her voice had become strident. "I want to purify the air."

"Get rid of them." He turned to tell Audrey to take them back, but she was gone. The stairs behind him were empty.

"Call Audrey back. Tell her to return them."

"She'll still charge us for the delivery and for her time to take them back."

"So, I'm stuck with a bill I didn't authorize." He was sick, *sick,* of being treated like an addendum to the business, as though his authority meant nothing.

As though he might as well have not bothered coming back to town to help out, even though he worked his fingers to the bone to make things better and to fix all of the mistakes that Dad had been making.

"Your father gave me free rein to make sure his office ran efficiently," Hilary asserted, getting into his face. "He *liked* the things I did to make the place warm and welcoming for his employees."

"Times have changed. I'm in charge now."

"Are you?"

How dare she? He vibrated with fury.

"In the future," he said, his tone as cold as dry ice and every bit as capable of burning, "bring your ideas to me for authorization before you spend Turner money. Understood?"

"Yes, *sir*." She stomped away to her desk. Only then did he realize the entire office had been listening. He needed to talk to her about adjusting her attitude, especially in public.

He entered his office and slid the walls closed, craving privacy, a few moments away from the opprobrium of him ripe in the office like the stink of old cheese. He hung up his coat and opened his briefcase.

A second later, one of his walls banged open, the sound jarring in the hush of the office. "What—?"

Hilary marched into the room with a paper in her hand. Once again, Gray had the sense that everyone in the large outer office listened, that the office itself, the very walls, floors and ceiling were holding a collective breath.

"My resignation," she said, slapping the sheet onto the desk. "I worked for your father for thirty-five years, and I have never, ever been treated with the disrespect you've given me in the past three months. I'm sixty-two years old. I don't need this shit."

In all of his years growing up, running in and out of the office with his parents and working here as a teenager, he had never heard Hilary use profanity.

She stormed out of his office, leaving him with his mouth hanging open.

"Wait." He jumped to his feet, sending his chair rocketing across the office. "Are you serious?"

"You betcha, mister."

"Why did you call me if you didn't want this company saved? Because that's what I'm trying to do here, Hilary."

"I no longer care."

"And these?" He pointed to the plants. "You caused this problem. Who's going to take care of it?"

"Whichever poor sucker takes over my job. Goodbye, *boss*."

She left the building amid stunned silence. Gradually, like the hissing of an angry snake, the whispering began.

He knew how destructive gossip in the office could be.

All of those visits he'd had here when he was a kid had been happy ones. The atmosphere and the work culture Dad had cultivated had been stellar.

Remembering what he'd heard while fishing with

Dad and Jeff yesterday, he realized that he had just rent a gaping hole into the fabric of the company Dad had woven with care.

He ran a hand across his forehead. He was sweating again. When Jeff had said that Hilary was formidable, he'd been right. Who would run the office now that the only woman who knew *everything* was gone? Who would take her place? Gray didn't know the other employees well enough to appoint one of them as office manager.

In the larger room, someone sneezed. A second later, so did he.

What the heck?

He remembered Arnie wiping his nose a lot during their meeting in his office last week.

Sam Power entered his office, nose bright red. "She's right, you know. The reno stirred up all kinds of stuff that's been irritating us. I've had a runny nose for weeks."

"Why didn't anyone tell me?"

Sam shrugged. "I guess we all thought that Hilary would."

No. She'd just decided to handle it herself, which, when he thought about it, was exactly what a good employee, a self-starter, should do.

"Hilary bought some air purifiers and then called Audrey to bring in plants."

Bloody hell. She'd even bought machines?

Hell.

Had he just screwed up?

Hell, yeah.

Where had the guy gone who used to handle anything that life threw at him with skill? He was disappearing, bit by bit, the undertow of his nerves, anxiety and guilt clutching his feet and pulling him under.

He had the best intentions. They weren't working.

The problem today hadn't been the plants. It had been his perception that Hilary had been undermining him again and spending money the company shouldn't put out at this time. Employee health was important, but she should have talked to him first.

But the idea that he should have absolute control over every penny was archaic, too. There was a middle ground that he hadn't negotiated with Hilary.

He shouldn't have taken her to task publicly. While he'd planned to lecture her on her disrespect toward him in public, he'd hauled her over the carpet in front of a room full of employees.

Hypocrite.

He would have never done it in his business. Another sign of how he was letting control slip away from him, of how he was letting life lead him around by his fears and anxieties rather than him leading his life where he needed it to go.

Rather than him getting past the anxiety to make healthy choices.

He knew a lot about business, but Hilary had more experience in *this office* than he had in his baby finger. He needed her back.

To be fair, he was trying. Why wasn't it enough? Arnie said his ideas were sound. Were they? Was he improving anything? Not while Dad undermined him. Today wasn't about Dad, though. The way he'd handled today's argument had been his mistake. Completely.

Okay, he was the one who had to fix it.

His goal here was to save the company, but he was losing individuals to the cause. One thing Dad *had* done right for years was to keep individuals happy.

He phoned Audrey. "Get back over here and arrange these plants in my office."

"O-*kay,*" she said. "If you insist."

Ten minutes later, she walked into the office. "Can I borrow a couple of the men from the lumberyard to help me move the bigger palms?"

"Sure."

She turned to leave, but he had a thought. "Wait. I saw your Dad at the gym with Teresa."

"You did?" Her smile lit the room. "That's awesome."

"Yeah, but I also saw his pickup there. How did you get all of the plants over here without the truck?"

"I used a Turner Lumber pickup and a couple of the guys helped me load the big plants."

"Who authorized this? Never mind."

"Hilary," they said at the same time.

He brushed past her closely enough for her perfume to stroke his neck with its comforting hands.

"Why are you frowning?" she asked. "You aren't going to give me hell like you did Hilary, are you?"

"Groveling. I hate groveling."

"I wasn't!" she retorted.

"No, but I will." He strode toward the stairs. "Hilary resigned. Now I have to get her back."

Her laughter trailed him to the first floor. He asked for Hilary's address from one of the cashiers.

A couple of minutes later, he stood on her veranda, trying to get past his roiling emotions to figure out what smart things he could say to get his employee to return to work.

When Hilary opened the door, she wasn't pleased to see him. "What do you want?" she asked none too graciously.

"Come back. Please. You were right. We need the plants."

She crossed her arms over her chest and said nothing.

"All right," he admitted. "You were right. More than right. We need to clean the air."

A huge chunk of humble pie lodged in his throat, and he forced out the words that needed to be said. "You make an incredible contribution to the company. You're irreplaceable. I will endeavor in the future to always treat you with respect, and I will never disagree with you in public again."

She seemed to be considering coming back. Dared he hope? "Please?"

Hilary smiled. "Okay, I'll come back." When he

would have returned her smile, she raised one finger. "On one condition."

Oh, boy, here it comes, he thought. The demands for money, for a longer vacation, for more sick days. Didn't matter. He'd pretty well give her anything she asked.

"I want more say in how the new office is arranged."

That's it? She'd surprised him. He was used to more greed.

"There are a number of ways in which the new setup works—" she inclined her head toward him as though conceding a point "—but an equal number of ways in which it doesn't." She wagged a finger at him. "Instead of dismissing my concerns, you should be taking advantage of my experience."

"You have a point. I want one concession from you."

Suspicious, she asked, "What?"

"We both have the same goal, to keep Turner Lumber in business. We need to work together to do that and find some middle ground that will work for both of us."

"Fair enough."

He stuck out his hand. "It's a deal."

She hesitated, as though gauging whether or not to trust him, and then shook his hand.

"Deal. I'll come back in at my regular time tomorrow morning."

Gray nodded and went back to the office.

Audrey was just putting the last plant into place.
"Did Hilary agree to come back?" she asked.

Gray nodded. "She was very reasonable."

Audrey smiled. "She always is."

She propped a hand on one of those gorgeous hips.
"What do you think of the office?"

"It looks good, great, wonderful." Hilary had been
right. The plants warmed up the space.

Audrey didn't leave, but neither did he head to
his office, both poised as though to say more but
not knowing what that might be. Finally, she slipped
around Gray and down the stairs.

Gray walked into his office with the cloud of Audrey's perfume keeping him company like an old
friend.

He didn't get home until well after six that evening, but the moment he walked into the house, he
knew something was wrong, as though a super-
charged electricity vibrated in the air.

He found Mom and Dad in the living room.

"What have you done?" His father's voice was
quiet, disbelieving. Dad stood beside the coffee table,
his stature diminished by age, but his outrage a lion
springing from his shoulders. Dangling from his fingers was what looked like a legal document. "They
want to have a psychiatrist interview me. To evalu-
ate me. So you can have guardianship. Of me and
my property."

John Spade was efficient. He did quick work.

They finally knew. Thank God.

The illness in Gray's stomach, a hard, burning ball of self-disgust, threatened to explode out of him. He wanted to cry, to literally fall to the ground and bawl like a baby for what he knew he'd just lost—Dad's trust and Mom's faith in him.

Mom sat on the sofa, face pale, eyes as wide as the Eastern Plains of Colorado, her equilibrium and her confidence in the goodness of the world, her unshakeable belief in her son, shattered.

He wanted to claw his way out of the guilt and shame, to place the blame on Dad's shoulders where it belonged, to shout, *this is real life, Mom. I did it for you.*

He would save the company and get the money from the sale of the land to pay off Shelly, and Mom would never know that Dad had fooled around on her. Because he knew what the DNA test would say— that Dad *was* Shelly's father.

At the same time, he needed to defend himself, to tell them that he'd had no choice, but to do that, he would have to admit what he knew, and that would devastate Mom. He had no defense that could be uttered aloud, that would ever see the light of day.

"What did we ever do to you to deserve this?" Gray heard his father's shock and wanted to calm him but couldn't. His anger with his father for bringing all of this on to the family choked him.

What he wanted to say, to yell, to spew, was, *You*

screwed another woman while you were married to Mom, and now we all have to live with the consequences.

All of us, including you.

He hadn't admitted to himself until this moment how deep his anger with his father ran for doing this, that underneath all of Gray's guilt and distress, there was such profound disappointment in his father that it almost eclipsed the scalding anger.

He could say nothing, couldn't explain a thing, without incriminating Dad and exposing what he had done to Mom.

Despite his anger, he still loved his father, but even more, he adored his mother. He would do anything to protect her.

Since he couldn't address that issue, he opened his mouth to address the other—how Dad was running the business into the ground—but Dad stopped him.

"Don't say a word. There's nothing you can say to defend this action."

"Yes," Gray bit out. "There is. Ever since I came home, you've countermanded every order I've given at work, every change I've made, even though my intentions have been the *best*."

He faced his mother, forcing himself to ignore how pale and fragile she looked. "Mom, you said that Dad was tired and that he wanted to quit the business. If that's so, then why won't he let go? If he wanted me to come home for so many years, why won't he let me run the business as I see fit?"

"He won't?"

She looked at her husband, who said to Gray, "Because you're running it all wrong. You want to cheat my employees out of everything."

"You're going to lose the company," Gray shouted. "You're going to go bankrupt without significant changes. I've tried to tell you every way I know how. The company is going to go under unless we take drastic measures. You won't let me take those measures."

"So what?"

"So *what?*" Gray couldn't believe Dad's nonchalance. "Do you *want* to lose the company?"

"Maybe I do. *You* never cared for it."

Gray shook his head in genuine bewilderment. "Why would you say that?"

"You didn't come home after college to take over. You started your own business."

"I needed to know that I could. I needed to prove that I was more than just your son, that I had a sound business sense of my own. That I could be a success in my own right."

He stepped forward, but Dad stiffened and he stopped. "Dad, it's normal for a young guy to want to be his own man and not an extension of his father."

"So why not come home after you'd proved your point?"

"Marnie." That one word said it all. "I loved Marnie, and she didn't want to live here."

"But a woman should follow her husband where he needs to live."

"Dad, that's old. Men and women negotiate. They do what they can to make each other happy. I tried to make Marnie happy. I met her in her hometown. It wasn't fair to ask her to leave Boston."

He was struck by a suspicion. "Were you deliberately running the company into the ground?"

With one quick nod, his Dad confirmed it.

Stunned, Gray asked, *"Why?"*

"If you didn't want it, then what was the point of holding on to it?"

"For the employees. If you thought I didn't want it, you could have sold it. If it goes bankrupt, your employees are out of work."

"But I've given them so much. They'll be okay."

"They won't if there's no money in the company to give them."

Harrison faltered and stared at the paper in his hand. "Go," he said. "Just go."

Gray left the room and trudged upstairs. Numb, he packed a bag with a few essentials and left the house, passing the living room without looking in, the mood of the place he'd once loved a black hole sucking the life out of him.

He drove away, toward the new condo building at the edge of town, where he found one furnished unit available to rent, but not until the end of the month. Tomorrow. He booked a room at the B and B and

got the top floor suite. Good. He needed privacy.
Needed to be alone.

He fell into bed and slept through until the following morning. Eyes gritty, he squinted against the
sunlight streaming through the window, past curtains
he'd forgotten to close, like a happy harpy singing,
"Good morning!"

What the hell was so good about it?

I've lost my family!

He didn't shout it, but he wanted to.

In the shower, he let water pour over him in nearly
scalding waves to cleanse the grime of shame he
imagined coated his skin like dirt.

He punched the wall. He'd had no choice, dammit.
He'd had to take Dad out of the equation.

Not that he was yet. John Spade had a long way
to go before that was done.

He'd just finished dressing when someone knocked
on his door. He opened it. Audrey stood on the landing, hands in fists on her hips, her lips thinned, a
white line of fury around her mouth.

Jeez. She'd heard.

"Abigail called," she said. "You're having your
dad evaluated?"

He nodded. "I tried to avoid this. I really did."

"How could you?" The warm voice that usually
bathed him with honey sounded raw, as though her
throat was so choked with anger it hurt to speak.

"I can't—" She studied him as though he were
a science experiment gone horribly wrong. "You

couldn't have changed that much. You used to be sweet. Did business, did your MBA, really change you so profoundly you would betray your parents?"

"No!"

"Then *what?* Why did you do this?" She scrubbed her hands through her hair. "Abigail called in tears."

His gut did its churning thing, now so much a part of everyday life he missed it when it wasn't happening. *Mom.* He'd been trying to avoid seeing her hurt, but there was no way this situation would ever go down well.

Still, he'd made his choice. Save the company. Save Mom. He and Dad no longer mattered.

Audrey's violet eyes flashed fire. "Is money so important to you that you have to take your dad's company from him?"

"*No! I* don't need the money. The company does. And She—" He'd almost said, *And Shelly does.* That was family stuff. Private. None of Audrey's business.

Fed up with how unfair life was, he ground out, "Listen, I'm tired. I'm sick of being the bad guy. I was called home to help out and I've tried my damnedest to make things right. If you don't like how I've done it, tough."

He slammed the door in her face.

Well, he thought, *that's that.*

CHAPTER NINE

AUDREY PRESSED HER finger against the Turner doorbell. When Harrison opened the door, she barely suppressed a gasp. He'd aged ten years in a day.

He stepped aside to allow her to enter.

Abigail sat on the sofa, her eyes red-rimmed, her demeanor defeated.

Oh, Gray, look what you've done to two of the best people on earth.

Dear God, she was angry. Furious.

She should go back to the B and B and kick his ass. Instead, she stayed where she was, because Harrison and Abigail needed a friend.

It also looked as though they needed comprehension of this disaster, but that she couldn't give. Even after seeing Gray only a few minutes ago, she had no better understanding of his motives than before she'd confronted him.

He'd been recalcitrant and unhappy. He might have committed a horrible disservice to his parents, but he hadn't looked the least bit pleased about betraying them. In fact, he'd seemed almost as ravaged by his actions as his parents were.

So why had he elected to try for guardianship over his father? What was in it for him?

Audrey sat beside Abigail and took her hands in her own. They were icicles. Audrey chafed them.

"I'll make tea," Harrison said.

"I can do it," Audrey offered, but Harrison stopped her with a sad smile.

"I need to keep busy. Stay with Abigail."

After he left the room, Abigail said, "This is killing him." Her voice hitched. "I don't know what to do for him or how to help him. We gave Gray everything, and now this."

Her bewildered gaze delved into Audrey's, as though she could find answers there. "I don't understand."

"Me, either," she said, her need to fix this undermined by helplessness and ignorance. "There has to be a reason. Did Gray need money?"

Abigail shrugged, the gesture more eloquent than words at indicating how at sea she was.

"Perhaps it had something to do with his life away from Accord. Tell me what happened to him back in Boston." Maybe between the two of them, she and Abigail could find hints. "I heard rumors of a car accident."

"Yes. His fiancée died in the crash."

Oh, God. She hadn't heard. She'd had no idea. "That's horrible."

"Yes, it was very sad. Devastating for Gray. They'd been engaged for five years."

There were no words. Even something like *devastating* couldn't possibly say enough.

"He loved her?"

"He adored her," Abigail said. "So much so that he stayed in Boston when he really wanted to move back here."

Oh. She'd thought he hadn't cared enough—about the town, his parents or Turner Lumber, to come home. She thought he'd become an urban snob.

Things weren't adding up. "Could he be so, I don't know, deranged by sorrow that he isn't thinking clearly?"

"I don't think Marnie's death caused this, Audrey. When he'd returned home, he'd seemed...diminished, but not bitter. I know he loved Marnie, but how could it relate to what he's done here?"

"I don't know." She held Abigail's hand and said, "I have to find out. I can't leave this. One way or another, I'll figure it out and get back to you."

"How?"

"I don't know. Any ideas?"

Abigail thought about it. "Ask him."

"I don't think it's going to be that simple."

"Try. Please."

How could she not? Her only thought was to go back to see Gray and to show no mercy, to bash away at him until he gave her answers.

ISOLATED AND VILIFIED, Gray did a strange thing.

He called Shelly Harper.

If Marnie were still alive, he could talk to her. She would comfort him, support him, and he wouldn't feel so alone.

But she was gone.

So thinking, maybe still hoping, that Shelly might be family, he phoned her.

She sounded cautious when she heard his voice. Rightly so.

"I, ah, just wanted to know how you're doing." More like he wanted to touch base with someone for whom he'd done something good and, judging by their faces when they'd opened the bags of groceries that he'd left, had been *recognized* as good.

Not vilified.

Not questioned.

Not undermined.

Not stonewalled, or smirked at or talked about behind his back.

He brought himself under control. It was all water under the bridge now.

He listened to Shelly talk about her kids, and his mood shifted, lightened. He'd met those children. He'd pictured Joe's smile while the boy's body betrayed him. He didn't know how was it possible to still smile, but Joe had. Gray had witnessed Tiffany's joy when she'd seen those silly flip-flops.

So, while Shelly talked, he got to know them better. Finally, too soon, he ended the conversation.

Shelly had to get breakfast for her children.

And Gray had to figure out where to go next.

HE SHOULDN'T HAVE come home to Accord. None of this would be happening if he hadn't.

Stop. Of course it would. It just wouldn't be happening to you.

True.

So, where did he go from here? Into work, he guessed. Just because his world had caved in and his parents would probably never talk to him again, and the only relatives he had left might not really be relatives, didn't mean that the world had stopped spinning on its axis or that time was standing still.

There was still work to be done and a company to be saved. If Dad wanted to call the cops to have him ousted from the place, fine. Until then, he was going to do his job.

When Gray entered Turner Lumber at nine, his anxiety level breaking records, he expected there to be coldness, expected to be shunned, but there was no more hostility than usual. Maybe Audrey was the only person her parents had told.

Hilary greeted him as though yesterday had never happened, as though she hadn't quit and been persuaded to come back.

Her presence reminded him of something he'd said to her yesterday about finding middle ground.

"Hilary," he said, "can you have Arnie meet me here as soon as he can?"

"Sure thing, Gray."

Gray? Not *boss,* or *sir?* Hmm, a good sign, maybe?

He and Arnie worked all morning, circling the

layoff issue, which Gray still resisted. Yes, he understood compromise, but not on this. Not yet.

He asked Hilary to have everyone meet in the main office after work again. Before she could ask, he said, "I would appreciate it if you would get baked goods."

"You got it."

At ten after six, he stood beside Arnie in front of everyone and told them about his dad reinstating the benefits, which of course everyone already knew.

And then he did something most business people would think insane, the business equivalent of hara-kiri. He gave the employees numbers. He told them how much the company owed. He told them how much the benefits were costing.

"Our largest expense, as with any business, is in the payroll."

Panicked muttering filled the room.

He expelled a breath and waded in. "You all need your jobs. I'm still fighting to keep everyone, but here's how it's got to go down *if you want to keep your jobs.*" His finger jabbed the air to stress his point. "We have to cut benefits. You can call my dad. You can have him override this decision, *and* you can walk out of here tonight and not come back."

They grumbled. "I don't mean that I'll have a fit and fire the snitch. I mean that if we keep handing out money for all of the benefits as they currently stand, we will lose Turner Lumber and every one of you will be out of a job. There's no more money."

He studied the faces around him. They were finally taking him seriously. "I'm learning to listen, to moderate in the middle of working to preserve what we have here, so this is the deal. We're purchasing a new benefits package. Gone are the orthodontics. Gone are the massages. Gone is chiropractic or physiotherapy without a doctor's certificate." He ticked them off on his fingers.

"All of your children will be covered for medical and dental. Anyone over the age of sixty will have prescriptions covered. Pregnant women will have their deliveries paid for."

Just as on a sinking ship, Gray was putting women and children into the lifeboats first.

"Banking sick days is off the table. No negotiation on that. I can't keep it. It's either that or lay off half of you. I can, however, upgrade you to twelve sick days a year instead of ten. That's the *best* I can do."

He turned to Arnie. "Anything else?"

Arnie shook his head.

Gray said, "As I told you last week, my office will be open at any time if you want to talk. I need help here, people. We're in this together. Let's make this company work."

He walked away, exhausted despite last night's heavy sleep.

"Hilary, I'm moving into that new condo building today." He gave her the address and left to pay up at the B and B.

He then bought bedsheets, towels and food and

drove to the condo. He opened the door, put the food away, and went straight to the bedroom where he made the bed, crawled in and fell asleep.

A persistent pounding on Gray's door refused to let him drift any longer in the gathering gloom of twilight.

He flung open the door, groggy and angry as hell.

Audrey stood in the hallway. She wore a deep yellow dress with big red poppies splashed across it. Springtime on steroids.

She wasn't smiling, but neither did she look as angry as she had this morning.

"What do you want?" he asked.

"May I come in?"

"It depends. If you're here to give me shit, I'm in no mood to take it."

"I'm here to listen." She looked sincere.

He stepped aside, and she brushed past him, her perfume waving a familiar hello. She stood in the center of the room and watched him. And waited.

Her serenity pissed him off.

"Don't you ever hurt?" he asked, not caring that he sounded as belligerent as a bully. "Don't you ever have bad days, or is life just one big dress-up party for you?"

A soft gasp reflected her shock.

He'd wounded her, and immediately pulled in his claws, feeling as guilty as if he'd stolen her lunch or punched her best friend.

A militant look crossed her face. If frowns could be lethal, he was a dead man. But so what? He was already dead, hollowed out and gutted like a fish for dinner. He'd lost everything that mattered to him.

"You were there when I had more than one bad day in the past week."

He deflated, then threw off his sour mood like a dog shaking off bathwater. "You're right. That was so far past fair. I'm sorry. Please, sit."

She did, on the sofa. He sat opposite her on a ridiculous little armless chair.

"We need to talk," she said. "I've been to see Abigail."

He found himself craving information about his parents. "Is she okay? Is Dad okay?"

What if his drastic solution had caused health problems?

"How are they? Are they sick? Dad hasn't had a heart attack?"

"No. Nothing like that, but they don't understand what happened." Her violet eyes thoughtful, as though trying to figure out a conundrum, she said, "Neither do I."

"Dad's running the company into an untenable position. Without real change, it will fold."

"I didn't know that. It's really that bad?"

He nodded.

She wrapped her hands around her knees. "I don't think that's all of what's going on."

She was too perceptive by half, damn her.

"What happened to you back east, Gray?"

Wariness gripped his throat like an old enemy. "What do you mean? This has nothing to do with Boston."

"What you did to your parents was so far out of character, I can't fathom it. When you first came back, you were cold, different, but people don't change their fundamental characters."

"They can."

"Really? Do you suddenly have so little respect for your parents that you would do what you did for money?"

He shook his head.

"Then why? What did you hope to gain?"

"Ironically, money."

"Something isn't adding up, Gray. This whole affair is fishy. You said your business is successful."

"My own company. Yes."

"Then you don't need your parents' money."

"I need cash. A lot of it. Quickly."

"Why?"

Audrey loved and respected his parents. How could he destroy that respect? Stomach acid, his old friend, put in an appearance, scalding him.

"I can't," he whispered. God, his head hurt.

Audrey approached and knelt on the floor in front of him. She grasped his wrists to urge his hands away from his face, to force him to look at her. This close, her eyes resembled pretty jewels, like amethysts with dark veins of purple running through.

Her honest goodness, her purity, made him feel dirty.

"Tell me why," she urged.

"I honest to God can't." Lord, he was miserable. He wanted to tell her, desperate to redeem himself, at least in her eyes.

"I—" He almost blurted the whole thing, but held himself back in time. A potent curse whooshed out of him. "I can't. If I could I would."

Her tongue made a clicking sound of frustration. She got up and returned to the sofa, crossing her arms, as though settling in for the long haul.

"Okay, then tell me what happened in Boston. Abigail said you were in a car accident."

When he didn't respond, she said, "You might as well confide in me. I'm not leaving here until you do, even if it takes all night."

He almost smiled. After the little he'd learned about her in the past ten days, he didn't doubt she meant it. She would probably sit here for a week. She would wait him out.

He nodded, not sure he could say anything without falling apart. He'd never spoken about that time, had never shared with anyone what it had done to him, about how poorly he'd handled the aftermath. How the effects still lingered, giving him strange ideas, dreams and memories, turning him into one sick puppy afraid of his own shadow.

Here goes nothing.

"I'd gone to a party with my fiancée, Marnie, and had too much to drink. No problem. Marnie was designated driver for the evening. She wasn't much of a drinker and didn't mind." Even to his own ears, his voice sounded dead. "I fell asleep. Marnie must have, too. She missed a bridge, we rolled down an embankment and ended up crashed against a boulder, the car on its roof. She must have been speeding. Doctors said she died on impact."

Thank God. He couldn't have borne it if she'd suffered or been maimed or, worse, paralyzed. Marnie would have hated that.

He pressed his thumbs against his temples, trying to block images of that night.

What he saw was blackness...the lack of all breathing, living creatures but himself. He felt the void that had nearly driven him mad sucking him down.

"I don't know how long I was unconscious. When I came to, the car was upside down and Marnie was dead. She'd taken the brunt of the collision on her side of the car. I was trapped in the darkness, my left arm broken. I couldn't move. Could barely breathe because of the weight of my body on the seat belt holding me in place."

He wished it wasn't nighttime, that the sun was streaming through the floor-to-ceiling windows to warm him.

"I couldn't reach my phone. I don't know how many hours we stayed like that before a passing car saw us and called 911. It was hell." He recalled his bone-deep fury. The ranting. The rage against life and fate. Marnie was gone, and he was trapped and could do nothing for her. Couldn't cut her out. Couldn't cradle her in his arms.

Audrey watched him with wide eyes. She might as well know all of his weaknesses.

"All of my life, I've disliked darkness, hated tight spaces and being trapped."

Recognition flickered in her eyes.

"You feel the same way?" he asked.

"No. I like the darkness. I like tight spaces. Caving is a cherished hobby."

"I couldn't do that." The thought of being underground left him clammy.

He scrubbed his hands over his face then dared to meet her eyes. "I've always been claustrophobic. Hanging in that car? In the darkness, with Marnie dead beside me? I cried. So you see how weak I am."

She'd been pleating her dress, not meeting his eyes, as though hiding something, but her gaze flew to his. "Weak? I've never thought you were weak. Of course you cried. You'd lost the woman you loved. I understand a lot now that I know about the accident."

She approached him, resting her fingers on his shoulder, their warmth a balm to his aching soul. "Since you came home, you've been brittle, on the edge of shattering. Now I know the final part."

"The *final* part? Of what?"

She glanced away, expression guilty, as though

she'd said too much. Then she said, "You might as well know the rest. I don't know whether Harrison and Abigail would approve of me telling you, but then, that relationship is over, isn't it?"

Regret scorched him. God, it had only been one day, yet he missed his parents as though an eternity had passed.

That relationship is over.

Had she meant to sound so callous? Then he twigged to what else she'd said. His parents had secrets. At least, separate from Dad and his indiscretion. Yes, he'd already guessed they had.

It was time to find out what they were.

"What *rest* is there, Audrey? Don't even consider holding back. Whatever you all know about me needs to be told. I'm a grown man." He wagged his fingers in a come-hither gesture. "Spill."

Her decisive nod relieved him. He was too tired to fight, but he meant to have answers tonight.

"It's long past time to tell you. Everyone thought it was a godsend when you forgot, but maybe not. Maybe keeping it from you was a mistake."

Audrey looked too serious. "Do you remember that we used to be friends?"

"Nope. In high school, we hung out with different crowds."

"Yes, I know. I'm talking about earlier. When we were very small. Five or six."

"Nope. We were never friends," he insisted. "I

would have remembered if we were." Where was this going? Why did the air around him feel so thin?

"We used to play together all the time. After my mom died, Dad used to bring me to work. You loved the hardware store and were always there, too."

Yes, when he was *older*. Not when he was little more than a toddler.

"We were inseparable," she continued, barreling forward when all he wanted her to do was to, for God's sake, *stop*. Yes, he'd wanted answers, but not when they filled him with dread.

Vague images surfaced, ephemeral but possible, of a small buddy beside him as they hammered and sawed using pint-sized plastic children's tools.

That hadn't been a pal he'd made up to replace the sibling he never had? Those vague feelings had actually been memories? That imaginary friend had been Audrey?

"When we were six and seven, they used to let us run in the fields out behind the store by ourselves. We'd be out there all day and only come back for lunch." Her tone had become wistful. "We had so much fun in those days.

"You," she said, her face full of the blessing of fond memories, "loved the outdoors, loved the wind and the sun and even storms. You adored racing across the fields at full speed. You loved life. You used to laugh a lot."

He couldn't force his gaze from her face. How

could he have forgotten all of this? A huge chunk of his life had always felt missing.

"One day, your parents took us to visit Abigail's parents who owned a ranch in Montana. It was just shy of your eighth birthday. They let us out the back door of the house and we ran off across the fields. They warned us to keep away from the fenced-off cattle and we did.

"We'd been outside for hours and were running and laughing and holding hands when the earth gave way beneath our feet."

Darkness. Suffocation. No! Gray surged to his feet, his heart beating frantic wings to escape his chest. "Stop. Don't say another word."

"We'd fallen into an abandoned well."

Terror. Helplessness.

"I don't believe you."

"It's true, Gray."

"No. I couldn't have forgotten something like that."

"It was traumatic."

Entombment.

He tried to swallow, but had no moisture in his mouth. He'd forgotten. Had forced himself to. Now it was forefront. He saw everything. "How…how long were we down there?"

"Ten hours. When we didn't return for lunch, they came looking. When they couldn't find us, they set up search parties. Finally, they heard my singing."

"Singing?"

"Well, half humming, half singing. All of it off-key." She laughed, but there was no true humor in it. "I'm a terrible singer, Gray."

He had a memory of a song. "'Up Where We Belong,'" he whispered.

Audrey smiled sadly. "I know. Dumb symbolism, but it was all I could think of at the time. I was so young. I'd been hearing it a lot on the radio."

He knelt in front of her. "You sang it for me." Over and over. He heard it. Saw it all, images on top of feelings on top of sensations.

"You hated being down there. You cried. I tried to comfort you."

"I should have been comforting *you*," he said, vehement in his frustration with his own weaknesses.

"No. Stop. Don't beat yourself up. I was the quiet one. Introspection, reading, sitting quietly all came naturally to me." She laid a cool hand against his cheek. "*You* were all about fresh air and action and daring feats. And…and *hurtling* through life. I loved that about you. You took me outside of myself. You gave me the world.

"Singing to you and holding you while we were trapped was my way of giving back to you."

He could see light so far above, as though it were heaven, and the dark chilling well they were in was hell. But he had warm little arms around him. Audrey had been his buddy. His other half. She'd probably saved his sanity that day.

How had he forgotten all of this? Was it possible

to hide a huge chunk of experience from yourself? To suppress so much?

Apparently.

She'd meant so much to him. He'd forgotten. He thought of how he'd treated her since she'd handcuffed herself to the greenhouse: sometimes well, but sometimes with disdain, and he felt ashamed.

They'd lost time and experience. They could have been friends all of their lives. No wonder he'd longed for a sibling. For a few years, he'd almost had one.

"They finally came after dark." She took her hand away from his cheek, and he missed the warmth.

He remembered—light diminishing, weakening, dying until it was gone, taking hope with it.

Then someone big came down on a rope and rescued him. Aboveground, they were separated, and he was welcomed into his parents' arms. Then...she was gone from his life.

"Why?"

She'd been watching him, and answered as though she'd followed his memories with him. "After that day, every time you saw me, you became hysterical. My presence reminded you of what you'd been through. Abigail and Harrison decided we should separate. Almost immediately, you buried the memory of the well and of our friendship. After that, when we met in town, it was as though we'd never been friends."

He couldn't believe he could bury a memory that profound. He'd heard stories of people repressing memories, and had scoffed, full of cynicism and doubt. Now he knew it could happen. "So that's why I'm claustrophobic."

"Yes. Abigail once told me that you spent your childhood years sleeping with the light on."

As he did now. He'd started his old habit again after the accident.

"No wonder the car crash affected me so badly."

"You lost the woman you loved."

"Yes. I was grieving, but there was so much more in me that I couldn't understand." He stared at her. "I thought when I left Boston that things would get better, but they didn't. I came home to Accord and started to get all of these awful feelings. I think memories were trying to surface, but I was repressing them. It made me crazy. I couldn't figure out why the accident was affecting me *here*."

A thought occurred to him. "Why wasn't it in the newspapers? I mean, a pair of kids trapped in a well is big news. Why didn't I hear about it later?"

"It happened in Montana. It was in their papers, but your dad managed to keep it contained and out of our local news. That would never happen these days with the internet."

He understood so much now. It all made sense.

"We can fix this," Audrey said. "I can help you to overcome your fears of the darkness. Your claustrophobia."

"What are you talking about? I don't need to overcome anything. I'm fine." Now that he knew the truth, he was sure he could handle his fear of close spaces. With his new understanding, he'd be okay.

"Did you listen to yourself when you told me about Marnie's death? About you being trapped? Utter detachment. You are so *not* dealing with this."

"Maybe it looks and sounds that way, but I'm unemotional because I've already dealt with it. I've had an entire year to deal with it."

"A year isn't that long."

"It's long enough." If he was too forceful, so be it, with Audrey insisting on things that weren't true.

"You're hurting, Gray."

"I'm *fine*."

"Come into the caves with me."

His heart lurched, flat-out just about jumped out of his chest. Go into a cave? "Are you insane? I don't have to prove anything to anyone."

"I'm talking about healing."

He wouldn't entomb himself.

He couldn't see clearly. Couldn't think. Had to get out of here. His vision narrowed as debilitating panic grew, turning his world dark, until he had to run. To escape the box of his fears.

He strode to the door. "This conversation is over. I'm leaving." He stepped outside, slamming the door behind him, gulping air.

Who did she think she was, believing she knew what was best for him? Bullshit.

He heard the door open behind him. "Gray?"

"Don't talk to me. I'm going home."

He stalked to the elevators, punching the button. "Come on. Come on." He clawed at the snug neck of his T-shirt.

"Gray—"

"I said I'm leaving."

"Gray," she shouted. What was her problem? He spun around.

"You live *here,*" she said. *"I* need to leave. Not you."

Coming to his senses, the black haze of panic, fear and anger cleared. He glanced around. He was standing in his own building.

He leaned his forehead against the wall and sucked air into his lungs until the dizziness gave way to reason and sanity. His denial was going too far. He'd ignored his problem for too long.

From the moment he'd buried his memories and had given up his little friend for the sake of his own mental health, he'd carried a burden—and today, at this moment, he'd reached his limit.

Good thing he was a man in control of his emotions, or he'd be punching a hole in the wall.

You're hurting, Gray.

He wasn't.

You're hurting, Gray.

Yeah, he was.

Badly.

He had to fix himself.

She watched him with so much tenderness, he came undone.

"I'll think about it," he said, capitulating because, in some strange way, he was helpless in the face of Audrey's compassion.

Heaven help him. He really would think about it.

He touched her cheek. He'd wanted to touch her since the day his foreman had summoned him to handle a weirdo causing trouble, and instead he'd found the most strangely beautiful, unique woman chained to his father's greenhouses.

He'd stolen those kisses because he wanted his hands on her all the time.

Jackie O meets Betty Boop. Audrey Hepburn meets Elizabeth Taylor.

The lush softness of her skin welcomed him, made him consider possibilities, made him want to follow through on those stolen kisses that had felt like lust and salvation rolled into one.

Those possibilities were *not* possible, though, and reality a persistent bitch. "I still have to follow through on the sale of my father's land." His voice sounded foreign to him, tinged with too much affection. She was his opponent. He had to bring her down to save his mother and the company and all of its employees. "I still need cash. I will file to have the sale of the land dismissed if I get guardianship of Dad's property. I'm getting that land back."

Her expression shifted, hardened.

"You can try." She punched the elevator button.

"You still want to take me caving?" He turned hard, cynicism a shell against her disappointment.

"Yes."

"You planning to take me into one of those hell-holes and leave me there?"

With a bittersweet smile, she stepped into the elevator and said, "While the temptation is strong, I'll resist." She touched the button for the ground floor, the compassion back in those lovely violet eyes. "I'll take care of you, Gray."

A promise. A benediction.

The doors closed, taking her away along with the warmth of the day, so chillingly similar to another time he'd completely forgotten about until today.

Cold, he returned to his condo and sat on the sofa holding his head in his hands, about as lacking in energy as a wrung-out washing rag.

If only he could talk to his parents.

No more hiding.

He'd been through the emotional wringer, but Audrey had been there beside him. She was willing to go even further if he was willing to take her help.

First, there was healing he had to do on his own.

If Audrey had enough faith in him to trust him with his past and to think he could be cured of his fears, then he owed it to her and himself to pull himself together, to give the future an honest shot.

He called his office in Boston. When the receptionist put him through to his chief financial officer, he ordered him to sell the business in Boston.

"You want to sell?" Bob Craven asked. "I had no idea you were thinking of this, Gray."

"I wasn't. This is new. Find me a buyer as quickly as you can. I want good terms—retain as many employees as possible. We'll provide attractive severance packages to whoever isn't offered a job, or whoever decides not to stay with the new owners."

"You know this will take a while. Months. Six. Maybe seven."

"I know, but get the process started."

He called a real estate agent next and put his Boston condo on the market.

It was time, past time, to say goodbye to Marnie. When the dust had settled, when papers needed to be signed and the condo emptied, he would make the difficult visit to her grave for the final goodbye.

JEFF HAD LIFTED weights again yesterday and was better for it, not as grumpy or as helpless. It felt good to be active, for his body to move again.

He wasn't ready to be an old man yet.

He didn't know where Gray was. Even though he'd committed to being there for Jeff, he hadn't shown up. Teresa had helped set up the machines. The gym was adding raised figures to some of the weights so he could load the machines himself.

"Jeff," Teresa said shortly after breakfast, "I want to go out to that nice-looking bakery in town."

His mood fell. He was getting used to having her here. *Liked* having her here, even though only one week ago, he'd hated the very idea of a therapist. Teresa wasn't what he'd expected. She taught him a lot, and she did it with patience and humor. "For how long?" he asked. "Will you be back by lunchtime?"

"No," she answered, "I didn't mean I want to go out alone. I want you to come with me."

Walk on Main Street? Eat in front of strangers when he had trouble finding his mouth? What if he spilled coffee on himself? He didn't at home anymore, but what if he got rattled in public and got messy? The place was always crowded.

"There'll be lots of people there. More than at the gym."

"That's the point. You need to talk to more people than just me."

"No." He fell right back into his old recalcitrant self. He couldn't do this.

"I don't know anyone in town, and I want to get to meet people." She touched his hand where it sat on the sofa arm. "You could introduce me to them."

He softened.

"Please," she said, and it clinched the deal.

Jeff stood. "Okay. Let's go."

Teresa parked the truck on Main Street and walked around to Jeff's side. His pulse beat hard in his veins.

Lord, what had he gotten himself into?

After he got out, Teresa twined her fingers with his. He was getting used to the feel of her hand, to the reliability of her touch, as though her hand belonged in his. They walked down the street together. He was walking on Main Street for the first time in, what? A year?

"Are people staring at me?" Jeff asked.

"Nope." She opened the door of the café. "Oh, my goodness, it smells incredible in here. I'm gaining weight just inhaling."

"Do you worry about your weight?"

"Jeff, every woman of a certain age worries about her weight."

"How old are you?"

"Fifty-eight."

Jeff didn't remark on that because someone called his name.

"A bunch of men on the far side of the room are waving you over," she said.

"Who are they?"

"I don't know." She laughed. "That's why you're here. To introduce me."

He didn't like that, but so what? She could see whoever she wanted to. "Are you looking to find yourself a man?"

"No. I just want to meet people, and the people beckoning to you are men." His grip relaxed. He didn't own her. "Let's go over there."

She led him to the table, and all of the men greeted Jeff, their voices warm, and it felt good.

He introduced Teresa, maybe a little reluctantly because he hadn't figured out yet who all was there. That Angus was a good-looking man. Jeff thought women found him attractive.

After a bit of shuffling, they found a couple of chairs and made room for Jeff and Teresa.

"What do you want, Jeff?"

"A coffee and one of Laura's cinnamon buns, if she has any left. If not, carrot cake."

"You got it. Any of you gentlemen need refills?"

After a round of nos, Teresa went off to place their orders. By the time she came back with the food, Jeff was immersed in a conversation about local politics, feeling as if nothing had changed since the last time he'd sat here with his friends.

A man didn't need to be able to see to express opinions or to listen. Jeff's mind hadn't changed. He was as sharp as ever, still interested in debate.

A revelation.

After Teresa set up Jeff's food in front of him, she said quietly, "Coffee's at three o'clock and a cinnamon bun at twelve."

"Jeff, how does that macular degeneration affect your eyesight?" He recognized Walter's voice. "What can you see?"

Jeff stiffened, because he was afraid of pity, of well-meaning sympathy.

Teresa elbowed him. "Answer the question."

Bossy woman.

Jeff explained because he wanted to, because he'd known Walter all of his life, and *not* because Teresa told him to.

"That's the pits, Jeff." He recognized Harold's voice. "Is it operable?"

Jeff explained that an operation might not work.

"At least with me," Harold said, "once I get my

hip replacement, there's a pretty good chance I'll be able to walk again without these damn crutches."

"Wish they had an operation that could fix the arthritis in my hands." Louis. He remembered Louis had hands and knuckles the size of pineapples. "They're becoming a pair of claws. Useless."

Jeff relaxed. They were treating him like one of them. "When is the hip operation scheduled, Harold?"

"Next month. Can't wait."

Harold might be brave enough to risk an operation, but Jeff wasn't. No way, no how.

They stayed for an hour and a half.

At the house, Jeff walked hand-in-hand into the living room with Teresa, but before he sat he squeezed her hand.

"Thank you. You're a lifesaver."

"Go on, Jeff. I haven't done much."

He squeezed her hand harder. "I'm saying that you're saving my life, and I mean it."

"Well, okay. Thank you." Her voice sounded different, warm and maybe shy.

He smiled all the rest of the day.

CHAPTER TEN

IT TOOK A few days, but Gray finally gave in to the inevitable. He decided to go into a cave with Audrey.

The memories she'd brought back of their time trapped in the well fractured his equilibrium and changed the way he viewed the world and his parents. Had they been justified in hiding so much from him, in not forcing him to deal with what had happened? He'd carried a burden of grief for nearly thirty years, underground, in shadows as black as the well in which he'd been trapped, and hadn't had a clue. How many times in his life had he been controlled by fear and not known it? How many decisions had he made that could have been different with knowledge and an understanding of what drove him?

Today, he chose a new path. He might not get rid of his fears easily, but he would at least start.

Audrey humbled him with her purity and strength and vitality.

Worse, she shamed him without even meaning to. Compared to her, to the unusual mature grace she'd shown that day in keeping him calm, imagining those small arms wrapped around him and those tiny hands patting his face, that sweet voice singing to comfort him, he saw himself as weak.

That was the only reason he would go into a cave with her—not to heal, not for anything *feel-good* like closure—but to know inside himself that he could be brave.

He'd grown into a strong man, dammit, and he intended to prove it.

He could do this.

First, he had to get the proper gear.

NOAH'S SHOP SMELLED like mothballs and incense. This wasn't usually the kind of place Gray picked up his clothes, but Audrey had suggested he buy hiking boots at the Army Surplus.

When Gray tapped the bell on the counter, Noah stepped out of the back room with a smile on his face, which dropped the second he saw Gray.

"What can I do for you?"

Oh, Lord, a businessman-hating hippie. Noah hadn't changed much since high school.

"I need hiking boots. Audrey's taking me caving. She told me you could show me the right boots to buy."

"Yeah." He walked, bobbing onto the balls of his feet, to one side of the store to the shoes and boots. "You need something with a really good tread, like these." He picked up a pair of sturdy hiking boots.

Noah fitted Gray into the right size, and they strode to the counter, with Gray snagging a pair of thick socks on the way. After he paid, he turned to leave.

"About Audrey," Noah said.

At his cold tone, Gray stopped and raised one eyebrow. It had been known to leave employees quaking. Not so with Noah.

"You hurt her in any way and you'll have me to answer to." All traces of professionalism were gone, and the gloves were off. "Are we clear?"

"We're clear." Gray walked out, knowing that a showdown was inevitable, because, yes, he would be hurting Audrey, exactly where it would do her the most damage.

He had no choice.

THERE TRULY WAS a hell and Gray was in it.

On Monday morning, Audrey's shop was closed and they stood at the mouth of Fulford Cave in White River National Forest in Eagle County, the beauty of the surrounding Rockies stunning but almost lost on Gray.

"I'm insane," he whispered. "I never should have agreed to do this."

Gray glanced dubiously at the entrance to the cave, a metal culvert. The descent looked maybe forty-five degrees with a ladder for climbing down. The metal tube had a circumference of maybe two feet.

"I never thought you would be sadistic, Audrey. Why choose this?" He swallowed bile. "Caving is already trial by fire without making me climb down that." At least it didn't drop straight down.

"I know," Audrey said grimly. "It's a lot like going down into a well, but the natural entrance won't work for a first-timer. We would need climbing gear. There is another entrance, but that one's tricky, too. This culvert is the safest way in and an easy cave for you to start with."

Gray glared at her. "To *start* with. This is a one-time thing, Audrey." His voice shook, not surprising, given that his hands and legs did, too.

"You'll get the bug," she said. Maybe she didn't get how deeply disturbed he was by darkness, or maybe she was just so high on her own enthusiasm that she'd lost sight of why they were here.

She took his hand and squeezed, compassion lighting her face. She was aware.

"This is a wild cave," she said. "There won't be any lights or paths, but I've been in here many times and know my way around."

"There are caves with lights and paths?"

"Yes. They've been set up so tourists can walk through and experience some of the beauty of the caves."

"Why didn't we go to one of those?" Desperate to get away, he said, "Let's go now."

"One of those caves wouldn't do you any good. They're too well-lit."

"Sounds great to me. I don't have to bury myself to heal."

"Yes, you do, Gray."

"At this moment, I hate you, Audrey."

She winced.

Gray bit down on his tongue. That had been nasty. But maybe true.

They'd suited up in insulated coveralls, as well as helmets with headlamps.

"I'm about to die of heatstroke," he said. It was the first week of September, and a beautiful sunny day. Summer moved inexorably forward while he had yet to get that land sold.

"It will be a lot cooler underground," Audrey said. "You won't get too far down the culvert when the temperature will drop to forty degrees." Audrey handed him gloves. "You'll need these." She also gave him extra light sources for his backpack—an extra lamp, but also a candle.

"A candle?" Gray asked. "Really? Not very high-tech."

"We'll use that while we eat lunch to conserve the batteries in our headlamps."

Gray swallowed, but, mouth dry, nothing went down. "We'll be eating underground?"

"Yep."

"I didn't know we'd be down there that long."

"Gray, your fears have been moldering inside of you for years, rotting. It'll take more than ten minutes underground to get rid of them."

He had his doubt they'd get rid of anything today outside of his breakfast and his dignity.

Audrey stepped onto the ladder and climbed down, casting him a reassuring glance before disappearing.

He put his foot onto the top step of the ladder and his brain exploded.

Murkiness. Shadows. A melancholic, endless, persistent gloaming. Mind-shattering panic.

Hunkered forward, he breathed through his nose.

"Gray?" Audrey called.

Too winded to answer, he concentrated on controlling his hyperventilation so he wouldn't pass out.

"Gray?" Audrey called again. "Are you okay?"

Facing the inevitable, he moved forward, but the second he stepped into the culvert and put his foot onto the ladder, he stopped breathing. He'd have to start again soon or he'd keel over.

Breathe. He couldn't.

Light-headed, he took another step down into the bleak interior, into the suffocating restriction of the cold corrugated metal.

There wasn't enough room for him to descend with his pack on his back, so he held it above him while the culvert swallowed him whole like a baby being sucked back into the womb, but a hostile one.

He couldn't take another step into that greedy darkness. A moment later, he felt a hand on his leg, Audrey reassuring him without words that he could do this. She'd climbed halfway up the ladder to meet him.

Nearly thirty years later, underground together

again, she was still the strong one and he still the sniveling little boy—and that was unacceptable.

He refused to repeat history.

Forcing himself, he descended the rest of the way. On the bottom rung, he stopped and leaned one hand against the cool rock wall, and concentrated on gulping great inflated balloons of oxygen into his lungs.

His heart already pounded hard enough to feel like a heart attack. But of course, he wasn't dying. Only badly hurting. In extreme fear.

It's only fear, Gray. It isn't death.

"This is the eighth largest cave in Colorado," Audrey said, her face barely lit by rays from her headlamp reflecting from the rock walls around them. "We're at an elevation of almost 10,000 feet."

He didn't give a hoot about elevation or the size of the damn cave in which Audrey wanted to entomb him!

He was dying. He had to get out.

He grasped the ladder and pulled himself back up a couple of rungs before Audrey stopped him by grabbing his calves.

"You can do this, Gray."

Could he? Maybe he wasn't strong enough. Maybe he was a coward through and through.

"Stop," Audrey said. "Breathe."

He hung suspended but did as she instructed. He wasn't dying. This wasn't the end of the world. This was only fear, and fear could be controlled.

He dropped to earth with a graceless thud.

Slowly, as though afraid to spook him, Audrey reached to his forehead and switched on his headlamp. He could see her clearly now, rather than as a shadowed entity below the lone circle of light of her own lamp. Her calm face became a lifeline, something dear to hold on to in his panic.

Her faith in him calmed him. A bit. Enough for him to say, "Let's do this," his voice not as confident as he would have liked, but them's the breaks. He was here, wasn't he? That was the best he could do.

Audrey smiled, bringing light and love to this underground prison, as she had all of those years ago with her songs and her comforting hands in the well.

Lord, he was falling hard for this woman.

"Give yourself time to adjust. Look up."

He saw the ceiling was white. "What kind of rock is that?"

"Moonmilk. Aggregates of fine crystals. It never hardens to stone. Much of the walls should look like that, too, but there's too much human traffic that comes through here for it to develop."

They strode forward into the cave. Audrey strolled, at any rate. Gray inched along, his hand on the cold wall. At least, he could walk upright. At least he wasn't jammed in beside Audrey like two fragile little square pegs into one round hole.

In the past few days, a floodgate of memories had broken loose, horrible and frightening.

He shook his head to clear it of those dark images, and concentrated on other revived memories, good ones, of Audrey, and what a sweet friend she'd been, and the hours of happy play they'd had together, in their homes and at Turner Lumber. And in the wide-open spaces around Accord.

She was right. He had loved to run, to be free. He'd embraced all of nature.

Once, they'd found an injured rabbit and had taken it home. Dad had gotten it fixed up at the vet's and had built a small home for it, and Mom had taught them how to feed and care for it. Then one day, when it was healthy again, they'd held a release party in a field and sent if off into the wild again.

Gray used to be a half-wild creature, too, loving the outdoors and freedom. He could get some of that back. He should add balance to his life. Work less. Live more. Get outdoors again. Run free.

The memory bolstered him. He wished he could share it all with Mom and Dad. But he couldn't think about them now without sadness. "Look," Audrey said, pointing to a small hole behind a large rock. "There's a small room in here."

She leaned forward. "Put your head beside mine, so both of our lamps are pointing into the room. See the stalactites and stalagmites?"

He did, their eerie beauty almost making up for what Audrey was putting him through by dragging him down here. Almost.

"Which are which?"

"Stalactites grow down and stalagmites up."

She launched into a travelogue of the cave, mentioning minerals—baryte, manganoan calcite, dolomite. "There's also quartz down here, but it's not that exciting. It's kind of dull."

He didn't care, just wanted to inhale and exhale normally for a few minutes, but the walls were crowding him.

"Audrey?"

"Yes?"

"This isn't helping."

"Oh. Sorry." She walked ahead of him, and he couldn't see her face, but she sounded sheepish. "I know. I'm geeky and weird."

"You're...okay." He sounded winded, as though he'd run a marathon.

Audrey touched his hand and he jumped.

She grasped his fingers. "Inhale, Gray. Deeply."

"Hard."

"I know." She did know. Her compassion, her empathy, astounded him, especially considering that his plans for her were no secret. She knew he would destroy her. He had no right to her goodwill and her generosity. He had no right to her.

But he wanted her, all of her, including her respect. He had to do this.

He followed her farther into the darkness and emotion blindsided him.

Darkness and silence you could cut with a scythe. Smell of gas. Scent of earth, of damp moldering.

"I hate this showing of weakness. I'm not much of a man right now. Maybe I never have been."

"You're strong, Gray. You can be a man when you want to be, when it matters."

She stopped walking, and he bumped into her.

"Yeah? When is that?" he asked.

She paid an unreasonable amount of attention to the rock face, picking at a sliver of something silvery in the wall before saying, "When you kiss."

He wasn't sure he'd heard her. "Say what?"

She cleared her throat. "When you kiss, you're all man, okay?"

A slow smile spread across his face. "Yeah?"

"Yes," she hissed. "Okay? Can we move on?"

"Nope. Let's explore right here a little longer, especially what you just said. You like the way I kiss?"

She harrumphed. *Interesting,* Gray thought, *that really is a sound. Onomatopoeic.*

"You haven't answered my question."

"Yes," she said with a repressive grimace. "I like the way you kiss, but don't get your shorts in a knot. It isn't going to happen again. Ever."

He grasped the back of her neck and planted a doozy on her unadorned lips, using everything in his experience to convince her that, oh, yeah, they were going to do it again. And again. And again.

When he pulled away, he was breathless and gratified to see that she was, too. "How can you deny what's between us?"

"I can."

She smiled suddenly, a blaze of sunshine underground, and he realized he'd been had.

"You did that on purpose." He marveled at her deviousness. "You *got* me to kiss you, to distract me from my fears."

"It worked, didn't it?"

"Yeah. I'm good for the moment."

He couldn't help returning her smile because that kiss had been pretty amazing.

They moved farther into the cave. The kiss had helped. For now.

The path they were on narrowed, and Gray tensed.

She felt the change in him, back to fear. "Is there anything I can do?"

"You could kiss me again."

"That was a one-time thing because I was afraid you wouldn't go any farther."

"I might not now."

"We're pretty far in, Gray. No sense turning around. Face your fears. Let me know how to help."

"Keep—keep walking so we can get out of here sooner."

She chuckled. He tried to laugh, too, but couldn't.

"This is the Big Meander," she said. "You have to bend over a bit. Okay?"

He followed what Audrey did, aware that he was moving farther and farther into the mountain. He slipped on the floor and slammed his hand against the rock wall to steady himself.

"Careful," Audrey said. "The rocks are slippery."

"Are they wet?"

"Yes. That's why I had you buy hiking boots instead of wearing your jogging shoes."

She reached an arm to him. "Careful on this ledge."

He swallowed his pride and gripped her hand.

"Now we'll crawl through this passageway. I'll go first."

She went through, and he bent forward to follow her, but it became too much. Bending over, his breath gusted in and out of him like a mini-hurricane. When he pulled himself together, he moved forward. At the top of the passageway, he found Audrey sitting on a large rock. Gray plopped down beside her.

"We're going to take a break," Audrey said. "We're going to turn out our lights for a minute and sit in the darkness."

"Are you out of your mind?" Gray nearly turned and ran back the way he'd come. "No way."

"I think this will help you, Gray."

Audrey reached up to Gray's helmet and shut off his lamp, so only hers illuminated a tiny corner of the cave around them. "Don't do this," he pleaded.

"Shh. Trust me, Gray." He found himself helpless against the tenderness shining in her eyes.

She removed her glove and one of his, and held his hand in hers. Then all went black when Audrey turned off her lamp, too.

Stygian darkness. The bowels of hell. A black darker than black. Deeper than onyx. A stifling vacuum swallowing undeserving boys and girls too young to be alert, too innocent to know that such darkness existed, but learning too early.

Lifelessness. Nothingness. Hopelessness. Death.

He sank into despair.

"Shh. Listen." Audrey's disembodied voice arose out of the hush of the cold, damp cave like a ray of hope. "What do you hear?"

"My heartbeat," he wheezed. "Too strong. Heart attack."

Audrey squeezed his clammy hand. "Try again," she said. "There's another heartbeat here. It belongs to the earth. Step outside of your fears. Listen to the cave around you."

He did, straining to listen outside of himself, to not drown in the thundering of his pulse in his ears.

He heard something...musical. "Water," he blurted. "There's water running somewhere."

"Yes," Audrey said, her voice hushed with reverence. "There's a stream that runs through this cave. That's creation, Gray. That's the ever-freshening renewal of life."

Slowly, his shuddering eased, and the fear inside of him shifted, morphed into an emotion less harsh, less debilitating. Hope grew. Despair retreated.

He sat here in the darkness, and his heart still thundered. His fears hadn't killed him.

That first fall down the well hadn't killed him because a sweet girl had kept him alive. This sweet woman had just gifted him with an easing of those fears that had held him captive for most of his life.

Audrey switched on her lamp. Her lips touched his cheek and her mouth on his skin couldn't be sweeter or more profoundly welcome. "Well done, Gray," she said softly.

"Why? I behaved like a baby."

"It takes a lot of guts to face a fear as big as yours. You didn't run from here screaming. You've got *cojones,* buddy."

Really?

"It was amazing to share your overcoming your fears with you."

Gray drank in her praise, not sure he accepted all of it, but taking in what he could. He'd survived. He'd wanted to run, to scream, to weep, but he hadn't. He'd stayed through his fears. He smelled like a construction worker. He'd been sweating. He didn't care. He'd survived.

They stood and continued on. He barely noticed the names that Audrey called out as they moved farther into the cave. Devil's Washboard. The Register Room. Upper Register Room.

"Take a minute to look around, Gray."

"Wow," he said, noticing an impressive rock formation that looked like a wavy sheet hanging from the roof and walls, impossibly thin to still be rock.

"They're called cave curtains."

When he looked, *really* looked and opened his mind and his fearful heart to the splendor of the cave around him, his breath backed up in his lungs. His chest expanded.

He hadn't expected such beauty, not underground where he thought all things bleak, forsaken. Passing through caves, he'd seen things in the beams of their headlamps that had taken his breath away, but these cave curtains stunned him.

Audrey chatted about stalactites, calcite deposits, dripping water and carbon dioxide, but Gray registered none of it. She pointed to great white lightning strike formations, which she said were buildups of gypsum, a too-ordinary word for otherworldly grandeur.

"Well," she said, studying his face and smiling. "We might have a convert."

"Audrey?"

"Yes, Gray?"

"This is all awesome. Outstanding. But I'm exhausted. I need to get out of here."

"Okay. We can go back and eat up top."

"First, I need to take a whiz. Point me to a private corner."

"No!" she shouted.

She shrugged off her backpack and rummaged inside until she produced a bottle. "Here. Use this."

"Seriously? We're underground. We're in the earth. It's organic. Cavemen didn't use bottles."

"We don't sully caves in any way. We don't leave our sewage for others to walk on later."

Their helmet lamps sent light and shadows bounding around the walls.

"There's a Caver's Creed. It goes like this. Take

nothing but pictures," Audrey recited. "Leave nothing but footprints. Kill nothing but time."

Gray stared at the bottle in Audrey's hand. "I can use that if I have to, but it's a narrow opening. What do you use when you have to go? You don't have the luxury of being able to aim."

"A wide-mouthed Mason jar."

Gray burst out laughing.

"I'm just joking. I use this carefully."

"I can hold my water until we get outside," Gray said. "I'm not going in *that*."

Audrey led Gray back the way they'd come. He had come to terms with his fears, yes, but he needed to bask in sunlight and fresh air. His body followed Audrey's like a heat-seeking missile.

They reached the culvert and climbed up and out. Gray shot his fists into the air.

"Yes! Yes!" He'd survived. He'd faced down his fears and had lived to tell the tale.

He turned to Audrey and kissed her, in celebration of life, to impart his eternal gratitude, her spirit vibrating with energy and commingling with his. Their bodies became fluid and pliable.

"God, I'm glad to be out of there," he breathed against her hair. He felt new, fresh, vibrant. "I'm reborn. I'm a new man."

He grasped her arms and shook her, careful to be gentle, holding in check the violent, life-affirming emotions running through him. "*You* did this. You gave me life."

He kissed her again, an ecstatic hard smack of his lips on hers. She stepped away from him, as though she, too, restrained feelings that threatened to run amok.

The sun shone like a brilliant gem, turning the forest into a green carpet, bringing their surroundings into sharp focus and carving the evergreens above them into relief against the azure sky.

Life became so brilliant, it hurt his eyes. After years of having a huge part of him locked away, *all* of him was alive and engaged. His body hummed. His psyche sang.

Audrey laid out lunch for them—granola bars, cheeses, nuts and protein drinks—her actions mundane in contrast to his newfound radiance.

He *loved* life. Joy coursed through his veins, enlarging them, filling his heart with boundless verve. He laughed for the pure pleasure of hearing it echo against the rocks.

"Squirrel food," Gray said, studying their lunch.

"*Healthy* food," Audrey replied.

Gray found a private spot to relieve his bladder then returned to Audrey. They ate. Gray couldn't get enough of it.

After lunch, while she packed up, quietly, thoughtfully, Gray said, "I understand."

She stopped. "What do you mean?"

"I understand how you turned to rock collecting and caving. I understand what draws you."

Audrey smiled. "You do?"

"Yeah. I won't ever do it again. I'm not cured, but I'm better. I don't like darkness, but I see now how you could turn to it."

"And do you understand why you didn't?"

He nodded. "Yeah, I do. I love the outdoors. I love sunlight and fresh air and weather. I get juice from what's above ground."

"You're air and I'm the earth."

"But I don't see you that way. I don't see you as earthbound. I see *you* as air."

He leaned his arms on his knees. "You have a stunning lightness of being, a bright light that hasn't been diminished by anything."

Audrey's violet eyes shone warmly. "Thank you, Gray. I'm so proud of you. You did well."

He wasn't sure what was going through her head, but she seemed to have been nearly as strongly affected by today as he'd been. She deserved honesty. "I nearly cracked when you turned out all the lamps."

"I sensed that. But you didn't. That's the key."

"Thanks to you."

She turned away, almost as though she were shy with him.

He felt the same way, inexplicably shy, but unwilling to let this momentous event pass without celebration.

"Come back to my place. I'll make dinner."

She didn't look at him, but her quiet yes spoke of acceptance of more than dinner. Just as his invitation had been for more. So much more.

They drove to the city in silence. Audrey dropped him off at the condo and drove home to change.

Gray checked his refrigerator, realized he had nothing for dinner, and ran across the street to the organic market, where he bought steaks and salads and a box of Godiva chocolates for dessert—dark chocolate with fruit and liqueur fillings.

Back at the condo, he quickly got ready.

Audrey arrived at six. She walked across the room, an exotic bird against the neutral backdrop of the generic furniture in a black dress with lime-green polka dots. Before she sat, he spotted a big pink bow at the back of her waist, drawing his eye to how small it was compared to her hips.

Elizabeth Taylor.

Those wide eyes, though. That porcelain skin. That fresh face.

Audrey Hepburn.

She turned him inside out with her contrasts.

Before he lost control and dragged her into his bedroom, he offered her a drink. They drank wine and ate broiled steaks and wild rice salad. Audrey ate like a real woman. She didn't pick, didn't pretend that she didn't have an appetite.

After dinner, Gray opened the chocolates. Heads together, they studied the legend. She chose an orange-and-Grand-Marnier filling and bit into it, leaving a smear of dark chocolate on her bottom lip.

Gray groaned. "Do you have any idea how tempting you are? How beautiful?"

She shook her head.

"Let me show you." He reached to drag her across his lap.

"Gray, I don't think—"

"No," he whispered. "Don't think."

He licked her lip, tasting the fruit and the liqueur and the flat bite of dark chocolate. Sinking his tongue into her, he tasted more, her lips and the skin inside her mouth silken with erotic welcome.

He wanted her more than he needed air. More than sunlight. She *was* sunlight. And purity. And sex. More contrasts.

You don't deserve her. You shouldn't have her.
Be quiet.

You know what you'll do to her. You'll betray her any day now. John Spade will make sure of that.

His desire for her nearly submerged his conscience. Nearly, but not quite. His overwhelming gratitude and a deep abiding tenderness drove him to love her, but his innate decency said no.

He pulled away slowly, tempted to take what he wanted, what she seemed willing to give, but he would hate himself afterward. Maybe she would, too.

He sent her home because it was the right thing to do. Beyond the lovemaking, he had nothing to offer her but heartache.

CHAPTER ELEVEN

JEFF HAD STOPPED SWEARING. Teresa had that effect on him. She lightened him. Dispelled the gloom of his spirit that the darkness of his eyes caused.

He walked into the parish hall with his hand in her grasp, where it now seemed to belong. He knew she meant to guide him, but he held hers for more than that. He enjoyed touching her, even in so small a way.

Teresa had nagged him into attending an after-dinner social organized by volunteers at Jeff's church. After his first outing to the coffee shop where he'd had so much fun and stimulation seeing his friends, he hadn't resisted doing other things Teresa wanted. He got a kick out of giving her a hard time when she made suggestions for outings, though. He liked how she used her humor and wits to talk him into things.

He didn't want her thinking he was a pushover.

But he was. Where Teresa was concerned, he would walk on water if she asked him to. How could a man change so much in such short a time? How could he go from not wanting a stranger living in his house to dreading the day that stranger would leave? And not only because of what she was teaching him, but for her?

He'd grown used to her habits, to having someone else in the house all day and to the sounds she made when she read. He called them her "musing" noises, her judgments on what was written.

She read the paper aloud every day and debated the news with him, informing him stridently when she didn't agree and even more when she did.

How could he let her go? How could he not? He was nothing more than a job to her, a client.

After all of these years without a woman, with only casual relationships with women in town, he wanted more. He wanted it all, with Teresa. He trusted his rapidly developing feelings. It had happened this way with Irene, too. Hard and fast.

He heard voices he recognized calling his name. They joined a table and Teresa introduced herself.

"Who's here?" Jeff asked, having learned there was no shame in admitting he couldn't see.

Everyone spoke up, so Jeff knew who was at the table. Teresa left to get food.

When she returned, she said, "Coffee at three. Date square straight ahead."

After she sat with her own coffee and snack, someone asked, "What do you think of our town?"

"I love it," Teresa replied. "Jeff told me how it used to be, and how city council decided to upgrade to bring in traffic on the weekend. I really like Main Street. Accord makes a great travel destination for people wanting to get out of the city for a few days."

"Think you would consider staying here?" Jeff

wasn't sure whose voice questioned Teresa, but he was glad the man had asked it.

The answer mattered. A lot.

"I don't know. There might not be enough work here for me to be able to support myself."

While the topic shifted, Jeff thought, *she could live with me permanently.* Then it wouldn't matter how large her paycheck was. The thought stunned him—he wasn't an impetuous man—but it felt right.

Shortly after ten, they drove home.

Jeff's thoughts tumbled like acrobats. *Should I tell her how I feel?* Years ago when he'd first started dating Irene, he'd known that she loved him because he'd seen it shining in her eyes.

Not so now. He couldn't gauge Teresa's expression, couldn't guess her emotions.

Should I say something? What did he have to lose? His life was short and getting shorter.

"I wish I could see you," he said, his voice quiet in the hush of the truck's dark cab.

"Why on earth would you want to do that?" she scoffed. "I'm not a looker, Jeff."

"I don't care. I just want to see you."

"You could if you had the operation."

"We don't know for certain it would work."

"We don't know that it won't unless you try it."

They'd had this argument before.

Tonight, his resistance softened.

"I might have it if it meant I could see you." There.

He'd put everything out in the open. She knew how much he feared the operation.

He heard a soft gasp. "I..."

Jeff laughed softly. "I never thought you'd be speechless, Teresa."

"Me, either." She sounded subdued. He'd screwed up. She didn't know how to let him down gently. He should have kept his mouth shut.

"I'm sorry," he said. "I shouldn't have said that. I'm just a client. I understand."

She didn't respond and his hope deflated.

At home, they went through their bedtime routines, but when Jeff finished up in the bathroom and returned to his room, he sensed her there.

He sat on his bed and waited.

"I shouldn't say this. I shouldn't say anything," she admitted. "I'm a professional. When my clients are men, I'm careful with them. I don't become involved."

He waited. Was there a *but* coming, or was he a foolish man, too hopeful when she had given him no signs and had made no promises?

"You are argumentative and stubborn," she said, and his heart sank. "But you're also highly moral and ethical and honest. I like your hardheadedness. I like arguing with you. I've learned from your friends that you used to do anything asked of you for anyone, purely from the goodness of your heart. I admire those traits."

He sensed her moving toward the door. "I work

hard to maintain my professional distance. It's important to me. So I will never have an affair or sleep with a client, but I want you to know something. I'll say this only once and then we won't ever talk about it again."

She stepped into the hallway and whispered before she left, "You are more than just a client."

THE NEWS CAME on Wednesday morning. Good thing Gray was sitting down because it shocked him, even though he'd known it was coming, had known that John would be able to pull it off. It destroyed him nonetheless. John must have used some powerful persuasion, or maybe some of Gray's own money, to get everything pushed through so quickly. Dad's psych evaluation had gone through, and it had been determined that his behavior was erratic—and the threat to the livelihood of everyone at the company substantial—enough to warrant Gray's concern.

Gray now had guardianship over Dad and his property, and could do whatever he wanted with the company. What's more, the sale of the greenhouses to Audrey had been made null and void. Turner Lumber owned that land again.

Gray should have rejoiced. He'd won. He felt no victory. No triumph. He felt nothing.

AUDREY WALKED INTO the Army Surplus and straight into Noah's arms.

"Hey. Whoa. What wrong? Is it your dad?" He rubbed her back.

"No." She started to weep, silently.

"Hey. You don't cry easily. What's happened?"

He led her to the counter and pulled out a cotton handkerchief from a drawer.

She wiped her eyes, smearing makeup across her temples and cheeks.

"Come on, babe. Tell me what's going on."

"The greenhouses."

"What could you have done that has you this upset?"

She broke into loud sobs. "I lost the greenhouses."

"Lost?" Noah swore. "Gray got them back?"

"He had Harrison declared incompetent." In the cave, there had been a breakthrough with Gray. She'd thought she'd prepared herself in case he still went through with this, but she hadn't even come close.

"Oh, Jesus," Noah said.

"I hired a therapist for dad. How will I pay her?" Disaster. Her mind couldn't process past that one word. "How can I win the competition without my plants?"

She couldn't control the sobs that made talking difficult. "If I move them now, they'll die. I planned to move them only once to take them to the competition."

Her despair eclipsed her good nature, her willpower and every ounce of strength she'd used to push herself forward through adversity, through the really hard times with Dad. She'd hit a wall.

"I have nothing, Noah. Nothing."

"You still have the store."

"I know, but it isn't paying me a living wage. Not yet, anyway."

"You'll get back the money from buying the greenhouses."

Small consolation for an aching heart. "Yes, I will, but they represented moving forward, taking huge strides toward becoming well-known in the Denver market and farther afield than just Accord."

"I know, but if you can hang on, you can still make a go of it. Look at me. I manage to hang on with the Army Surplus."

"But Dad's operation. His eyesight that just keeps getting worse. I can't live off my blind father."

That's what this amounted to. Pride. She'd really thought she could pull it off. She could bring home an award that would take care of Dad's medical expenses and his therapist's salary. Yes, she could pay Teresa with what she got back for the greenhouses, but that was only a down payment. She'd been paying a small mortgage on them, as well. The win would have been a steady income for the upcoming year.

"He's going to tear down the greenhouses." None of the good things Gray had done for her and Dad lately diminished her profound disappointment in him.

"I'll make you dinner tonight at my place and take care of you. You need a friend right now, okay?"

She nodded.

"You need to eat now, too. Go to the washroom

and clean up your face. I'll pick up lunch from the bakery and bring it back here."

She couldn't dredge up a smile. Noah was trying so hard, but nothing was going to fix this.

He bent his knees so she would meet his eyes. "Are you going to be okay while I'm gone?"

"Yes. I think I'm all cried out."

"Good, 'cause I'll be gone for a while. There's something I have to do before I pick up lunch."

GRAY SAT AT his desk at work, unable to get a thing done. He'd always reveled in his business victories in the past, but they had never felt so dirty.

His sliding wall flew open and Noah strode into his office, looking like a thundercloud had taken up residence on his face.

Crap. Trouble. Gray stood.

Noah's fist met Gray's chin before Gray had a chance to prepare.

His head snapped back, then rocked forward, and pain exploded through his jaw. For a peace-loving hippie, the guy packed a lot of power.

"Fair enough," he said, rubbing his jaw. "If it's any consolation, I feel bad."

"It isn't. What are you going to do for Audrey? She's at my place crying her heart out."

Dear God, that pained him more than the fist in the face. He'd known all along she would be hurt, but when he'd started this process three weeks ago, he hadn't cared about her.

Now he did, too much, and there was nothing he could do for her.

Noah said a couple of truly nasty things and then stormed out. Gray closed the walls of his office because everyone and his uncle were staring at him, and he needed time alone. Buckets and buckets of time alone.

GRAY STOOD IN front of the greenhouses and watched the backhoe pull into position and raise its bucket to smash through the buildings.

For the first time since arriving ten minutes ago, his gaze lit on the interior, barely visible through humidity-coated glass. It wasn't empty.

He raised a staying hand and stepped to the door.

Inside, every plant to which Audrey had introduced him, every *baby* she'd talked to, still sat in colorful rows waiting for her, confident in their patient green finery that she would be there soon to flood them with water, nutrients and love.

Gray's throat ached. Why hadn't she taken them?

He called her, but her phone went to an answering machine.

"Audrey, if you're there, pick up. You need to get these plants out of here."

He heard a click and then, "Why?"

At the sound of her rough voice, his resolve faltered. He hadn't spoken to her since the day she'd taken him into the cave to start him on a journey of healing.

He thought of Joe, therapy and a wheelchair, and Sam and Tiffany, ruthlessly triaging one person's needs over another's.

Audrey was an adult. She would survive. He didn't doubt that she'd pick up the pieces and make a better life for herself.

"*Why?*" he echoed. "Because they'll be destroyed. I'm pulling down the greenhouses today. Now."

"They will die when I move them. I made that clear to you the first time you tried to tear down *my* greenhouses."

He didn't miss the emphasis.

"Most of them are exotic plants," she continued. "They're too delicate to move until they are fully mature."

She cleared her throat. "Do your dirty work. I can't save them." She hung up.

Gray stared at the phone.

Envisioning twelve-year-old Joe on the sofa, his body folding in on itself, and Shelly's admonishment that it would get worse, he knew he had no choice. Stepping outside, he nodded to the backhoe operator.

It edged closer to the building. Its bucket rose, tipped toward the delicate glass, but Gray didn't see the greenhouse. He saw Audrey.

She might as well still be chained to the front door. Her spirit was here, on the land, in the building.

She would have nothing to use to enter the flower show. She would never win that monetary award for her beautiful flowers. Her store would never get the boost it needed to bring in more customers than just those who trickled in from Accord.

The backhoe screeched when it navigated into position.

Teresa already worked for Audrey, already tended Jeff. Audrey had gone into debt to bring Teresa here. How was Audrey going to pay her salary in the future if she couldn't bring in enough money from the flower shop?

The bucket glanced off the glass as the operator maneuvered it into position.

The bucket came in for the kill.

How would Audrey—?

In his mind's eye, he imagined her beauty, selflessness and magnificent spirit, all destroyed by one ugly decision.

He couldn't do this.

He wasn't destroying Audrey's work. He was destroying *her*.

He couldn't.

"Stop," he shouted, but the operator couldn't hear him.

The bucket would hit.

"Stop!" he yelled.

It touched the glass. With an ominous crack, the glass split.

"Stop!" Gray sprinted to the machine and reached in, grabbed the man's arm and hauled him out of the backhoe, dumping him onto the ground.

"Hey!" the operator shouted. "What's wrong with you?"

I'm insane. Crazy. Stupid.

Sentimental.

In love.

Whoa. Really?

No. Just serious, serious like.

He couldn't love and lose again. He suffered the memory of Marnie hanging upside down in the car, her body lifeless, her once beautiful spirit gone.

"I said, what's wrong with you?"

The construction worker's voice brought Gray back to the present. "You couldn't hear me. I was telling you to stop."

He helped the man to his feet. "Sorry, man. I changed my mind. Load the backhoe onto the truck. We're through here today."

His foreman approached. "Are you serious? Not again."

"Again," Gray murmured, sick, unable to believe what he'd just done. What would happen to Turner Lumber?

He watched the construction equipment, the *de-*struction machinery, make its way back to the trucks and drive away.

He fell onto the front step and hung his head.

What would happen to Joe now?

What would Shelly do? He could pay her rent for her, barely, considering that he paid a monthly mortgage on his condo in Boston until it sold, and now his monthly rent on his condo in Accord.

But what would happen to Joe?

When no great bolt of inspiration tumbled from the sky, he entered the greenhouse and wandered the aisles, struck by how warm and welcoming the old building felt.

Maybe humidity was good for the soul. More likely, it was the bountiful life around him, the exotic beauty that fought for its survival every second of every day. It might be pampered by Audrey, but it would perish in a heartbeat without her in a matter of a day or two.

Already, many plants drooped. He stuck his finger into the soil of a couple of them. Dry.

He phoned her again, but she wouldn't answer. She needed to get out here to water these things.

Still, after repeated calls, she didn't answer.

How could he blame her?

She'd given up.

He'd destroyed her spirit. Had killed her hope.

Gray took off his suit jacket, rolled up his sleeves and went in search of a water spigot.

Some plants he sprayed using a hose and others he watered by hand with water he hauled around in buckets, hoping like crazy he wasn't killing them with too much moisture. What he knew about plants could fit into a thimble.

While he worked, he thought and thought until he

devised a plan—a slow one, because nothing was going to get him money faster than selling this property to a company that was greedy for land and had plenty of money in hand.

He would have to lay off some of Dad's employees, but maybe he could get a couple to agree to early retirement. As soon as the sale of his Boston condo went through, he'd give the money to Shelly with a promise of more to come.

She would just have to trust him.

He knew he also had to do what he'd been avoiding. He needed to pick up the results of the DNA test.

An hour and a half later, he finished, rolling his sleeves down and donning his jacket, more at peace than he had been in years. He'd come to a decision, a momentous permanent decision.

He would stay here in Accord and keep the company alive as best he could, with as little carnage as possible.

Once his company sold, he would plow his money into Turner Lumber and run the business. He wanted that company. It was his legacy, and he'd been gone too long.

As well, one way or another he was going to repair his relationship with his parents. He didn't know how, but it had to be done.

He loved them and he missed them.

First, he had to mend his friendship or whatever it was that had developed between him and Audrey.

He left the building and strode to the car he'd rented now that he didn't have access to Dad's Volvo, unsure what his next step would be for Shelly's family, but certain he had to see Audrey first.

At The Last Dance, he peeked in through the front door. She was alone in the shop. Good. He stepped inside, and she turned at the sound of the door opening and closing.

When she saw him, her eyes widened—her red-rimmed, teary eyes.

I'm so sorry.

He'd caused her so much pain.

"Did you come to gloat?" she asked, her throat raspy. "That's low, Gray, even for you."

"No." He stepped toward her, and she shifted away, but a few cells, a tiny ephemeral portion of her soul, strained toward him. He didn't know how he detected it, but he knew. She needed comfort.

He moved closer, and she must have seen the compassion on his face, but she stayed her ground.

"I didn't do it." He needed her to stop crying, to stop breaking his heart with her pain.

"Didn't do what?" It sounded like *Dind do wud?*

"Stop crying." Her weeping made him ache physically. "Please, stop. You're killing me."

Her shoulders shook.

"I didn't do it," he shouted, and she stared at him, the violet of her eyes almost purple with brimming moisture, her mouth open, her full lips moist.

He kissed her fiercely, pouring his regret, his apology, his comfort—and his aching lust—into her.

She pulled him hard against her, rammed her fingers into his hair and devoured his lips, consumed his mixed emotions and gave of her own.

When Gray came up for air, she asked, "Do you mean it?" her voice dangerously low, afraid to believe, he guessed.

"I didn't tear down the greenhouse. I sent the equipment away."

She closed her eyes and screwed up her face into a tight ball. She murmured, "Thank you, thank you, thank you," a novena of gratitude.

"I'm selling the land back to you."

"What?"

"Same deal as you had with Dad."

"Why?"

"Because I can't hurt you."

Leaning her head against his chest, she whispered, "I didn't know who you were anymore. In the cave, you had a breakthrough, came back to yourself. Then you let Spade go through with taking my greenhouses away. I thought the boy I used to know was dead."

Maybe he had been for a while, for years, but Gray felt parts of his old self stirring, rousing back to life, and all because of Audrey Stone.

"Just because I went into a cave doesn't mean I'm cured. I'm a long, long way from healed, Audrey. But

I'm getting better. I'm making decisions that won't hurt the people around me as much."

To fully understand what had driven him to go so far, Audrey needed to meet Shelly and the children.

"Do you have anyone coming in to pick up orders today? Can you close the store?"

"Yes, I can close for the day. Why?"

"We're taking a day trip."

"Okay. Again, why?"

"Can you wait for an explanation until we get there? Seeing with your own eyes would be better for you than anything I can say. You won't believe me otherwise."

When she didn't move quickly enough, he said, "Come on. Now. We need to go shopping."

"Shopping?" she echoed. "You're behaving strangely."

They shopped at the organic market on Main Street, and Gray bought a lot of the same foods he'd picked up before at the convenience store on the corner of Shelly's street.

This time, here in this upscale store, they were better brands and cost a heck of a lot more than at the convenience mart. In addition to juice, cheese and cold cuts, he also bought treats, the kinds of things Shelly would never be able to afford for her children, like fresh cherries, chocolate and healthy chips made from sweet potatoes, beets and taro. Then, because Sam would hate him for buying healthy chips, he bought bright orange cheese balls. He purchased fresh fruits and vegetables. He picked up a whole roasted chicken and potato wedges.

It felt good, amazing, fabulous to buy them food again, but it wasn't enough. He wanted to buy them toys. *New* toys.

Throughout, Audrey watched him with curiosity but also restraint. She didn't ask what the groceries were for. Maybe she thought he was filling his larder.

She peered at him strangely, though, when he drove onto the highway that led to Denver.

Just outside of the city, he stopped at a big-box department store and asked, "What would a four-year-old girl like? Pretty clothes? Dolls?"

"What kind of girl is she?"

"She's perfect. Tiny and precious and lively." He smiled. "She likes pretty things." He described the flip-flops he'd bought and Tiffany's squeal of delight.

"So you want to buy her a present?"

"I want to buy her a *lot*. She has nothing."

"I know exactly what to get. How much money do I have to spend?"

Gray mentioned his top limit, which wasn't a fraction as high as he really wanted to go, but he had to be smart. Inside the store Audrey picked up pretty clothes, but fall items rather than summer.

"It's only August," he protested.

"Which means she already owns summer clothes. She'll need cold weather things." She picked up a pink jacket and held it open. "A good lining to keep out autumn winds. Pretty, but also practical."

She found a turquoise leotard and a pink tutu and tiny pink leather ballet flats, and Gray could imagine Tiffany as a dancer. Maybe he should pay for ballet lessons.

Whoa, don't get ahead of yourself. You don't know what kind of involvement Shelly wants you to have in their lives.

It hurt to think she might *not* want him involved. His attitude toward them was shifting, from hostility to acceptance to a desire to be part of their lives, to almost an ownership of them as family. And he needed to be careful about that. Nothing had been settled for certain yet. They still barely knew each other.

In the toy section, she picked up a Barbie doll and murmured, "I wish I had time to make doll clothes." She looked at Gray. "I also wish they made a more realistic figure, without this huge bust and mile-long legs. Curves would be nice."

Audrey walked ahead of him, and Gray thought, curves *are* nice.

"You know what? Let's skip Barbie. Let's get her books and puzzles and—look!" Audrey's squeal was almost as high-pitched as Tiffany's. "Fairy wings. Oh! Every girl needs fairy wings." She placed the gauzy things on top of everything in the cart.

"One last stop," she said. He followed her to the boys' toys and picked up a tiny suede tool belt filled with tools. "Every girl needs to learn to fix her own things. Look, here's a little tool bench. Let's get her that, too."

She looked over what she'd picked up and grinned. "I've spent all of your money. Let's go."

"Not yet." Now it was time to shop for Sam—a bike helmet, skateboard, ice skates and a heavy winter jacket.

"I hate to do this," he said, "but I guess I should get the kid clothes."

"How old is he?"

"Nine."

"How big?"

"Average."

"That's a good jacket, but there will be four months when he'll need something in between."

They picked up a fall jacket, sweaters and jeans, and a pair of Vans skateboarding sneakers.

"Are these kids in need?" Audrey asked.

"Like you wouldn't believe."

"Let's get him a scarf, warm mittens and a hat." She led him to the shoe department and spread her arm. "Winter boots."

"Good thinking."

Throughout it all, his heart grew bigger, stretching his chest to the max.

"Okay," she said. "Now, can we go?"

"No." What to do about Joe? He described Joe's medical condition. "His mind is in perfect working order, but his body is failing. What do you buy a kid like that?"

"How old?"

"I think twelve."

She nodded and considered.

"Okay, electronics. Can you afford an iPod?" When he nodded, she said, "An eReader or tablet?"

He nodded again. They picked up an iPod and decided on a small tablet, because Gray didn't know what kind of weight Joe could hold over an extended period of time, if he wanted to play games or read books. Gray loaded up with gift cards, so Joe could download from the internet.

"You said these kids don't have much. Do they have internet?"

Gray swore. No. He charged everything to his credit card and then they went to an internet café to register the devices and download books and music while they ate.

"What books should I get?"

"Is he smart? Bright?"

Gray shrugged, ashamed that he hadn't paid attention. Was Joe often ignored by strangers because he wasn't *normal* and didn't *look* as easy to approach as other children?

"Okay. Get *The Hunger Games*. All three. Also, there's an author who's perfect for his age. Gary Paulsen. Get everything, but especially *Hatchet*."

They scoured websites until they found more books and also added half a dozen games.

Then they turned to music and downloaded a lot, using the gift cards Gray had bought.

Joe had no one to show off for, no peers to whom he had to relate by listening to the right music, so Gray was free to choose music according to what he thought Joe might like. As much as he could guess, anyway, without knowing the boy.

They downloaded Maroon 5, Mac Miller, AWOLNATION, Classified, and then, because Gray loved them, he threw in AC/DC and Led Zeppelin.

"Time to go." Gray packed up the electronics. "We have one more stop."

They visited a holistic store where Gray picked up supplements that were supposed to help people with Duchenne. He'd researched extensively online. No way would Shelly be able to afford this stuff on her own. His credit card groaned when he used it again. This would have to be it. No more treats for Shelly's family for a while.

When Gray parked in front of Shelly's house, Sam rode up on his bike and watched them get out.

Gray held out his fist, and he and Sam bumped knuckles, watching Gray with a speculative expression.

"Who are you?"

Gray understood he wasn't asking his name, but exactly how he fit into Sam's small orbit. So...Shelly hadn't told the children anything.

"I'll explain inside."

He took the groceries out of the trunk and carried them to the front door. The boy followed.

Sam opened the door and called, "Mom."

Shelly stepped out of the living room. Gray turned to introduce her to Audrey and realized that Audrey hadn't come in.

CHAPTER TWELVE

HE WENT OUTSIDE and spotted her leaning against the car, skin ashen, and approached her. "Uncanny how much he looks like me as a kid, isn't it?"

Audrey glanced over his shoulder toward the house. All but Joe stood on the veranda, watching. Eyes bleak, but a spark flaring, she asked, "You expect me to just accept this?"

"Yes. It is what it is."

"You want to introduce me to your family?"

"Yes. That's why we're here today."

"And you make them live in squalor?"

"I'm trying to fix that. It's why I needed to sell the land, but I've come up with a different plan."

She marched away down the sidewalk.

"Hey!" He ran after her, but she refused to stop walking. He grabbed her arm, but she pulled out of his grasp as though he were infectious. "What's wrong? I know it's a shock, but—"

"That's what you call this?" She rounded on him. "A shock? You call kissing me and pretending to have loved a fiancée in Boston while having fathered someone else's kids a shock? It's a travesty. It's dishonest. You couldn't have shared that with me? Is she your wife? Or is she just a mistress?"

Gray's jaw dropped. "You think Sam is *my* son?"

"Isn't he? How else do you explain the resemblance to you?"

"He's my nephew."

She frowned. "You don't have siblings."

"Apparently, I do. I have a half sister."

"But that's not possible. That would mean that your dad...or your mom..."

"My dad. Mom doesn't know."

"How old is she?"

"A couple of years older than me."

"I don't believe it."

"It took me a while, too. Come meet them."

He took her elbow to urge her toward the house, but she resisted.

"Harrison would never have cheated on Abigail. He has always loved her. I refuse to accept this."

"Dad's name is on the birth certificate."

"Anyone can put anything on one of those. This is impossible."

"It's true, Audrey."

"Your dad wouldn't have done that to Abigail. If he adored her a fraction as much when she was young as he does now, he couldn't have fooled around."

"She has my smile."

Confused, Audrey asked, "Abigail?"

"Shelly. My sister. Half sister. She has the *exact* same smile as me."

He'd managed to get her as far as the pathway to the house, but Audrey balked, staring at Shelly as though she were an interloper, the first sign Gray had seen that Audrey's generosity had limits.

Worse, the glare Audrey directed toward Shelly could cut steel, shatter glass. Audrey wasn't angry. She was furious. In her denial, she was taking it all out on Shelly.

But it should have been directed toward Dad. He was the real culprit. So, why did she, and Gray himself, find it so hard to do? To place blame where it truly belonged? Because it was impossible to turn your back on a lifetime of love and admiration.

"Audrey," he said, voice low and urgent, "do this for me. Keep an open mind for me. I've only just found out I have a sister."

He ran his finger along her drum-tight jaw. "Relax. Please. I've given you precious little reason to trust me, but I'm asking you to now."

He kissed her. "You helped me in the caves. I need your help again."

She softened. "I'll try."

At the steps, Gray said, "Audrey, I'd like you to meet Shelly Harper. Shelly, my friend, Audrey."

Shelly stuck out her right hand and smiled. Gray watched Audrey, saw the moment that she understood that smile was indeed his. She shook Shelly's hand and braved a returning smile, but only Gray realized what it cost her. Underneath her bravery was a certain defeat in accepting that this woman truly was Harrison's daughter.

With a despair he hadn't anticipated, he witnessed the death of Audrey's innocence. He should have warned her. In bringing her here, in wanting to expiate, to explain his actions, he'd hurt her. He should have kept her as ignorant about this as he had his mother.

Only now did he realize how much he cared for Audrey, and that her pain was his. He should have protected her from this every bit as much as he was protecting his mother.

They trooped into the house, and Audrey sat in an armchair. Shelly propped Joe up with cushions, so he didn't take up the entire sofa. Gray sat beside him.

Shelly offered refreshments. "I don't have coffee, but I can offer…" She trailed off, perhaps realizing that water was all she had.

"You have coffee," Gray said. "I brought some. Sam, can you get the bags I left in the hallway?"

Sam carried them in. Shelly didn't look happy, and Gray realized how much easier on both of them the charity had been the first time when it was anonymous, when he wasn't here to witness her acute and real loss of pride.

Shelly might not have any pride left when it came to begging or blackmailing for her children, but accepting this was hard on her nonetheless.

Gratified that Audrey noticed her embarrassment, that maybe Audrey wouldn't suspect Shelly of being a gold digger, Gray took the bags from Sam and rummaged through them until he found the coffee and handed it to her. "I'd love a cup, it you don't mind."

Shelly looked at Audrey, who hadn't yet lost her cold shield, but who nodded nonetheless.

Gray handed the bags to Sam. "There's cream and sugar in there, too."

"You didn't have to do this," Shelly said, "but thank you."

"Shelly," Gray said quietly, halting her progress from the room, "I really enjoyed doing it."

Shelly smiled. "Thanks...bro."

Bro. Brother. Holy cow.

Shelly and Sam left the room, and he heard her putting things away. Moments later, he smelled coffee brewing.

Tiffany sat on a tiny stool in the corner, staring at Audrey, studying every aspect of her from her toes to the top of her hair. Audrey wore her springtime-on-steroids dress again today, the red flowers popping against the deep yellow, and the yellow crinoline rustling when she crossed her legs.

Shelly returned with a plastic tray and three steaming cups. They doctored their coffees.

The silence stretched, and Gray had no idea how to break it, how to ease Audrey's shock and anger. He was coming to terms with what a monumental mistake this had been when Tiffany came to the rescue. As had happened with him on his first visit, she was the icebreaker, the melter of hearts, disarming with her big eyes that cut through resistance straight to affection.

She stood and smiled at Audrey, patting the armchair beside her and cocking her head to one side. "I can sit here?"

Gray watched Audrey fall, realized the moment when she lost her heart, and recognized that she would eventually accept all of this.

Audrey squished to one side of the chair, and Tiffany squeezed in beside her with those cheap little flip-flops he'd bought her still on her feet. Had she taken them off at all since he'd bought them?

"Does she sleep in those?"

Shelly laughed. "Almost. She won't wear anything else on her feet."

Tiffany fingered Audrey's dress and the inch of crinoline showing at the hem. With one tiny finger, she traced the beads of Audrey's bracelet. "Pretty."

Audrey glanced at Gray with a wry, but still wary-around-the-edges acceptance, and said, "Get the rest of the bags from the car." A quiet but firm command.

Gray grinned and followed orders, taking Sam with him. Back inside, he handed out the gifts.

Tiffany, of course, squealed multiple times, making everyone laugh.

When Sam saw all of his gifts, he high-fived Gray and fist-pumped the air.

"Mom, I got a helmet."

Gray squatted in front of Joe. "We brought gifts for you, too. Do you want to see them?"

While the other two children had opened their gifts, squealing, clapping, whooping and hollering, Joe hadn't said a word, almost as though he'd thought the world had already dished out all it had to offer him, and there wasn't any more coming. Ever.

When Gray mentioned there were gifts for him, a lopsided grin split his face, and he nodded, too vigorously, setting himself off-balance.

Gray's vision threatened to mist over. He blinked hard and righted the boy, pushing the cushions in more tightly to bolster him, then retrieved the bags with Joe's goodies in them.

Taking out the iPod first, he handed it to Joe, whose grip was weak, but he managed to hold on.

"We already loaded it up with a bunch of music. We guessed what you would like. We got Maroon 5. Sound good?"

Joe nodded too hard again, and Gray laughed and righted him. With his less-than-perfect dexterity, Joe had trouble putting the buds in his ears, but Gray stopped him.

"Not yet, buddy. There's more." He pulled out the tablet and passed it to Joe. Joe's eyes got huge.

"Mine?" he breathed.

"Yours." Gray turned it on and explained everything they'd put on it, describing every game and naming every book. "We bought the mini tablet because it's light. You should be able to hold it for hours with no problems."

"What's *Hatchet* about?"

"I don't know. That was Audrey's idea."

Joe looked at Audrey.

She stopped playing with Tiffany. "It's about a boy close to your age who's in a small plane that crashes into a lake in rural Canada. The pilot dies, and the boy is stranded with no way to let anyone know where he is. He's miles from civilization without food, water or blankets. The only thing he has to use for survival is a hatchet. It's an awesome story."

"I want to read it now, please."

Gray opened the story, Joe took the tablet and started to read, so intent he blocked out all of the noise around him, his scoliosis a nonissue with the small tablet.

Shelly didn't respond. Only then did Gray realize how quiet she'd been.

"What's wrong?" he asked.

She inclined her head toward the kitchen, her mouth tight. Gray knew that angry-woman look and wondered what he was about to catch hell for.

In the kitchen, he asked again, "What's wrong?"

"I wanted to be the one getting my kids that stuff."

"You would have been buying it with money from my dad. What difference does it make if I jumped the gun and picked it up today?"

She whispered fiercely, "I want to make you take it all back, but I can't do that to my kids."

Only when her voice broke did Gray realize that she wasn't just angry, she was also sad.

"Whether or not it was your dad's money, I wanted

the pleasure of buying things for my kids, of seeing them open something from *me* at Christmas." She swiped tears from her eyes. "I know it would have been an illusion, but it would have been *my* illusion. I'm their mom."

That responsibility, the knowledge that she couldn't provide for her children, weighed heavily on her, made her look older than her years.

"I'm sorry," Gray said. "I wish I'd been thinking clearly. I got excited about buying things for them."

Mollified, she nodded. "Nothing can be done about it now." Shelly's sudden smile was wobbly and wet. "Thank you for buying gifts for Joe. He's not always treated like a child. People tend to forget him, as though Duchenne makes him unaware of what's happening around him."

"No problem. I really enjoyed buying everything."

They returned to the living room where Tiffany was dressed in her tutu, slippers and fairy wings, dancing around the room, singing off-key.

Gray retrieved the small bag from the holistic store and explained what it was, but Shelly was still watching her son read.

"This is so much better than him staring out the window for hours. It will keep his mind occupied."

"We need to get him to a therapist to get his body moving."

"I can't until I get the money from you."

"I'm working on it. Before I leave today, I'll write another check for next month's rent."

He explained about putting his condo in Boston for sale and getting the money to her then. She would have to trust him that the rest would come in time.

AUDREY CARRIED THE empty mugs to the kitchen. Shelly took them from her to wash. No dishwasher, Audrey noted.

"How did you first know?" she asked.

"My mom told me who my dad was long ago."

That was a problem Audrey would have to wrap her head around at some point, but that hadn't been what she'd been asking.

"No, I mean Joe. Was he born that way or did it develop?"

"He seemed normal at birth. His symptoms didn't show until he was five. Maybe earlier, but I think Tom and I were in denial that anything was wrong with our perfect little boy."

"How did you finally figure out something was wrong?"

"Muscle weakness in his legs. He couldn't run or jump properly. He fell down a lot. We thought he wasn't much of an athlete." Shelly dried the mugs and put them in the cupboard. "Plus, he was always tired. We could no longer deny it, though, when he had trouble climbing the stairs to go to bed at night."

She closed the door with a restrained click. "Then we got the diagnosis, and our world fell apart."

Audrey sighed. "How did you deal with it?"

"I cried for two weeks. Maybe more. I went into a

depression that lasted months. Finally, I picked myself up and went to the library and learned all I could about it. I went there a couple of times a week, researched online, joined chat groups and learned all I could from other parents."

She crossed her arms over her chest, essentially hugging herself. "We'd already had Sam, and I worried about him, but as you can see, he's fine."

"He won't get it?"

"We had him tested. He doesn't have the gene, thank goodness."

"And Tiffany? Can she get it?"

Shelly shook her head. "Girls don't get it. She can carry it, though."

Audrey sat in a chair at the spotless kitchen table.

Shelly sat across from her. "When I realized I was affecting Sam, as well as Joe, with my depression, not to mention my marriage, I entered life again and threw myself into making everything work."

"You've done an amazing job. Your kids are great."

"Thanks. The thing is…" She tapped her fist against the table. Her face screwed up, but she stopped herself from crying. "I can't make it work now that Tom is gone. I can't go to work and still care for Joe. I can't make enough money to pay for a caregiver." She took a tissue out of her pocket and dabbed at her eyes. "I never had a career that paid much. I couldn't afford college, so, after high school, I worked in a retail store. When I met and fell in love with Tom Harper, we married and started a family right away."

"You could have had Harrison pay for college."

Shelly shook her head, a hard, emphatic denial. "When he didn't care that my mom was pregnant and never sent her support, she didn't ask him again, and I decided I never would."

That was so unlike the Harrison Audrey knew. There was no denying that Shelly was a Turner, but something felt wrong about all of this. She didn't think it had anything to do with Shelly.

When they'd first arrived today, Audrey had thought Shelly was scamming Gray. No more. Shelly was as honest as the day was long.

But she would have sworn that Harrison was, too. The whole idea that Harrison could have…that he might have…

No. It was beyond the realm of possibility, beyond the stretching of her imagination. Maybe she was still in shock.

Abigail. Oh, dear lord, what would this do to Abigail? Before the day was over, Audrey was getting to the bottom of this.

Shelly spoke. "I contacted him now only for the children's sake. Otherwise, I never would have."

"If it's any consolation, in your shoes, I'd be doing the same thing. Harrison has a lot to make up for." Audrey stood. "Time to leave, I think."

Gray sat on the floor in the living room playing

Go Fish with Sam and Tiffany, looking very much like an oversize kid himself.

When Audrey and Shelly entered the room, and Audrey picked up her purse, he understood that it was time to leave.

There were hugs all around.

Anger underlay Audrey's shock, simmering while she hugged the children. They were not a part of this. Harrison had always seemed to be honest. All of these years, had Audrey—*and Abigail*—been such poor judges of character?

"HOW DOES SHE COPE?" Audrey asked.

They were in the car, and Gray was driving them to the lab. They'd left a happy home, but Audrey had been subdued until now. At the house, Gray had thought she'd been coming to grips with Harrison's dishonesty, but maybe not.

"Shelly?" he asked.

She nodded. "Tell me more about Duchenne."

"The only research I've done is on the internet, but what I've learned is that it's a form of muscular dystrophy that progresses and worsens quickly."

"I was afraid to ask Shelly what the future held. Worsens how?"

"The muscle weakness will continue to get worse. He'll eventually have difficulty breathing, and heart disease will begin to set in at about age twenty."

"So young," Audrey whispered. "It makes me sick to my stomach."

"It gets worse," Gray said, grimly staring at the road ahead. "He'll probably be dead by the time he's twenty-five, most likely because of a lung disorder. Between now and then, there can be a whole slew of complications. Cardiomyopathy, decreased mobility, pneumonia or lung infections."

"Shelly will need every penny you can give her."

"Yes. More than money, too. She'll need emotional support. Her mom is dead, and she has no other family."

"Why did you buy all of those gifts today?"

"Guilt, mostly. I had such a great childhood. My parents gave me everything. I had a college education that allowed me to become successful in business."

"Guilt is a great motivator. Is that why you're giving her money?"

"No. She's blackmailing Dad."

"What?" Audrey sat up straight.

"That's why I had him declared incompetent. To void the sale of the land to you so I could sell to a huge agricultural conglomerate. They were willing to pay a fortune."

He glanced from the road for a second to look at her profile. "Don't judge her harshly. She's desperate. She'd run through her husband's savings since his death and didn't even have the rent for September. If I hadn't given it to her, those kids would be on the street. Can you imagine Joe in a shelter?"

"Or worse," Audrey said. "They would have taken

him from Shelly and institutionalized him. It would have killed her. It's obvious she loves him."

"Yeah, I've had the same impression. That's why I had to wrench that land back from you. It wasn't worth a fraction as much with you and those greenhouses sitting in the middle of it. Shelly wanted one lump sum that she could use to support the children until they grew up."

He pulled into the lab's parking lot.

"So, what will you do now?" Audrey asked.

"Sell my business in Boston."

"Are you serious?"

"Yes. I'd held on to it thinking I would someday return there after Mom and Dad…passed away. They're healthy, though, and could hang on for years. I hope they do."

"They're fragile now, Gray."

With a sharp glance, he noted her frown. "Do you think this did them any permanent damage?"

Audrey hesitated, and he hated it, terrified that he might have diminished them so deeply with his actions that they might fail.

"Tell me," he demanded.

"When I visited, they didn't look good. I'm worried about them."

"Can you see why I couldn't bring this to them? Why I had to handle it myself? It would break Mom. Kill her."

Audrey was quiet for so long, he thought she wouldn't answer, but she nodded.

"I know you're going to think I'm being paranoid, but I paid to have a DNA test done here. I need to run in to pick up the results."

Five minutes later, he returned.

"This is it," he said. "The moment of truth."

He tore the top off the envelope and pulled out the papers, and what he read took his breath away.

"What is it?"

Gray handed the results to Audrey.

"What on earth?" She handed them back to him. "You need to talk to your parents. There's something really strange going on."

He drove out of Denver, and neither he nor Audrey said another word until they reached Accord.

"I'm going with you to see Harrison and Abigail," she said. "We need to find out what this means."

"We? You would help me with this?"

"I love Abigail as though she were my own mother. When I was little, after Mom died, Abigail treated me like a daughter. I want to help her get through this."

Gray nodded. "Okay. Let's do it."

When they drove into his parents' driveway, his nerves skittered and danced. He hadn't seen either of his parents since that awful day when Dad had kicked him out of the house.

Man, he loved them. He didn't want this tornado barreling down on his family to demolish what he'd only ever known as a loving relationship. Mom and

Dad were devoted to each other. He didn't want this huge change to destroy a once-happy couple.

Audrey knocked on the front door.

Harrison answered, shocking Gray with his appearance. He'd aged more in the past week than in the past five years.

Oh, God, Dad, what did I do to you?

Gray's knowledge that his dad was lost to him overwhelmed him.

"What do you want?" Harrison asked, his once hale voice now a whisper, his gaze on Gray both hungry and angry.

"We need to talk," Gray said, his tone not quite as confident as he'd hoped, not when he wanted to wrap this frail man in his arms and beg his forgiveness and swear his undying love.

Harrison frowned. "What is there left to say?"

"May we come in?" Audrey asked. "Please? There are things you need to hear."

For the first time, Harrison registered her presence.

"Audrey? You're with Gray?" He seemed to mean, *You're* siding *with Gray? Supporting him in this?*

"Gray is right, Mr. Turner—you need to talk. He has something important to show you and Abigail."

Heaving a sigh, he stepped aside. "Come in."

Gray stepped past him and into the living room, where Mom waited. She'd aged, too. More than anything, he wanted to take her in his arms, to cherish and protect her from the tornado.

Everyone sat but Gray. He couldn't settle, just

needed to get this done quickly. While his parents were too well-bred for outright hostility—no vulgar cursing or screaming here—their unhappiness burrowed under his skin.

"There's no easy way to say this. When I came home, I started to handle all of your correspondence. Last month, I received a letter from a woman who was trying to blackmail Dad."

"I remember," Dad said. "I told you she was full of nonsense."

"Yes, you did, but I went to visit her anyway. Dad, she looks like me. She has my smile. Her son is the spitting image of me at that age."

"Would someone please explain who and what you are talking about?" Abigail asked.

"Did you ever know a woman named Edie Kent?" Gray asked.

"No, I've never heard of her." Abigail sat up straighter. "Is she blackmailing Harrison? Why?"

"No, not her. Apparently, she's dead."

"Oh. Sorry to hear it. Then who's blackmailing my husband?"

"Her daughter."

"Why?"

"Because she thinks she's Dad's daughter."

"That's absurd," Abigail said.

"As it turns out, it is impossible, but I didn't know that until this afternoon."

"Tell us everything, Gray," Mom ordered.

Gray explained it all—the photo of Sam, his visits to Denver, the family resemblance and the DNA test.

"Here's where it gets interesting. The DNA test says that she isn't Dad's daughter. *But* she is family. How can that be? You are both only children."

Harrison and Abigail exchanged a significant look.

"What?" Gray asked. "What did that look mean?"

"Craig," they said together.

"Craig?"

Dad nodded. "Craig. Another one of his tricks."

"Who is Craig?"

"Your uncle."

"My *what?* I've never heard of him. Why not?"

"He died before you were born. This is no doubt his daughter."

"He envied your father his success something fierce," Abigail said, "and played tricks to subvert him wherever he could."

"Including," Harrison said, "pretending to be me on occasion. Used to go into Denver and impersonate me, throw around money, pretend he was a bigshot owner of a big company."

Knees weak, Gray fell into an armchair. Delayed shock. Dad truly was the man Gray had always thought him to be. What a blessed, awesome relief. The larger part of the shock might be that Gray had an uncle he'd never known about.

"We stopped seeing Craig just before he died," Abigail said. "Sort of booted him out of the family."

"Why?"

"Because he made advances toward your mother."

"Mom was beautiful. That's enough to get angry about, but to cut him off from the family?"

"He was…" Mom looked away. "He was forceful about it. If Harrison hadn't shown up when he did…"

Okay, for that, Gray might have killed the man.

"Craig grew up terribly indulged by my mother. He wasn't evil, just—" Dad shrugged eloquently "—spoiled. He thought he could have whatever he wanted in life."

"He was Shelly's father." Gray took the paper back from his dad. "I've been giving her money."

"Why?"

"Because of this." He handed his father the photo of Joe. "He has Duchenne muscular dystrophy. The woman's husband is dead. She has three children, and the care of this one child is a full-time job. She has no family to help her. She's desperate for money.

"Plus," he continued, "I thought she was my half sister." He hadn't meant that note of regret to slip into the statement, to be said aloud, not when it might sound like a rebuke against his parents for ever having had only one child.

He'd always felt alone as a child, as though he'd once had a special relationship with someone who'd died. He understood now it had actually happened, and it had been Audrey.

"I've met her twice. She's legitimate, Dad. She isn't a gold digger. She has genuine needs."

"I met her today, too," Audrey said. "She's an honest woman. Her children are charming."

To Abigail, she said, "You would love them. She's a stellar mother."

Gray glanced down at the photo of Shelly. He almost wished it had all been true. Then a thought occurred to him. "She's my cousin."

"Yes," his dad agreed. "She is family."

One sister lost and found. And lost again.

Audrey came up beside him, uncanny in her ability to understand what was going through his mind—the terrible disappointment, the sense of loss, the grief.

"She's still related to you. She's still yours. She's your cousin. Those children are still yours. They're family, Gray. You haven't lost that."

He nodded, slowly. "Yes, they are still family."

To his father, he said, "That's one of the reasons why I took guardianship of your property—to boot Audrey off the land. I was crazy to sell it, to get Shelly the money so Mom would never learn about this. I'm so sorry, Dad."

"I told you I was never unfaithful to your mother."

"I know." At some point, he would have to talk to Dad about the company and what Gray planned to do with it, but not right now. He had a more burning issue to discuss at the moment.

He explained to his parents about the claustrophobia, the panic and all of the unexplainable feelings that flooded him whenever he saw Audrey. "Since coming home, I've felt like I was going crazy. I was still grieving for Marnie and then I was acting like a nut. Then I got this letter and freaked out. I haven't been thinking straight since coming home."

Abigail and Harrison exchanged glances. "We have a confession to make," Mom said. "About something that happened when you were a child."

"I already know about it. Audrey told me everything."

"Sorry," Audrey said. "He was in a bad way and needed to know where his feelings were coming from."

She stood and took Gray's face between her hands, her palms dry and cool on his cheeks. "I'm so sorry we handled things the way we did."

"I'm angry, Mom. I wish you'd done it differently. I missed out on a lot. Why did you keep the fall down the well a secret?"

"You seemed to want to forget. You never talked about it. Never acknowledged it. We thought it best to leave it that way. We were wrong."

"I have to come to grips with the lies in this family."

Mom's eyes brimmed with tears. "I've never forgiven myself for not finding a better way to help you. I would change it all if I could." She straightened, and Gray knew she was hanging on to her composure by a thread. "I'm going to make tea."

She and Audrey went to the kitchen. Gray heard Mom murmur, "Thank you. I'm glad he knows."

Dad watched Gray with a rebuke on his mobile face. "How could you believe that of me?"

Gray scrubbed his hands through his hair. "I didn't, at first. When I initially went to Denver, I planned to expose her as a lying cheat."

He went to the window and stared outside. "Her son answered the door, and he was the spitting image of me. Then I met Shelly and she smiled."

He turned. "It was my smile, Dad. *Exactly* my smile. I still couldn't believe you'd done it, and I didn't know anything about an uncle Craig.

"I planned to handle the whole thing quietly so no one in town would ever know about Shelly."

"Speaking of the town, does everyone know about the guardianship? You made me a *dependent adult*."

Gray shook his head. "I don't think so. We have a lot to talk about, but can we do it tomorrow? I've had enough drama for one day."

"I suppose so," Harrison said.

"I'm still going to help them, Dad. They're family. I've put my business up for sale."

"You love that business."

"Yes, but things have changed. I really care for Shelly and her children. I'm beginning to think my life is out here, in Accord, and near Denver."

"You think you can take Turner Lumber from me?"

"We can talk about that tomorrow, too." Once Dad heard what was in the evaluation, Gray didn't doubt they could work things out. Somehow.

"That's another reason why I want to be here. For you and Mom. I thought I'd lost you." When his voice cracked, Gray stopped talking, overcome by emotion—love and affection, relief that it was all out in the open, and gratitude that his dad truly was the man he'd always thought him to be.

THE FOLLOWING DAY, Gray returned to the house to talk to Dad alone. They settled into the living room while Mom napped upstairs.

"Dad, how can we make things right between us?"

"I don't know." He was still cool. Gray had a battle ahead of him. "I'm stunned by your actions."

"I had good reason. I needed to void the sale of land to Audrey to get the money for Shelly." He laughed without humor. "For all the good it did me. I couldn't tear down the greenhouses and destroy Audrey's work. We're selling the land back to her."

"As it should be," Dad said.

"The other reason I had to take control was for the company. I know you think I didn't want it and that's why you stopped caring about its success, but I've learned something since I came home."

Gray realized how important Turner Lumber was to him, and what a tragic loss it would be to the town if it folded. He had made his point in Boston. Yes, he'd proven he could start and run a successful company of his own. But Accord, his family and Turner Lumber were *home*. He belonged here.

"I *want* to run the company," he said. "I'm here

now because I want to be, not because I have to be. I want the business to flourish and I want to be part of making it happen. I want the employees to be happy. Audrey has taught me so much. Has made me see where I was held back by fear."

Since going into the cave with her, he'd stopped his obsessive counting and frantic gum chewing. His stomach had settled. He still hated darkness. Tight spaces freaked him out. But understanding where it all started was the key to getting better. And the healing had begun. He'd turned a corner.

When Dad didn't respond, Gray said, "You did an amazing job starting Turner Lumber and building it into a solid company that employs a lot of people. But times have changed. I want to show you how to turn things around. I want to share my ideas with you, Dad, but I also want your mentorship."

Dad's decisions might have been erratic lately, but Gray was certain Harrison still had a lot to teach. And with Gray controlling the business, Dad wouldn't be able to sabotage sound decisions.

"What do you mean *mentorship?*"

"I want you to come into the office with me tomorrow and we'll go over everything together, we'll crunch numbers, we'll talk ideas. We'll make this a *family* business. I know you said you're tired. You can do as much or as little as you like. But I mean this from the bottom of my heart, Dad. I want to be part of the heritage you started."

Dad's eyes looked suspiciously moist. He nodded. "Okay. Let's do that."

THE NEXT WEEKEND, Gray drove his parents to Denver, organizing the day with Shelly, who insisted on
making them dinner. They arrived at noon. Shelly
was making a traditional Sunday dinner for lunch.

"We're having roast," Sam announced as they
entered.

"Roast," Tiffany repeated, twirling to show off
her tutu, ballet slippers and fairy wings.

"We never have roast." Sam.

"Never." Tiffany.

"I can't wait." Sam.

"Can't wait." Tiffany.

Shelly laughed. "Go into the living room, you two.
Shoo. Out of the way."

Gray watched her extend greetings to his parents,
and could only imagine what was going through her
head right now. Embarrassment that her mother had
gotten it wrong. That Harrison was not her father,
but his brother, Craig, was.

The evening Dad had told Gray that he had an
uncle Craig, Gray had phoned Shelly and explained.
He'd renewed his claim on her as family and his commitment to helping her out.

They sat in the living room, and before they could
socialize, Shelly said, "I need to clear the air."

She looked at his dad. "I'm so, so sorry I sent you
that letter. I thought you'd abandoned me and my

mom, and that you owed me. Now I find out you didn't owe me a penny of child support." She looked stricken. "Gray has still offered to give me money. It's outright charity. I can't accept it."

"You can and you will." Dad used his business voice, the one infused with enough authority to cow the strongest man. "You are part of our family now."

Harrison stood and offered Shelly his hands. She took both of them in hers. "Our family—" Harrison glanced from Abigail to Gray "—is too small. We would like to welcome you into it."

Shelly's hesitant smile grew. "Give me a minute in the kitchen. I have to put in the Yorkshire pudding."

"I think I might swoon," Mom said, easing the intensity. "I adore Yorkshire pudding."

They all laughed.

Shelly left the room, and Gray thought it had more to do with having a good cry than with getting pudding into the oven.

Gray waited five minutes while his parents chatted with the children, getting to know them, then he joined Shelly.

Her eyes were red. "Your parents are really good people."

"Yes, I think so, too." He touched her arm. "Are you okay? I know you thought you were meeting your father today."

She tented a rib roast with foil. "Yes, only to find out he's been dead for years."

"I'm sorry."

Her shoulders lifted in a poignant shrug. "It wasn't what I wanted to hear, but it is what it is."

"If it's any consolation, you can still call me bro. That is, if I can still call you sis."

She turned around. "I would really like that."

Gray held her until Sam barreled into the kitchen to ask when lunch was *finally* going to be ready.

Shelly laughed, dished it up, and they ate in the living room so Joe could be part of the celebration.

On the drive home, Mom said, "You were right, Gray. Those children are delightful. I'm so glad they will be part of our family."

GRAY COULDN'T SEEM to stay away from Audrey.

He entered the shop to talk to her, maybe to touch her if she'd let him. Did she like him any better now? He didn't know.

I don't like you.

A lot had happened between them since that night.

He heard banging out back. He stepped around the counter, and Jerry came forward to nudge his hand, then followed him to the alleyway behind the store.

Audrey wore a pair of overalls, and she was hammering away at a wooden box. Things jiggled while she wielded the hammer.

He enjoyed the view for a while and then asked, "What are you building?"

She jumped, jamming a hand against her chest.

I can do that for you.

"You scared the daylights out of me. I thought I was alone."

"Sorry. What's all this?"

"I'm building a series of boxes, stands, for my plants for the show. Since my space is so small, it will have to be three-dimensional."

"Good idea. Want some help?"

"I would *love* help. I want to get this finished tonight so I can spend a bunch of time in the greenhouse tomorrow, getting all the plants ready. The show's on Sunday."

Gray stayed for hours, building boxes with Audrey and *for* her when she had to serve customers.

When they finally finished, he took her out for a quick dinner because they were both famished, and kissed her when he left her at her car to drive home, the kiss as natural as breathing. And as essential.

CHAPTER THIRTEEN

TERESA TOOK JEFF fishing, tiptoeing into his room to wake him at five in the morning.

"I'm awake," he said, hearing her.

"Okay, I'll go put on the coffee and oatmeal."

"Add a couple of boiled eggs to get us through to lunchtime."

Jeff showered and then went downstairs, feeling good. Happy. Even if nothing could happen in the way of a personal relationship with Teresa, he enjoyed that she was here. And he remembered her whispering, "You are more than a client," and it warmed him.

He'd been getting out with Teresa. They went out most days, either to the café or to the gym—she'd gotten her own membership.

Only two months. She'd already been here for two weeks. Someday she would be gone. He couldn't think about that. He had to find a way to convince her to stay.

Today was their second time going fishing.

With her help, he was learning to take care of himself.

Jeff entered the kitchen.

"Oatmeal's in the middle of the placemat, and your egg is on your left. Coffee's on the right."

He followed her instructions without exception. They'd become a team.

"What do you want to do in the winter?" she asked. "Snowshoeing?"

"You still going to be here then?" He heard the insecurity in the question.

"I like Accord better than Denver." She bustled around the kitchen making their lunch while he ate his breakfast. "I like the people. I like the scenery." She laughed, and music filled the kitchen. "I love the fishing. I heard there's a long-term care facility for seniors in Accord. I wonder whether they need caregivers?" Her voice sounded wistful. A good sign.

Maybe she would move here. Maybe she wouldn't be too far away.

They drove to the lake in silence. Sometimes they talked, and sometimes they just…were. Teresa was easy to be with.

"Well?" she asked.

"Well, what?"

"If I'm still planning to be here in the winter, what do you want to try?"

"Snowshoeing."

"Sounds like fun." Was he imagining the satisfaction in her voice? "I've never done it."

"We will, the second there's enough snow."

At the lake, they wrestled the canoe off the roof

of the car, Jeff not needing a whole lot of help from Teresa. His strength was coming back.

Out on the lake, Teresa rummaged through the tackle box, through flies that Jeff had tied years ago. A momentary sadness passed through him that he wouldn't be able to do that again.

"Oooh, this one's a beauty," she said.

"Describe it."

"Woolly yellow neck above a hook eye."

"The marabou damsel."

"It's gorgeous. Does it work well with trout?"

"Yes. Let me show you a trick."

Jeff stood to step forward, but maybe his eyesight put his balance off. The canoe tilted and then turned over. Teresa screamed, and Jeff held his breath as he hit the water.

He came up for air and grasped the overturned canoe.

"Teresa," he shouted.

The silence of the settling water his only answer, he panicked.

God, no. Don't be gone.

"Tess," he screamed.

A pair of strong arms clasped him from behind.

"I'm here. I'm okay."

With one arm, he grasped the canoe and with the other reached for her.

"You scared me."

"I'm a strong swimmer."

"But I couldn't see you." Jeff's voice shook. "You didn't answer me."

"I was underwater looking for you."

"You were worried about me?"

"Terrified." She touched his face.

"Good."

"Good? Why you—"

His hand moved from her waist to clasp the back of her head. His mouth came down on hers, off-center. He kissed her, moving his lips until he squared up with hers and then slipping his tongue into her mouth.

It had been too long.

All of that crotchety passion that he'd put into railing against his illness and fate he transmuted into lust.

Tess kissed him back with an intensity that matched his own.

Was she fierce in her lovemaking, too? Honest and straightforward and fun-loving as she was in the rest of her life?

In time, they ended the kiss, Tess pulling away slowly.

"I like the way you do that," Jeff said.

"I like the way *you* do it."

"Good. We aren't finished, my Tess. We've only just begun."

They heard a motorboat from a distance away, one of the lake cottagers coming to rescue them, no doubt.

"How much did we lose?" he asked. "What was in the boat?"

"All of your ties. Our lunch. The life jackets we should have been wearing."

"It can all be replaced. You can't. I'm glad you can swim."

"Me, too. Water's cold, though."

He pressed his chest against her cold, hard nipples. "Yeah, I can tell."

Tess chuffed out a laugh. "You're wicked."

She drove them home in their wet clothes where they took warm showers, separately, to Jeff's dismay.

Afterward, he heard her drying her hair and called to her as soon as she turned off the dryer, from his bedroom where he sat on his bed leaning against the headboard, because he needed her there with him.

"Are you okay?" She neared the bed.

He nodded.

"I'm going down to make lunch. Do you need something first?"

"I need *you*. Now." He snapped out a hand and was lucky enough to snag her wrist. "Stay." A thread of emotion ran through his voice, something he hadn't felt in a long time—the love for a woman.

Giving her no chance to back away, he had her sprawled across him and his arms around her like steel bands.

He kissed her cheek.

"Where are your lips?"

She laughed and said, "Here," and he felt her mouth on his.

He kissed her with the passion and heat of a younger man. Jeff might be in his sixties, but he still remembered how to handle a woman.

She didn't resist. When he finally came up for air, she said, "I can't do this. This is unprofessional."

"Screw being professional."

"If I'm not careful, *you* will screw a professional."

Deep laughter shook him. He wished he could see her, but would make do with touching her.

"I love your sense of humor," he said.

He kissed her forehead.

"You're fired," he murmured against her hair.

"Jeff," she said, her voice thick with desire, but also with frustration. "I need this job. I have to support myself."

His lips touched the tip of her nose, as though he could learn the shape of her face with his mouth instead of his failing eyes. "Not if you marry me."

She stilled. He held his breath. The air in the room turned into billions of listening particles. She leaned away from him, and he could feel her staring at him.

"I beg your pardon?"

He watched her steadily, even though he couldn't see her clearly. "I need you, Tess. I know we barely know each other, but I want to get to know you better. As it is, I know enough to want you here all of the time, not as an employee, but as a cherished friend."

"I don't know what to say," she whispered.

"Say yes." He kissed her again, and her resistance melted into desire, want, need.

His hands roved her body, learning and coveting every one of those extra pounds she griped about.

They made love all afternoon and cuddled while the evening turned to orange and then to dusk outside the window, while they revealed all of their secrets to each other in the waning light through the window.

Tess loved Jeff back with as much intensity as he offered, a partner, taking his burdens as hers and transmuting them to joy.

They spent the night together, a glorious revelation of lovemaking and late-in-years sex that was passionate and fulfilling. He hadn't known his life could still hold this, not at his age, not with fading eyesight. In his heart, in his soul, he knew he was making the right choice.

AUDREY DROVE HOME late with Jerry on the passenger seat beside her, tired but happy with the progress she'd made on her show stand. Correction, the progress she'd made today with Gray's help. Like old times, he'd been a good buddy. Unlike in the past, the way she felt about him was all grown up, and the thoughts she had were not "buddy" thoughts at all. They left her itchy and aware and aching.

Was there a possibility of something more with him? Could she forgive him for what he had done to his father? Now that she knew about Shelly and her children, Audrey had a better understanding of what drove Gray, but the whole business had been so ugly. He had reneged on taking back the greenhouses. He'd saved them from demolition. Was he closer to the boy she used to know and adore? Or would the cold businessman raise his head if threatened again? He'd done so much healing in the cave, though. She wondered...was there possibility with Gray?

She got out of the car and was leading Jerry to his kennel when she noticed the house was dark. Dad and Teresa were home because his truck was in the driveway. Even though it wasn't quite eleven, they must have gone to bed early.

"Come on, Jerry. You can come inside tonight."

Inside the front door, she stopped and listened.

"All quiet. You're in for the night, Jer. You can sleep in my room and I'll put you out in the yard before Dad gets up in the morning."

She walked upstairs in the dark, Jerry's nails click-clicking on the steps behind her.

On the landing, she stopped because she'd heard something strange. Voices. In Dad's room. A woman giggling. Teresa?

Oh, my.

Dad's voice murmured something, then his deep laughter filled the bedroom behind his closed door.

Oh, oh, my.

Teresa's voice responded and, while Audrey couldn't catch specific words, the tone was warm, loving.

Oh, oh, oh, my.

Audrey smiled so broadly, filled with such joy, she was shocked it didn't light up the dark hallway. This was awesome, fabulous, more than she could have hoped for. Dad deserved happiness.

She crept to her room at the far end of the hall, washed, undressed and crawled into bed, all while her grin stretched her lips ear to ear.

Holy jumping jelly beans.

Jerry lay down beside her on the bed, and she buried her fingers in his fur.

When had this developed? Dad's surliness had eased and his temper had abated with Teresa's presence, sure, but Audrey hadn't seen this coming. Hadn't had a clue. She'd been too busy to notice.

She stared into the darkness, petting Jerry and happy for his company, but thinking about romance. The happiness for her father slowly morphed into longing.

She adored her job and her independence, loved her family, friends and dog. The challenge of starting a business and competing in the show excited her. She wanted more, though. She wanted a home of her own and a family.

Remembering how good it had felt to hold Pearl, to imagine that the baby was hers, longing filled her chest like a hard round balloon. Even more, she wanted someone to love and appreciate her. Someone who wouldn't try to change or pigeonhole her, but who would see her and accept her as she was, wholeheartedly. Lovingly.

That tentative wonder and hope after working with Gray today evaporated. She remembered his disdain of her clothing, her style. No. There was no possibility of romance there.

Sleep eluded her, as out of reach as the love and acceptance she craved.

GROGGY FROM LACK of sleep, but happy for Dad, Audrey filled a thermal mug with coffee from the pot she'd made and doctored it the way she liked it.

A few minutes ago, she'd heard movement upstairs and someone showering. Dad? Or Teresa?

She heard footsteps coming down the stairs too quickly to be her dad's. Teresa entered the kitchen, but pulled up short when she saw Audrey. Her face turned a becoming shade of pink. The woman was no beauty queen by any stretch of the imagination, but this morning, she glowed.

Audrey liked her. "May I ask what your intentions are toward my dad?"

Teresa, who was usually so calm and so in control, stammered, "I— He—"

Audrey laughed to ease Teresa's discomfort and wrapped her arms around her. "Thank you for making my dad happy." She pulled away and looked into Teresa's pale eyes. "You did leave him happy, I assume?"

Teresa's shy smile looked so out of character on her bold face that Audrey grinned.

"He asked me to marry him," Teresa said.

"Woot! Are you serious? That's awesome!"

Dad married? No longer alone to deal with the terrible changes in his life? After Mom's death so many years ago, Dad had found love again.

"You have my blessing," Audrey said, reveling in the joy that resonated in the house.

"WHAT DO YOU mean you can't come?" Audrey stood in the Army Surplus, shocked that Noah was backing out of his promise to attend the floral competition with her. "You promised me you would support me."

Noah looked harried. He ran his fingers through his hair. "I know, but that was before Monica Accord booked a fund-raiser to help me raise money to start a soup kitchen in Denver."

Audrey crossed her arms. "Which she just *happened* to book on the same day as my event."

"It was a mistake. An oversight."

"Didn't you tell her you would be busy that weekend? You were going to help me set it up."

"I know. I did tell her I was busy, but she must have misunderstood and thought I was telling her to book it for that weekend. You know how she gets things wrong sometimes."

Monica was her former sister-in-law, and, yes, sometimes she did get things wrong. "I can't believe you're defending her. Monica isn't as dumb as everyone thinks. She's dumb like a barracuda. She always manages to get her way in things." Audrey knew she was being mean-spirited but couldn't stop herself. How on earth was she going to set up all by herself?

The front door opened, but Audrey was too caught up in her panic and disappointment to care who had come into the store.

"That's not true," Noah said hotly. "She's been great. She's been giving clothes and makeup to local women for job interviews. She's not selfish."

"How do you know? You don't hang out with her."

He shrugged and avoided her eyes. Were...were Noah and Monica an item? "I had a prior commitment from you."

His eyes widened. "That's enough, Audrey. Cut it out. If you can't be supportive of the work I do, then just don't say anything."

"I've always supported your work to help the poor, Noah," she said. "I'd hoped for the same in return."

She turned to leave with as much dignity as she could muster while her nerves jittered. How was she supposed to do all of the work alone, transporting so many fragile flowers, heavy wooden boxes and a trellis, as well as setting up an exhibit that would take hours and hours?

A shadow fell across her. Gray.

"I'll help you," he said, his voice quiet but firm, and Audrey could have cried she was so grateful.

"I'd like that," she responded, her voice equally as quiet. She didn't say more because she didn't think she could. Her emotions were reeling. She'd always been able to depend on Noah.

She stopped Gray with a hand on his arm.

"Can I trust you?" She studied him while she waited for his reply, willing him to tell her the truth, to be the person she'd always believed he could be instead of the cutthroat businessman he'd become.

He touched her hand, oh, so briefly with his fingers, a feather touch, but it left an impression. "Yes, you can trust me."

She believed him. "Can you be at the loading dock of the store at eight on Sunday morning?"

"I'll be there." He turned and strode toward the counter.

Audrey left the shop.

GRAY AND NOAH faced off.

"You warned me against hurting Audrey," Gray said, "but it looks like you're the one guilty of that."

Noah's gaze slid away. "Yeah, you have no idea how bad I feel."

Gray's grunt must not have sounded too supportive because Noah said, "I do feel bad. What did you come into the store for?"

"Nothing now. I wouldn't give you a nickel to support this shop after what you just did to Audrey." When he left, he let the door slam behind him.

Sam's birthday was coming up and Gray had planned to give him a Swiss Army knife, but he'd find somewhere else to buy it other than from that hippie snake-in-the-grass Noah.

WHEN AUDREY DROVE up to the rear of her shop at eight on Sunday morning, Gray was already there, waiting. The weather had turned unseasonably cold.

For an hour, they loaded supplies from the shop into the bed of her dad's pickup and then drove to the greenhouses.

"Everything looks awesome." Gray grinned. "You're going to do well. Let's get the truck loaded."

An hour and a half later, they'd unloaded everything at the back door of the convention space.

She drew her plan out of her purse and outlined her ideas to Gray so he would know where to place things, starting with the six-foot sunflowers in the back, tucking them into the corner and lining them along the bland gray curtains.

In front of them, she set up the arbor she'd brought, and Gray helped her wrestle it into place. She curved and curled her clematis with their weird hairy seed-pods over it. Underneath the center of the arch, she put a small stone bench and tucked her orchids in and on and around it.

She arranged her boxes, covering them with the moss she'd ordered online and had had delivered two days ago. On one of the higher boxes, she arranged her larger mushrooms.

She placed the smaller boxes on the lower ones.

In and around everything, she tucked her animal topiaries—squirrels peeked out from behind orchids, and a hedgehog looked as if he was nibbling a puffball.

On the floor at the front of the display, she set up a fairy garden with small houses she'd made from birch bark and wild plants she'd found in the forest, including maidenhair fern that she'd divided to make miniature shrubbery around her miniature houses. With stones she'd hand selected from a stream, she created the tiniest walkways edged with small fences that she'd built in the basement and had painted pale blue.

From a doll's shop, she'd ordered chairs that she'd painted hot-pink. She put them in the middle of the tiny garden and placed the tiniest, jewel-toned mini-primroses that she'd nurtured in the back of her store.

"Voilà," she said, standing back and planting her hands on her hips. The display was whimsical and playful and original. She loved it. Would anyone else?

"Wow," Gray said. "This is incredible."

She wanted to believe it, but she couldn't judge her own work.

"Truly?" she asked, watching him to make sure he was telling the truth.

A gentle smile lit his face. "Truly. It's a wonderland. You've created something unique using your imagination. Children will love it."

"Adults, too, I hope. They'll be the ones voting."

Gray frowned. "How are you going to get people back here?" He glanced around the crowded showroom. "There must be at least forty displays."

"Forty-two, but who's counting?"

"So, you said you'd dress up like a clown to grab attention." His glance flicked over her.

She'd worn a hot-pink dress today with a fitted bodice and a hot-pink angora sweater on top. Her full crinoline made the skirt jut way out. She thought it way cool, but a temporary insecurity on such an important day had her blurting, "Do I look okay?"

"You look stunning." She did? Where was the disdain Gray had shown her when he first came home, when his scrutiny of her style spoke of harsh criticism, when he thought she was cuckoo to dress this way? Now he thought she was stunning? "Answer my question. How are you going to get people back here?"

A slow smile spread across her face as she reached for the box she'd picked up from the printer yesterday and opened it. Inside were a couple thousand hot-pink bookmarks, each one offering a prize to anyone who turned one in to her booth.

"What are the prizes?"

She bent over the one remaining unopened box on the floor.

Inside were hundreds of pink papers hearts. She'd made the paper herself, begging and borrowing used computer paper from all of the shops and businesses in town, shredding it and blending it at home, adding red tissue paper for color and morning glory seeds, and carrying the pulp to work where she shaped and dried the hearts. After she caught Jerry eating one, she learned to store them out of reach.

Come spring, anyone who planted a paper heart in their garden would soon be rewarded with morning glories.

Gray grinned. "Brilliant."

"Thanks."

He shook his head. "You've done so much work for this. You deserve to win."

"Thanks." She basked in his admiration. She might be a highly confident person, but Gray's support today mattered. "Let's check out everyone else's displays."

"You know what, Audrey? You go ahead. I'm going to stay here."

Audrey felt an odd jolt of foreboding. "Why?"

"While you were setting up, there was a guy watching everything you did. Didn't you tell me Bolton planned to win this thing?"

"Yes, but sabotage? I find that hard to believe."

Gray rested his hands on her shoulders, and Audrey felt a sizzle all the way to her toes.

"I've worked in the cutthroat world of business. I know what men are capable of." He crossed his arms over his chest. "I'm staying here to guard the display while you look around."

"But what about once the doors open and I have to stand at the door to hand out bookmarks? I can't expect you to stand here all day."

"I'll be here." His hard jaw, the determined, mulish set of his lips, brooked no argument.

"Okay, but I'll come to relieve you every half hour, so you can get a coffee or go to the bathroom."

"Every hour."

"But—"

He kissed her hard, full on the lips, and she flapped her hands.

"Oh, my lipstick. I'll have to reapply it before everyone gets here."

Gray burst out laughing. "Go fix it now."

In the washroom, she reapplied the lipstick that matched her dress perfectly and then took a quick walk around all of the other displays to check out her competition. When she got to the front of the room and saw Bolton's floral display, she stopped cold.

It was massive, stunning, every plant huge, every flower overblown and showy.

How had she ever thought that whimsy could win the day?

Downcast, she returned to Gray and stayed with her plants while he took a spin around the room.

He came back with a big smile. "Bolton's display is impressive, but over-the-top. Conservative. Predictable. You've got this in the bag."

"Oh, Gray, don't say that." For the first time in her life, she actually wrung her hands. "I'll get my hopes built up too high. God, I'm a mess."

"Audrey, chill. Everything will work out."

"Not if I don't win that prize money. I won't be able to keep Teresa on. What will I do about Dad?"

"Worry about that later. For now, put a big smile on your face, hand out bookmarks and enjoy the crowd."

"Okay. I'll do my best." She handed him a small hole punch. "People are allowed to keep the book-marks, because they advertise my store. When you give them their paper hearts, punch the bookmark and give it back to them. That way they can't come back more than once. I don't have enough hearts to hand out multiples."

At one o'clock on the dot, when the security guards opened the front doors and people rushed in, she handed out her bookmarks with the map on the back of the convention floor showing exactly where she had set up her display.

So many people entered, and she had such a good time chatting them up, she missed relieving Gray at the first hour interval. When she glanced at her watch, she realized it was almost three and literally ran to the back.

She found Gray charming a crowd of people in front of her display, telling everyone what all of the different types of flowers and mushrooms were. No wonder he was such a good businessman. He had an amazing memory.

"How is the promotion going?"

"See for yourself." He held up a small box that was

full of dots of paper that he'd punched out of bookmarks. "Tons of people are following the instructions and coming to the back to claim their prize."

He stepped close to avoid the crowd. The heat of his body soothed her nerves. "The best part is their reaction when they get here. Everyone loves it. Young and old."

Just then, Audrey heard a voice she recognized. "Wish to hell I could see it myself."

She spun about. Dad stood beside Teresa.

"Dad! What are you doing here?"

"I wanted to know what your work was like." He sounded gruff, as though the last place he wanted to be was here, but a smile hovered at the corners of his lips.

"But you hate my gardening. You hate that I work with flowers."

"Tess said it's beautiful." He nudged his chin toward the display.

Tess? How sweet.

"It's amazing, Jeff," Gray said.

"I haven't told you about the best part," Tess said. She described the miniature fairy garden.

"Where do you get your ideas?" Tess asked Audrey.

"I don't know. They just come to me, and I have to act on them. I sort of feel like they are part of the universe trying to come to life through me." She shook her head, frustrated. "That sounds dumb."

"No, it isn't," Jeff said. "Sounds like the kind of thing your mother used to say when she was trying to persuade me to spend more money on the garden."

He never spoke about Mom. "Did you ever say no?"

"Never. She always got what she wanted. Now, you are getting what you want in life, too. That's good."

Audrey's heart swelled. Dad was proud of her. This monumental moment would live in her memory forever. Discreetly, she wiped tears from her bottom lashes.

Tess winked. "We're going off for a coffee, and then we'll come back to visit some more."

After they left, Audrey explained a few of her plant choices to attendees, and then asked Gray whether she could pick up a coffee for him.

"I could use one." He punched a couple of bookmarks and handed out more seeded paper hearts.

Audrey went to the café at the other end of the room only to pull up short when she saw Tess carry a couple of steaming drinks in paper cups to a table where her dad sat, and then lean forward to kiss him. On the lips.

Oh. Oh, my. Oh, the look on Dad's face. Bliss. He touched Tess's cheek, bringing a smile to the woman's face, which almost made her pretty. Then he pulled her down for a deeper kiss. Audrey had never seen her dad as a sexual creature. But it was all good

In a cloud of happiness, Audrey bought a coffee for Gray and carried it back to her flower stand.

"What's up?" he asked. "You look strange. Are you okay?"

"I just saw my dad and Tess kiss."

"What? Like a peck on the cheek?"

"No. Deeply. Romantically. Full of lust. I know they've been sleeping together."

A satisfied smile spread across Gray's face. "Hey, that's really great."

"It's strange. I've never seen my dad in that way."

"It's good for him. It's good for Tess, too. I like her. She got him out of that house and out of his shell."

"You're right. I'm happy. I'm just in shock."

"Well, get over it and get back to the front door. You need to hand out more bookmarks."

She did, for another two hours before heading back to Gray and sending him off to get an early supper.

"What about you?" he asked. "You must be starving."

"I'm too nervous to eat."

"Listen, here's the deal. I'll go grab a bite, but only if you promise to let me bring something back for you."

"Okay, but keep it small. Honestly, my tummy's full of butterflies."

He left, and Audrey handed out plenty of hearts.

While he was gone, Shelly and the children showed up. Two of the children—Sam and Tiffany.

"Shelly, what are you doing here?"

"We came to see your show."

Humbled, Audrey considered the cost of bus fares and entrance tickets for the three of them.

"You didn't have to come."

"We wanted to," Tiffany piped up.

"Who's watching Joe?" Audrey asked.

"My neighbor is going to check on him every half hour."

"Mom's never left him alone for so long before," Sam said.

"He's twelve years old, but his needs are so special." Shelly bit her bottom lip.

Sam said, "He made mom come out. Said he's not a baby anymore."

"You're all still my babies. Always will be." Shelly hugged Sam hard enough for him to complain.

"Mom."

"I love your display." Shelly touched an orchid. "It's incredible. How do I vote for it?"

Audrey explained about the computer terminals at the exits.

"Do we all get a vote?" Sam asked.

"As long as you have your ticket stub, yes. Input the number on your ticket and you'll get to vote."

"Cool." Sam shoved his hands into the pockets

of his low-slung jeans. "I'm voting for you. This is awesome."

Tiffany squatted on her haunches, fascinated by the fairy garden. Audrey hunched down beside her.

"Do you like it? Who do you think lives in the houses?"

For the next five minutes, Tiffany spun a tale about fairies and goblins and a troll who resided under the tiny bridge Audrey had built out of toothpicks.

Audrey stood and said to Shelly, "I'm impressed. She's got a great imagination. Maybe someday she'll be a writer."

Gray came back with a tea and a croissant. "How's this?"

"Perfect. Thank you."

He handed over the food and turned to hug Shelly. "Hey, sis."

"Hey, bro." Audrey heard affection and satisfaction resonate in Shelly's voice.

"We have to go. I can't bring myself to leave Joe at home by himself much longer." She explained to Gray about the neighbor who was checking in regularly. "Half an hour intervals are too long for him to be alone. I'm worried."

Audrey held her for a moment, moved that Shelly would come all the way out to the convention center to support a woman she'd met only once.

Gray walked them out and then came back.

"I'll take over again. Go find a quiet spot to sit and eat."

She went to the back, behind the curtains away from the crowds. She needed a quiet moment to collect herself. There were computer terminals in place at the exit doors at which the attendees could cast their votes before leaving. At six o'clock, the organizers would tally the votes, and by seven, she would know whether she'd won. *How was she doing?*

"I told you to stop worrying." A disembodied male voice on the other side of a curtain sounded annoyed. "Cripes, how many times do I have to reassure you? Bolton will win. The software's been set up so if anyone comes close to beating Bolton, it will add more votes to keep Bolton on top."

Stunned, Audrey dropped her half-eaten croissant.

Sabotage? Of the voting system?

She held herself still and listened.

"How can you be sure it will work?" a female voice asked.

"I had my nephew set it up. He's a computer genius."

Anger, no *rage,* poured through Audrey. After all of her effort, hours and hours making boxes, trellises and seed-infused paper hearts, and backbreaking times hauling soil, planting seedlings and nurturing them to perfection, she might lose—no, *would* lose—because Bolton Florists decided that winning was so important they had to cheat.

No way in *hell* would she let them get away with

it. If she lost here today, she would lose to someone honest.

She left her tea and croissant and ran from the
back.

When Gray saw her face, he grasped her arms to
steady her.

She explained what she'd heard.

"There's no way I can win when the software's
been rigged." Her voice shook, because a fireball
burned inside of her. Ethics, morals, were important, *huge,* to her. "I have to find the organizers and
raise the roof."

"You need to concentrate on your booth and talking to attendees." He grasped her chin. "*You're* as
important here today as your flowers. You're beautiful and perky and passionate. People respond to
that. They love you."

In the middle of this whirlwind of tension and
anger, he had to go and say something wonderful
like that, and she couldn't respond? They were in a
room jam-packed with event attendees. But if they
were alone, she would throw her arms around him
and kiss him breathless.

"Let me handle this," he said.

"Okay. Give them hell, Gray."

He stalked away, pulling his cell phone out of his
pocket as he left.

GRAY REFUSED TO let this happen to Audrey, not when
she'd worked so hard. He called the local police and

was put through to the fraud division. He told them what Audrey had heard, urging speed to get this fixed before the end of the show.

They promised to send out a couple of detectives, along with a computer geek who did freelance work for the department.

They arrived forty minutes later.

Gray huddled with them, and they decided to hunt down the organizers. Gray left it to the cops to explain what was happening.

He knew they were right when one of the men and the lone woman in the group blanched.

"We'll be asking our computer expert to take a look at your program when the voting ends. He'll determine who the winner is."

The other detective said, "If he finds signs of fraud, we'll be taking all of you in for questioning and placing charges if they're warranted."

The woman looked sick. The one man who Gray was sure was the other guilty party fidgeted and bobbed around as though he had to go to the bathroom. Good. Let them stew.

Back at the display, he calmed Audrey's fears, updating her on who he'd called.

At six o'clock, when the doors closed, they broke down the display and loaded up the rental van.

AT SEVEN O'CLOCK, the florists and their families gathered in the auditorium of the convention center. Dad and Tess had stayed.

Now that the moment of truth had arrived, Audrey's nerves skittered. She didn't know what she would do if she didn't win. She'd seen pretty stiff competition in the other displays.

Gray stood on her one side, and her dad on the other.

Dad wrapped his arm across her shoulders and said, "No matter what, Audrey, I'm proud of you."

Knowing how much it cost Dad to finally accept her new career, the sentiment brought a lump to her throat. "Thanks, Dad."

The microphone at the front of the room squealed, and then the soundman got the levels right.

The head of the organizing committee, Walter Reed, stood behind the mic with the results of the voting in his hands. Audrey assumed at some point he would be investigated about the fraud.

Word had rippled through the florists that the detectives' computer geek had found the software Audrey had overheard the man talking about, and it had indeed been rigged in Bolton's favor. Two members of the organizing committee, a man and a woman, along with the son of Bolton's owner, had been taken away in handcuffs.

Audrey hoped they got the book thrown at them, and, if Walter were found to be involved, that they'd string him up by his thumbs and leave him to hang for a few days. Pompous ass.

Word had also come down that Bolton would not

be disqualified because the owner himself had apparently not known about the fraud. Yeah, right.

As Walter began to speak, Audrey gripped both Gray's and her dad's hands. She wasn't sure, but she might have been crushing bones.

"The jury's winner is Bolton Florists."

Audrey slumped. Surprise, surprise.

Grumbles ran through the audience, none of them too happy that Bolton was still in the race, given the fraud charges.

"The winner as determined by our attendees' votes is…Audrey Stone."

Audrey's knees buckled. Gray hauled her into a hug that nearly crushed her. Dad gripped her next, and his cheek against hers felt damp. Tess kissed her cheek.

As though she'd left her body and watched from a great distance, she registered the crowd's cheers and applause. Apparently, they liked her a heck of a lot better than Bolton.

"As you know—" Walter calmed the crowd and continued, "We used a points system to determine the overall winner, by adding points from both our jury selection and the attendee votes. I'm pleased to announce that our overall winner and the recipient of the $25,000 award is…"

Audrey grew dizzy. She'd stopped breathing.

"Audrey Stone!"

The crowd went wild.

Audrey had to sit and put her head between her

legs. "I don't believe it, I don't believe it," ran like an incantation from her lips.

Hands patted her back. Words of congratulations washed over her.

At length, she lifted her head and stood.

"It's really true?"

Gray's grin answered the question before his words did. "It's true, Audrey. You did it."

She laughed *and* cried, while Gray whooped and spun her about in his arms. Everything she'd hoped for was coming true and it was too much to take in. The work, the dreams and the chance she had taken starting her business had paid off.

She was filled with so much happiness she felt almost numb. The best part, though, was Dad's smile. Her heart overflowed.

After she picked up her trophy and the check, the four of them left the building together.

When they got to the parking lot, Dad said, "Audrey, I have something to tell you. I hope you think it's good."

Audrey waited.

"Tess and I are getting married."

She started to laugh and cry again, not quite sure how that was possible, but she was doing it. "Oh, Dad, I'm so happy for you. You, too, Tess."

Well. Times had changed. So much was working out for the better.

"I'll have to find a new place to live."

"No," Tess asserted, with the adamant pressure of

a hand on Audrey's arm. "That house is your home. You belong there."

"Not anymore. It's long past time for me to move on. You two will need your privacy. I'm so happy about this."

"I had to fire the woman to get her to agree to marry me," Jeff said.

"I'll still need to work, though. I talked to the owner of a care facility for seniors. She's going to hire me part-time so I can still spend a lot of time with Jeff. Now it won't be duty, though." She cast an adoring glance at him. "It will be pleasure."

"No, Tessie. It will be mine."

Love was in the air, and it was a beautiful thing.

"Come on," she told Gray. "Let's get these flowers back to the greenhouse."

THEY FINISHED UNLOADING the plants from the back of the rental van and then delivered everything else to the store.

Audrey locked the back door of the shop and turned to Gray, her eyes tired.

Strangely, he didn't want the day to end. Not yet, at any rate. Not when his heart was flying for Audrey.

"Are you hungry?" he asked.

She nodded.

"Come to my place for dinner." *Say yes.*

Her eyes widened. "Really?"

"Really. I'll do takeout. What do you feel like?"

"Beer and ribs."

He laughed. "Yeah? You're an earthy woman, aren't you?"

She nodded. "I have to return the van, though."

"Okay, do that while I go to the bar and pick up the food. Meet me at my place."

He turned to go, then had to make sure he wasn't imagining that Audrey was going to have dinner with him. "Okay? You're coming for sure?"

Did he have to sound so damn unsure of himself?

"Yes, I'll be there."

She climbed into the high seat of the van, flashing a little thigh.

CHAPTER FOURTEEN

GRAY PICKED UP half a dozen bottles of Corona, a couple of limes and two servings of barbecued ribs, potato salad and coleslaw.

Three quarters of an hour later, Audrey sat on the floor in his living room, a froth of hot-pink, dark curls and laughing violet eyes. The remains of their takeout feast littered the coffee table.

"You're a messy eater, you know that?"

She giggled and stuck a finger into her mouth to lick off the sauce.

Gray grabbed her wrist, because if he didn't seize this chance, he would never forgive himself. He thought about her all the time, his feelings still sometimes clouded with panic and fear from sharing that one fateful huge event with her, both good and bad emotions around Audrey inextricably wound together. Inseparable. He wanted her, though, more than he'd ever wanted a woman. Even Marnie.

When he licked her thumb, drawing it across his tongue, a shiver coursed through his body. When he sucked her index finger into his mouth, *she* shivered.

He tugged her across his body until she draped across his thighs, her face a mere fragment of space away from his. This close, he could drown in her eyes, in their unusual color, and in the endearing warmth in their depths.

An open book, Audrey couldn't hold anything back, or hide the tiniest part of who she was. He wanted to be part of her honesty.

Licking the sweet sauce from her bottom lip, he took his time loving her, savoring the soft skin on the inside of her mouth, laying her back with one hand holding her head and the other roaming her body.

He sucked the skin of her neck into his mouth, sure he was leaving a hickey and happy to do so.

With her boundless generosity, she'd granted him everything, had cradled and supported him through blinding fear, had given him back his self-respect.

He kissed the tender flesh behind her ear, felt her tremble in his arms, her body as giving as her soul.

His hand explored the hills of her wondrous breasts and the soft curve of her belly to the hot crevice between her legs. Her breathing hitched. She moaned, a small breathy exhalation of wonder.

He'd never wanted, craved, so much, to see a woman's body, to see *this* woman's being.

Slipping the pink buttons through their holes, he spread her dress open to reveal...perfection.

While he'd wondered often what feats of engineering held all of Audrey's glory in place, he wasn't prepared for the jolt of raw lust that burned through him.

French, sexy and incredibly un-PC, a corset in pink satin with white polka dots, trimmed with black lace, did insane things for her body, pushing here, nipping there.

He pressed one of the cups down, and her breast, with its large rosy nipple, popped out, generous and warm. He took it into his mouth. Nothing had ever tasted sweeter.

He cupped its feminine weight, and his thumb abraded the nipple. For endless minutes, he paid homage to her breasts, heating both Audrey and himself, leaving him edgy and aching.

He pushed up her dress and fluffy pink crinoline, crazy to see more of her voluptuous body. As he'd guessed, she wore stockings, but rather than a garter belt, they were held up by pink lace garters.

He grasped one and pulled it off her leg, along with the stocking. He caressed her shapely calf, her knee to her round thigh, so much beautiful skin softer than eiderdown.

A scrap of pink satin covered her mound, highlighted by one black velvet bow decorating her like a present. He unwrapped her as though she were birthday, Christmas and Valentine's Day rolled into one, the best gift given by the sweetest woman.

Without warning, he flipped her over, because he had to see more of her or die.

The panties were a thong, barely there on a behind more delicious than ice cream and apple pie, more decadent than chocolate, more lavish than the anemic stick figures that populated fashion runways. She moved, raised her bottom high, subtly enticing him with the swells of her body. He touched her, traced those waves with his palms and ran one between them until he pushed the satin aside and entered her with one finger, her silken flesh wet and warm and welcoming, nature's satin far softer than the fabric she wore, or anything man could manufacture. Velvety. Earthy. Home.

AUDREY STUDIED GRAY while he slept, brushing an errant lock of dark blond hair from his forehead.

He looked younger in sleep. Less severe. Less the successful CEO and more like a little boy. But he didn't love like a boy. He loved like a man. All man.

She wanted to make love again. To pleasure him. For some reason, when they'd made love, he'd insisted on doing all of the pleasuring, but if he thought she would be a passive partner in this relationship, he had another think coming.

What exactly was their relationship? Audrey didn't know, but she planned to do her best to make something lasting out of this. She'd wanted Gray for a long, long time. Even when she hadn't liked him, she'd still desired him, but had held herself back.

No more. In the past two weeks, he'd been behaving like a friend, a true friend, as though he really cared what happened to her.

Today, he'd given her immeasurable support. He accepted the way she looked and how unique she was. *You look stunning.*

Gray still loved his fiancée, but she would take as

much as he could offer, and she would work at making love grow, starting with a foundation of desire and the affection that had grown between them over the past month.

She already had a foundation. She'd known him when he was her little friend. Lately, she'd seen the ways in which the boy was still inside of the man, and her affection had grown into love.

She ran a hand along his arm, sighing with pleasure. She'd waited a long time for this.

Unwilling to wait until morning, greedy with pent-up hunger, she touched him until he moaned.

He came awake slowly with deep throaty murmurs while she loved him.

After he came, he kissed her, lingering for drugging moments, the man a secret sybarite under his proper business suits. What an unparalleled pleasure to experience Gray like this and a beautiful end to a spectacular day.

"Let's shower together," Audrey whispered.

"I like the way you think. Give me a minute to get my strength back."

They made it to the bathroom eventually, after many more kisses. Audrey soaped Gray's long, lean body, and he did the same with hers, finding pleasure spots she didn't know existed, turning all of her skin into one giant sex organ.

"Stop that," she whispered.

"What?"

"Making me so happy. I want to pleasure you, but I keep getting distracted by your hands."

An arrogant chuckle was his only answer, that and more delving of those talented hands.

"I said stop it."

"Not a chance, lady. Get used to it."

Oh, she could. She really could.

They returned to the bedroom and curled into bed together. Audrey turned off the bedside lamp. Gray tensed in her arms.

"Shh," she soothed. "I'm here."

She felt him ease into sleep and held him for a long time. A deep satisfaction filled her. *Gray.*

THE CALL CAME at 11:46.

"Gray." He glanced up from the document he'd been reading, still tired from last night.

Audrey had been stunning. Greedy. Generous.

And he loved the daylights out of her.

I don't like you.

She must like him now. She'd spent the night with him.

This morning she'd gone off to celebrate her floral competition win with caving for the day, but he had work that needed to be done. Not that he would have gone with her into another cave anyway. Never again.

Hilary stood in the doorway of his office wearing a worried frown. "I know you told me you didn't want interruptions, but you need to take this call."

Her expression sent foreboding through him, and he reached for the phone.

"Gray?"

"Yes, Jeff, what's up?"

"I got a call from a guy over near Glenwood Springs. Audrey went caving there this morning." There was a rough exhalation on the other end.

"Jeff, this is sounding ominous."

"My daughter… Little Audrey…"

Gray's chest constricted. Fear bit into his psyche. "Jeff," he barked, tone sharp. "What's wrong?"

"It's bad. There's been an earthquake. Ten people went in. There's no way for them to get out. The entrance caved in."

"That can't be true." His hammering pulse choked him. Panic cut off air to his lungs. He couldn't believe anything would happen to Audrey, not after losing Marnie. *He wouldn't allow it.* He couldn't lose another woman. How had he allowed himself to care so much? "There must be a mistake."

"No mistake. There's been no contact with anyone inside. We don't know whether they're still alive."

"I'm going out there. She *can't* be gone, Jeff."

"If you're going, I want to go with you."

"Can you be ready in fifteen minutes?"

"You bet. I'll be ready and waiting."

Scant minutes later, Gray pulled up in front of Jeff's house. Jeff waited on the veranda. He'd aged. Those crevices beside his mouth that grief had carved into his face after Billy's death, but had been filled in with Tess's love, were back as deep as caverns. Even his salt-and-pepper hair seemed more salt than pepper.

Standing beside him, Tess asked, "Can I come?"

"Yes, get in."

She had a bag with her. "I brought coffee and food. The drive's close to three hours. Here." She handed him a thermal travel mug. "It's black. I didn't know how you'd like it."

Thank God for women like Tess, always ready with a helping hand and a calm head. Gray settled Jeff into the front seat and took off the second Tess climbed into the back and closed her door.

"Head into Denver and then west on I-70," Tess said.

Gray cursed. Three hours just to get anywhere close to Audrey. She'd worked hard all summer and throughout September. She had earned a few days off with her caving buddies, but he'd missed her the second she'd left Accord.

He was a dollar short and a day late. He should have told her he loved her last night. He should have asked her to marry him. He should have begged her not to go this morning.

Gray drove fast, and halfway there was pulled over for speeding. The string of curses he let out was both inventive and comprehensive.

When the cop approached his window, Gray said, "Officer, I have to get to Glenwood Caverns."

The officer nodded. "The cave-in."

"Yes. I need to get there now."

"I heard they're letting only family through."

"My daughter's down there." Jeff sounded rough. There was no doubting the man's distress.

The officer worried his lower lip with his teeth.

"I'm her fiancé," Gray lied.

The officer said, "Follow me. I'll get you there."

Gray sat on the officer's tail until they reached the caverns.

Between himself and Tess, they pushed and pulled Jeff through a crowd of reporters, all while Gray issued a terse, "No comment," to their questions.

"Who are you?"

"Are you related to the people who are buried under the rubble?"

When Jeff sucked in a gasp, Gray shot that last reporter a dirty look and told him to shut up. He didn't care how rude he sounded. *Buried* was a stupid word to use if the guy had any suspicion they were related to the victims.

No, Gray refused to think of Audrey as a victim. He wouldn't believe she was dead. She was strong, dammit. A survivor.

The officer got them right up to the front, where rescuers worked on clearing the entrance.

"How long will this take?" He faced a man who looked as if he was in charge.

"Who are you?"

"My fiancée is down there." He brought Jeff forward. "This is her father."

"Okay. This is how things stand. We don't know what's happening underground. The earthquake was mild, but we're unsure how far back the cave-in went."

Jeff groaned.

"If it helps, this is a stable system of caves. We have hope the only problems are here at the surface. It will take a while to clear the entrance, though, because we don't want any more rock to come down."

Gray thanked him. "We'll wait and watch. Don't worry, we won't get in the way."

"I'm not worried about that. It's just that we're in for a long haul. This will probably take all night."

"That long?" Tess asked.

"Yes, ma'am. We're being very careful."

They stepped to the side where they sat on rocks as flat as tables.

"I wish I'd thought to bring blankets or heavy jackets," Tess said. "If we're going to be here all night, we'll get cold." She glanced at Jeff. "I can take you to a motel."

Jeff's jaw jutted. "Not on your life. I'm staying. I plan to be here the second my daughter *walks* out of that cave."

None of them wanted to consider the alternative—that she might be carried out on a stretcher, injured, or in a body bag.

"Jeff, come hell or high water, the second Audrey gets out of that cave, I'm marrying her," he promised, or threatened, depending on your point of view. "I shouldn't say this to her father, but then I'm going to love the daylights out of her until she gets pregnant so she can never go back into another one of these infernal caves again."

Jeff nodded emphatically. "Amen."

AT ELEVEN THAT night, long after the sun had gone down, while Gray, Jeff and Tess sat on rocks that leached the heat from their bodies, the rescue efforts moved forward by painstaking inches.

Huge lamps had been set up on sturdy tripods, and the efforts continued without flagging into the night.

Paramedics had come forward to hand out thermal blankets to the families gathered at the site waiting for word of loved ones.

They folded some and used them to sit on, and then spread others over their shoulders, huddling close, with Gray and Jeff insisting on putting Tess between them.

Tess was right. They should have brought jackets, but it had all happened too quickly.

She pulled out the sandwiches she'd made, but ended up putting them away when none of them could manage more than a few nibbles.

How could Gray eat when he knew that Audrey was underground, cold, hungry and maybe even hurt?

Was she hurting? Was she remembering that dark time in the well with him? He wished he was down there with her. *He* would sing to *her*. He would hold her. For Audrey, he would be the strong one this time.

She meant more to him than his own life.

Just before dawn, a cheer went up. They'd broken through.

Gray jumped to his feet. He clasped Jeff's upper arms. "She'll be fine. They'll get her out."

A few minutes later, the news spread that there was another blockage thirty feet into the passage, and hope deflated. Silence returned, despair a palpable presence on the mountain.

An hour later, they broke through again. For minutes on end, there was confusion and then shouts, whether triumph or dismay was hard to tell from the outside. The shouts echoed around underground until one of the diggers ran out.

"We found them. They're alive."

Gray whispered a prayer of blessed thanks. Jeff slumped against him.

The rescuer waved to the paramedics, his gestures frantic. "We've got one woman injured. She needs attention. Get over here quick!"

The paramedics rushed in with a stretcher.

Gray grasped Jeff's arm. "How many women went caving? Was Audrey the only one?"

"I don't *know.*"

Gray stared around at the other relatives.

One by one, they said, "I'm waiting for my son."

"My brother."

"My fiancé."

"My son."

Not one other parent or sibling waited for a woman.

Gray covered his face with his hands. "Audrey."

Endless, agonizing minutes later, the paramedics came out with an unconscious woman on a stretcher, her head swaddled in bandages.

Gray couldn't see. He couldn't, for the love of God, *see* whether it was his Audrey.

Too soon, he knew.

The other cavers came out in single file. All men.

The woman on the stretcher was Audrey.

Gray rushed to her.

"How bad is she?" he asked. "Is she going to live?"

He couldn't lose her now, not when he'd just come back to her after so many years. Not when he was finally finding himself.

"We need to get her to a hospital right away. Out of the way, man."

"Where will you take her?"

"We're going straight to Denver."

"A head injury?"

"Apparently, she was hit by falling rocks. The cavers took good care of her. There's no hypothermia. They did their best."

He closed the ambulance door. "Gotta go."

Gray returned to both Jeff and Tess, who waited stoically.

"We're not losing her," Gray said. "Come on. We need to follow that ambulance to Denver."

On their way to the car, Gray passed the same officer who'd given them an escort the dày before. He looked freshly shaven, his uniform crisp, and drank a steaming cup of coffee.

When he saw Gray's face, he sobered. "What's going on? I thought everyone was alive."

Gray pointed to the ambulance driving away, its siren wailing. "That's Audrey. She's unconscious. They're taking her to Denver."

The officer tossed his still-full paper cup into a garbage can.

"Follow me. I'll get you there."

In a terrible déjà vu, Gray trailed the cruiser with its flashing lights to the hospital in Denver.

Audrey had already been brought in, but no one could tell him what was going on.

"The doctors are still with her," a nurse said.

"Where can we wait?" Gray asked.

"I suggest the cafeteria. She was one of the trapped cavers, right? It's been on the news. You all look cold and tired. Go eat. If anything happens, I'll come get you."

Gray hated to contemplate what that *if anything happens* might be, but he took comfort from how calm the nurse was.

"Come on," he said to Jeff and Tess. "She's right."

The nurse found them an hour later.

"She's good. She'd conscious. She's got a concussion, so they're going to keep her for a couple of days."

"Days," Gray said. "Doesn't a concussion usually entail just an overnight stay?"

"Yes, but the doctors are being careful. Do you want to see her?"

Gray let Jeff go in first.

After Jeff came out, he entered the room.

"Audrey?" he whispered. She opened her eyes. "How are you?"

"Tired," she murmured. "I was so cold."

Gray stared at the woman he'd grown to care for with unsurpassed passion and thought, *I love.*

I love.

He was love. He was love.

He'd held back from giving completely to Audrey because of fear. More accurately, because of memories of fear.

There was no more room in his life for panic or anxiety. What was the opposite of fear? Not courage. Nor bravery.

Love. Love was the polar opposite of fear.

What was the absence of fear? Again, love.

His chest, his life, the universe expanded. He became part of all and every.

Audrey watched him, her smile radiant. She knew. She understood. He recognized a feeling that had always been a part of him, lost, submerged, but never conquered. There had been one person in his life who had known him better than anyone else, even better than himself.

Audrey was understanding. Audrey was love.

The paradoxes of his life, the worries, the vanities, became reduced to one word. Audrey.

Needing her more than food, water, drink, his heartbeat and the blood in his veins, he embraced her.

The air between them, the molecules that separated beings, the flesh that separates humans, dissipated. He breathed her into his soul.

"Welcome home."

"I never left."

"Love me," he whispered

"Always," she promised, her eyes as frank and bright as pansies in June. "I have loved you forever."

Her truth awed him, left him speechless, and he rested his head on her dark head and breathed.

Hospital noises outside the room, and reality, intruded. He pointed a finger at her. "You are never going caving again, do you hear?"

She smiled. "Yeah? Says who?"

"Says the man who's going to marry you."

"Marry?"

"You know, when you squeal like that, you sound like Tiffany."

"I can't help it. You just said the *M* word. Are you sure?"

"I've never been more sure of anything in my life. I love you. I adore you. I want to worship you for the rest of our lives."

"I like the sound of that."

"Yeah? And how about this? I want children. I

want to have them with you. I want you pregnant the second you're healthy."

"Caveman," she said, but softened it with a smile.

"You scared me." His voice wavered. "You terrified me. I thought I'd lost you. I can't go through that again. I want you for my wife, and I want a family and home in Accord. I'm serious, Audrey. I want to worship you. I love you."

"I've waited a long time to hear those words, Gray. I love you, too." She held his face between her small cool palms and looked into his eyes. "The boy I used to know is back."

Radiant, she said, "Gray, you're not the cold CEO anymore. You're *you* again."

"No, I'm no longer the cold businessman." He rested his lips on her forehead. "You brought me back to life, Audrey. Back to myself."

"I'm glad. I'm so happy to see *you*." She fingered the blankets and blushed. "I like the sound of babies. I'm already thirty-six, though. We might only ever have one."

"That's fine. Just means we'd better start soon."

"Gray?"

"Yes?"

"I'll stop caving while we have babies, but I'll probably do it again in the future."

"No, you won't," he said fiercely.

She laughed. "*Yes,* I will. You can't hold a good woman down, Gray."

He rubbed his cramping stomach. "Audrey, you're going to be the death of me."

A COLD DRIZZLE coated the cemetery with silver puddles in the late-September evening dusk. Gray had returned to Boston for a brief visit. Before he could marry Audrey, he had to say goodbye to Marnie.

The weather was unusually cold, chilly enough to warrant an overcoat on top of his suit, the mood of the day somehow fitting for the occasion.

He set the pale peach roses he'd brought into the small urn on the headstone of Marnie's grave, their color soft yet brave against the gloom. They'd been her favorite flower.

There was so much about Marnie that he remembered, that he would never forget, no matter how much he'd come to love another woman. Or had come back to loving Audrey.

For half an hour, he talked to Marnie, telling her about the twists and turns of his life over the past few months. Somehow, he knew she would understand if she were alive. She would support him in the difficult decisions he'd had to make with Dad. She would approve of the changes Gray was making to Turner Lumber.

Above all, she would like Audrey.

"She's different, Marnie. Not like you at all, but she matters to me as much as air or my own heartbeat. As much as you did. I hope that doesn't hurt you wherever you are."

He didn't know anything about the afterlife, reincarnation or religion. He did know that he was loved by two good women. He loved two amazing women. How many men could say they were that blessed?

The soft rain stopped and a sliver of pink settled on the horizon, the distant sun wishing the world good-night. Gray closed his umbrella and shook it.

"Goodbye, sweetheart," he whispered before leaving to start his new life, knowing a small but vital part of himself would remain behind with Marnie.

CHAPTER FIFTEEN

APPARENTLY, TIFFANY WAS going to be a flower girl at their wedding because, really, how could someone that cute, someone who adored dressing up so much, not be in the wedding party? Especially given how much she also adored Audrey.

In fact, she was rapidly becoming a mini-Audrey.

Sam and Joe, in his new wheelchair, were dressed in tuxes beside Gray at the front of the church. Jerry Springer Spaniel sat on their far side with a big red bow tied around his neck.

The physiotherapy was doing wonders for Joe, strengthening his arms and back, and easing some of the pain from the scoliosis.

Gray's business had sold remarkably quickly, and he'd put a lot of money into Turner Lumber. They'd lost a couple of employees to early retirement, but had managed to dodge laying anyone off. The mood in the building had improved and many Turner Lumber workers sat here in this church today.

He'd given Shelly a lump sum that she and her children now lived on. He'd given her back her pride, and it looked good on her.

Shelly sat in the front row beside Gray's parents. Gray still couldn't stop himself from showing up at her house unannounced with gifts, no matter how much Shelly scolded him.

He just had too much fun shopping for them.

Besides, the scolds had become good-natured, and Gray didn't mind them.

Tess sat on the other side of the church, waiting for Jeff to join her after he walked his daughter down the aisle.

They planned to get married after Jeff had the surgery he'd finally agreed to and his eyes healed, followed by a week of deep-sea fishing. They continued to lift weights together three times a week. Jeff's devotion to Tess was an inspiration to Gray, as was his dad's to his mom.

God, he loved them.

He would do everything in his power to make sure that his own marriage was as successful as theirs. By example, Dad had taught him how to treat a woman with respect and how to love one for a lifetime.

Gray looked out over the congregation and thanked his lucky stars for good friends and neighbors. In the past months, he'd become an important part of Accord, taking suggestions for updating the business from Hilary and many Turner Lumber employees— suggestions that suited the small-town business that it was.

He'd learned to listen.

The organist started the music.

Tiffany appeared at the back of the aisle in a pink dress and white shoes with frilly white socks.

She carried a white basket full of flower petals she strewed on the carpet leading to the front of the church. When she reached the front, she ran to her mother and said, "I didded really good, Mommy."

The congregation burst into laughter.

Then Audrey was in the doorway, the sun streaming through stained-glass windows behind her, so even though she wore a cream dress, she was still bathed in the colors that she normally loved to wear.

She started down the aisle on her father's arm, and Gray's heart expanded, grew and took flight. Was any man on earth ever as lucky as he was today?

She'd brought color and light into his life. She'd banished the grays and blacks, the fears and despair that had plagued him when he'd returned to Accord.

Audrey wore a homemade replica of the dress that Jacqueline Bouvier wore the day she married Senator John F. Kennedy. But it was a dressed-down, less busy version with fewer tucks and pleats. He knew this because Mom had been talking about it for weeks, mentioning portrait necklines and bouffant skirts and details he didn't understand.

To him, Audrey looked like an angel.

Judging the original bridesmaids dresses at the Kennedy wedding too plain for Tiffany, Audrey had designed and sewn a miniature version of her own dress in pink. Tiffany sat on the floor playing with the rosettes on the front of the dress.

On impulse, he picked her up and gave her a big kiss on her tiny cheek. Then he set her on her feet.

He'd never known that a heart could hold so much love without exploding.

When Audrey reached the front, she received a kiss from her father. Tess stepped forward to lead Jeff to the front pew.

The wedding vows Gray and Audrey had written and were now speaking humbled Gray with their earnest simplicity and honesty.

After the wedding celebration—and all of the food had been consumed and too many glasses had been raised in toast—Gray took his bride home.

He'd bought the condo, and they'd given the existing furniture to charity. Audrey had turned the rooms into bowers of color and texture using rich, bold fabrics, infusing her warmth and sense of quirky humor into the surroundings.

Gray loved it.

He carried her over the threshold, the tradition old-fashioned but fitting for a woman who reminded him of contrasting classics—Betty Boop and Jackie O, Audrey Hepburn and Elizabeth Taylor. He'd fallen in love with the things he used to find outlandish. Now? He wouldn't change a thing about her. He'd found his way back to himself because of Audrey.

When he set her down, letting her body slide slowly over his for the sheer pleasure of it, he whispered, "Welcome home."

* * * * *

*Look for the next story set in
Accord, Colorado, by Mary Sullivan!
Coming in June 2014
from Harlequin Superromance.*